"Where was you, Victorine?

Don't lie. You was with him, at the vicarage, wasn't you? *Wasn't you?*" Jeremy had taken hold of me by my shoulders and was shaking me.

"Let go of me! Of course, not. I was on the moor. Everyone knows that. Who are you to say otherwise? Let go, at once!"

"I will when you tell me the truth. When you stop these *lies.*"

"I'm not lying! Why do you accuse me? I've done nothing!"

"Because *this* was in Mrs. Flemming's hand when I found her. How did she come by it, if you wasn't there? Answer me that!"

Jeremy reached into his shirt pocket and threw a shiny object onto the bed: the seagull with its wings outstretched in flight.

I0601022

Gothic Spring

Caroline Miller

A
Rutherford Classics
Publication

www.rutherfordclassics.com

Gothic Spring

A publication of Rutherford Classics

A Rutherford Classics Book

Third printing
ISBN: 978-0-9981697-2-9 (softcover)
        978-0-9981697-3-6 (ebook)

Publisher's Cataloging in Publication
Gothic Spring/Caroline Miller
222 pages--1. Gothic--Fiction. 2. Suspense--Fiction. 3. Thriller--Fiction. 4. Mystery--Fiction, 5. Psychological--Fiction 6. Victorian--Fiction

Dedication

To my loving mother, Cristina Mattei

One

I DO NOT EXPECT anyone to understand the bizarre sequence of events that changed my life from its bucolic existence into a living hell, nor do I look for compassion. Suffice it to say, I grew up in the northern part of England, an only child who'd been orphaned since I was ten and, prior to the time of these mishaps which I am about to describe, I had been living for five years under the protection of an indulgent aunt—a plump woman in her mid-sixties, whose faded mouse-brown hair aged her beyond her years.

Growing up, I kept to myself much of the time. Being a bookish child, I fancied that I was brighter than my classmates at the Leland School for Girls, that ivy encrusted structure that looked more like a mausoleum than a center for learning. I imagined that they resented me for my passions, Shakespeare and Milton, while they contented themselves with chatter about bustles and garden parties given by the Queen. Further, because I suffered from a severe form of epilepsy and was subject to seizures, they thought me strange, or at least, unreliable.

No matter, by the age of thirteen, my seizures increased and the purgatives became more severe. No longer did I suffer mere episodes of faintness that could be remedied with the application of trinitrini. What followed were periods of complete collapse that began with a tingling in the limbs, then a stiffening and ended in bodily thrashings so severe that I had to be held down to prevent me from doing myself an injury. Not a pretty picture I suppose, though I never had any recollections of my suffering, being unconscious at these times. Certainly these seizures and the treatments that followed, pine baths and the application of leaches, were remedies alien to a classroom. I was forced to withdraw from school, my education assigned to the sometimes careless hands of a series of tutors, most of them so unremarkable that I can recall neither their names or faces—except for Mr. Huddleston, who was dismissed because he wrote me endless poems. The other whom I remember with some fondness was Vicar Soames who served not as my academic but as my Biblical teacher.

A cleric of advanced years, the vicar's frock coat reeked of the camphor he rubbed into his joints, and his asthma made him wheeze. Despite his impairments, he was faithful to me and tottered to my fireside each Wednesday afternoon so that, once grown used to him, I found him amusing. Toward me, he showed both patience and endurance, being neither alarmed nor repulsed by the excesses of my illness. In time, we two misfits grew together, each accommodating the other the way the earth accommodates a seed until it flowers.

On the occasions when his infirmities caused him to be absent, I missed him and was saddened when these lapses increased. His failing health affected his work in the parish, as well, and in time the church council called for his retirement. Aunt Julia was among them, though I suspect she had another motive. The extended length of our visits, the vicar's and mine, became an annoyance to her. "The man is forever underfoot," she would often complain. Nor did the gifts he brought me—flowers and sweet meats meant as rewards for my studies—win him her approbation. At the very least, she accused him of spoiling me. At the very worst, she may have spied him kissing my hands, my cheeks.

Whenever the subject of retirement was broached, however, the vicar argued against it. "One does not retire from God's work, Miss Ellsworth," he huffed once during a chance street encounter with my aunt. "I may not be a young man, but neither am I so enfeebled that I should be put out to pasture like an old cart horse."

His remarks did nothing to endear him to my relative who wielded considerable influence where church politics were concerned. In the end, her will prevailed. A railway ticket was purchased, lodgings arranged for in Breighton and in a matter of days, the old man was no more than a memory.

He, for his part, wrote faithfully to me during the early months of his exile. His first letters were restrained. He described the beauty of his walks along the seashore, the temperate nature of the breezes; but as time passed, I sensed in his descriptions a hunger for my company that bordered on the sensual. "Victorine, how I long to have you with me so that we might sit together on the beach, our fingers luxuriating in the warmth of the sand. The abundance of God's beauty here could open your heart, free you in ways that were never possible in that northern clime. If you could come to me, for a week, a day? Will you come?"

For a time, I considered accepting his invitation and even toyed with the wording of a response. "Dear Vicar, to walk with you upon the beach, to share the rhythms of the undulating waves, to feel the sun's glow warm upon our backs, our faces, that would be heaven, indeed. How I desire it and to hear your sweet voice pour wisdom into my ears again..."

Of course, his proposition was ludicrous. Aunt Julia, because of my illness and her dislike of the vicar, would never countenance the journey. Knowing that impossibility, my thoughts were bold, shameless, perhaps. But no matter. In the end, I made no reply. What was the good of it? Because of the distance, I would never see Vicar Soames again. He was as dead to me as my parents. I had to bury him with silence. Eventually, his letters stopped coming. It was no more than I expected. And yet, I confess to feeling betrayed. He should have prized me more.

Happily, a new man soon arrived to assume the community's pastoral duties, a man I thought to be interesting in that he reminded me of my father. Vicar Flemming was of middle height, a broad-shouldered man with a coarse beard and an uneven gait that suggested time spent at sea. His wife, Eva, by contrast, was thin and colorless, except for her mass of auburn hair.

I found her cloying. She insisted upon clinging to her husband's arm during the round of social receptions that were arranged upon their arrival. Perhaps she sensed the disparity in their talents and was afraid to lose sight of him lest he find someone more his match. Some observed this same behavior and thought her manners sweet—men, especially, for whom it would be natural to think that a woman should live in her spouse's shadow.

Aunt Julia's reaction, when she heard my opinion, was a disappointment. She defended Mrs. Flemming. "She strikes me as being a good and dutiful wife, Victorine. Someone whose demeanor you might study. You'll be a wife one day, God willing."

Being a spinster herself, I doubted that my aunt's advice was coinage but the words did make my skin crawl. I was fifteen with no desire for marriage, especially since most of the males in our village shared a common want of intellect!

My father had been an exception. He'd served as vicar of our church until his death five years earlier when he and my mother were killed in a house fire, whilst I was away, visiting my aunt. I had adored my father. Like our new vicar, he too had been of medium height, dark and craggy, and like him, seemed more framed for hard labor than for a life upon the pulpit. But, unlike the farmers and tradesmen who populated our community, my father had been a scholar, attentive to the Scriptures and preoccupied with questions of the eternal. Some thought him too serious, even moody, but he was never so with me. I could interrupt him whenever I liked—a privilege not afforded my mother and which, I suspect, raised her ire. I would often be accused of being spoiled, though not within my father's earshot. She held her tongue in his presence; though sometimes when he sat me on his knee before the evening fire, her expression verged on anger or possibly, apprehension. I was never sure which.

I only knew that I never could please my mother. If I brought her picked flowers, she'd dump them in water and forget to arrange them in a vase. A drawing brought home from school was her opportunity to criticize. "Cows aren't green, Victorine. Grass is green. Surely there are enough cows in Braxton for you to know better." Even her acknowledgement of my successes was faint. "I met your teacher on the High Street today. She was full of praise for the fairy tale you wrote. I wonder that you didn't submit a poem as we agreed. A poem requires more *talent*, surely."

If my father detected my mother's ambivalence toward me, he never spoke of it and I kept my silence, seeing no other recourse but to try harder to please her. The task sometimes plunged me into deepest despair, especially on those nights when the voices of my parents rose above their usual murmurings and my name filtered back to me. I hated to hear them argue, especially as I was the cause. On those occasions I would fall asleep, crying.

The new pastor's similarity in form and feature to my father did much to explain my immediate interest in him. I felt a kinship between us the moment we met. When he announced that he would soon resume his duties as my Biblical teacher, I was elated. And I confess that on the morning of my first lesson at Windmill Cottage, my heart and my head were filled with butterflies. I'd barely slept the night before and had risen early so that Aunt Julia would have time to plait my wild, black tresses with ribbons.

"Such a peacock," she teased, staring at my reflection in the mirror when she'd finished. Then she uttered a sigh. "Seeing you like this, I'm reminded of how much you resemble your poor mother. She was quite the beauty in her day, though I doubt it brought her much joy."

"I don't recall that anything did," I said, allowing the memory of her to pass through me like a shadow. Then I shrugged and took another turn before the glass, determined to let nothing spoil the day.

I confess to being satisfied with my reflection. I might have wished to be taller, not so petite, and that my complexion was less pale; but my eyes were a gift from my mother, large and violet and on this day, they sparkled with expectation. My sole regret was that I wore a serviceable gray gown instead of my blue one. Aunt Julia had insisted that I make a sober first impression, an idea completely foreign to my own; but when I saw what an admirable job she had done with my hair, I gave no complaint and followed her, meek as a lamb, down the stairs for a final inspection of the parlor.

There, the curtains were drawn back to let in the light and as it was a cold November day, a fresh fire had been set. The room was perfect. No detail had gone unattended. Greens, in lieu of flowers, filled the vases and stood out against the background of whitewashed walls and Tudor beams. On every chair, chintz cushions had been plumped to their maximum. Still, I continued to pace, fearful of some oversight. It seemed an eternity before the hall clock struck three.

Hearing it chime, I ascended the stairs to my room, hoping for a good view of the gate. A minute passed, then two, but there was no sign of the vicar—neither in the street beyond the picket fence, nor anywhere on the gray horizon. When a quarter of an hour had passed and he was still missing, I was beside myself.

"Do you see him yet?" Aunt Julia called up from the hallway. I told her no and despaired that he'd forgotten us. But no sooner had I spoken, than I caught sight of him. He came flying down the street like a man chased by dogs, his hat grasped firmly in one hand. The garden gate squealed its warning and before I had time to offer a warning of my own, his knock could be heard on the front door.

"Never mind, Vicar. Never mind," my aunt could be heard cooing. "Tucked away as we are on the edge of the moor, we're only too glad that you found us."

They commenced into the parlor and closed the door behind them to keep in the fire's heat, and I could hear nothing more. What were they were talking about? I wondered. Was it me? Was Aunt Julia amusing our guest with stories about my nervous flittering as I awaited him?

Knowing that she would be inclined to do so, I should have hurried downstairs. But a stronger impulse had prevented me. I wanted to make an entrance: I wanted to hear conversation stop, to enjoy the element of surprise as our visitor turned to gaze at me, his eyes taking me in, perhaps admiringly.

What I'd not reckoned with was that my guardian should take such a fancy to the vicar that for an interminable period my absence would go unnoticed. No call came from the stairwell. No voice chided me to hurry along. I feared that if I failed to make an appearance soon, I might be entirely forgotten! Horrified, I ran from my room without a final glance into my mirror.

"Dear child, I was wondering what delayed you. Not still primping, I hope." Aunt Julia turned a puckish face in our guest's direction. "She was in such a state earlier. Afraid you'd forgotten her."

Color rose to my cheeks as I shouldered past her, a frailty she was quick to note. "You seem a little flushed, dear. I hope you're not coming down with something. What do you think, Vicar? Doesn't she seem flushed to you?"

The man in the frock coat came forward, eyed me intently, and with much appreciation in his voice said, "If I'm to be allowed an opinion regarding the young Miss Ellsworth, I should say she's looking well. Very well, indeed."

I feared he might be making fun of me, but the effect of the shadow cast by his prominent brow, the mouth being thinly drawn and the jaw squared, led me to hope that here was a man of character who might be trusted. For what seemed an eternity, we peered into one another's eyes. I could feel my cheeks grow warm again and was forced to lower my gaze for fear he might read too much in my expression. He turned away, perhaps as a courtesy to me, and addressed my aunt.

"My prescription for the young lady, and I confess, for myself, would be a strong cup of tea. Could you manage that, Miss Ellsworth?"

At his question, Aunt Julia lept to attention. "Of course, Vicar. I've laid out a lovely tea. It's in the kitchen. I'll just bring it in, shall I?"

Without waiting for her guest to reply, my guardian disappeared behind a swinging door, leaving her apologies behind like a trail of fallen leaves. The vicar and I were alone. I was so nervous I could feel a slight tingling in my left hand. *Oh, God, oh, God,* I prayed, silently. *Please don't bring on an attack. Please don't make me appear grotesque before this man.*

I focused my eyes on the Oriental pattern of the carpet at

my feet. If I could concentrate, I might hold back the tingling sensations that were creeping up my arm. I knew that I should sit down. My thoughts were becoming sluggish, floating idly in my head like goldfish in a bowl of water. I moved toward one of the chairs by the fire and the warmth seemed to revive me. Perhaps I was not having an attack after all. Perhaps I was simply nervous.

Aunt Julia returned with a trolley at that moment, and seeing the vicar and I still standing, encouraged us to sit down, an order with which I was happy to comply. Our guest seated himself in the chair opposite me and stared with pleasure at the array of treats my aunt had assembled. How so many towers of biscuits, trifles and tarts could be piled upon on a single tray seemed a feat of magic. My guardian had outdone herself—and to such a degree that a person with a suspicious mind might have accused her of raiding the local pastry shop. However, the vicar and I were inclined to raise no questions concerning the source of this bounty. We dug into our tea and were profuse in our compliments.

Beyond being an excellent hostess, my guardian was also something of a raconteur and while we ate, clotted cream trickling down our chins, she regaled the vicar with the local gossip—meant only, she protested, to acquaint him with his new parish. The stories, however, were told with sufficient animation to keep him enthralled. He learned, for example, that Constable Mills, a sleek young man with a shock of red hair, had recently purchased a bicycle in London. It was glossy black with a padded seat and a bright, shiny bell which, when rung, was loud enough to be heard across the Commons.

"Regrettably," said my aunt, leaning forward as though confiding to a pair of co-conspirators, "young Mills took too great a fancy to his new bell. It could be heard late into the night. Everyone was annoyed by it. Then one afternoon, he went too far. He rang his contraption as he was passing Anthea, Miss Clemmons, a teacher at the Leland Girls' School. He was on the High Street at the time and I'm sure he meant nothing but a greeting by it. Still, she was so taken aback that she lost her balance, spun round and, as she's not a small woman, brought the pair of them crashing on to the cobblestones."

Tears of laugher formed in the corners of Aunt Julia's eyes as she recalled the incident. "Anthea, you will learn, Vicar, does not take humiliation lightly. She threatened to bring a charge of disturbing the peace against our young constable and would have, too, if it hadn't been for her friend, Elliot Pounder. He's the music teacher at the Chapman School for Boys. He promised to have a word with his former pupil and apparently his admonishment had its effect. The bell is seldom heard now, except on occasions — like that time, just before you came, when a crate bounced free of a lorry and spilled a load of chickens onto the Commons."

Aunt Julia sat wiping her eyes with her hanky. In a moment she would go on to snipe about Mrs. Snively's penchant of large hats or the ambition of her fellow Church Councilman, Robert Crowley, to be appointed as a local magistrate. She was prevented from it, however, by the chiming of five bells upon the hall clock.

"Dear me, where has the time gone?" said the vicar, returning a biscuit to the tea tray. "I shall be late for vespers." That said, he leaped from his chair and, giving his hostess a handshake with his thanks, he rushed from the cottage forgetting me, my lesson and almost forgetting his coat — which he was quick to retrieve before trotting down our gravel footpath in the direction of the church. Disappointed, I watched him go with his coattails flying behind him like a pair of crow's wings.

Afterwards, Aunt Julia and I returned to the customary silence of the parlor. The cushion upon which the vicar had sat still carried his indentation, but that and the extra cup and saucer, were the only evidence of his visit. For me, he might as well have been a dream as we had barely spoken.

With some annoyance, I watched my aunt, humming to herself, as she loaded the trolley with the empty dishes and headed for the kitchen. For her, the afternoon had been a success. For me, it had been a failure. Whether the vicar returned tomorrow or each week thereafter, I had been robbed of the present, and for me, given the vagaries of my illness, the present was all I could rely upon. Standing at the center of the empty parlor, I could feel my energy dissipate as if into a vacuum. Only the wind and the sound of a bare branch tapping against the window hinted at any signs of life.

❄ ❄ ✪

We received no other visitors until Saturday. Jeremy Simones made our deliveries on that day, bringing produce from his father's shop. He was a few months younger than I and didn't share my love for books, but we were close all the same, much to the envy of a number of schoolgirls who considered him handsome and wanted his attention for themselves. He had been kind to me since

8

early childhood, but I confess I took no romantic interest in him.

To his credit, the flirtations he endured never turned Jeremy's head. He remained modest throughout his life and could pass a mirror without pausing to admire his blonde reflection. Nor was he inclined to be like other boys his age, rowdy and full of mischief. What free time his father allowed, he spent designing gadgets or kites, which he flew along the cliffs at the edge of the moor. I'd often see him there during my solitary walks, chasing the wind with one of his paper birds. Sometimes he'd stop and we would walk together; but as he grew older a shyness, which I found amusing, took hold of him.

Aunt Julia was exceedingly fond of Jeremy and always had tea waiting when he arrived. They'd chat in the kitchen for an hour or more if his duties permitted, and could become so engrossed in their conversation that, if I joined them, which was not always the case, they could be slow to acknowledge my presence.

On the Saturday following the vicar's call, I made a point of seeking the pair out. I was hungry for news of our new cleric and hoped that Jeremy, as he made his delivery rounds, had collected some new information. By the time I joined them, their conversation was well underway.

"You mustn't think that because a man has manners that he's a fop or a dandy," Aunt Julia was lecturing. "That would be false. Very false, indeed. Learn by his example and you'll escape growing up to be a lout. You wouldn't want that, would you?"

"My pop's not like him and he's no lout."

"No. Your father's a fine man. A man of character and integrity. But you could learn from someone else all the same."

"Who?" I asked, by way of announcing myself.

Jeremy and Aunt Julia looked up from the table.

"We're having tea, Victorine. Would you like some?"

"Yes, please." I slid into the chair my aunt vacated and looked Jeremy in the eye.

"Who were you talking about just now? You sounded annoyed."

The blue-eyed boy opposite me colored a little. "I'm not annoyed. We was just talkin'."

"Jeremy thinks the new vicar's a bit affected," replied my aunt with her back to us. "That's because he's a man of good breeding. We don't see much of that in these parts. It makes him stand out."

"Maybe so. But what's the good of breedin' around a lot of cows? If he wants to put on airs, he's best off in London or Paris where they fancy that sort of la-de-da." Jeremy wrung his cap as he spoke.

"My, my. Whatever's got your back up?" Aunt Julia chuckled. "The man's not been here much more than a month."

"Dunno. It's a feelin', I guess. Like he can't be trusted. "

"Can't be trusted? What nonsense. He's a man of God! Victorine likes him. Tell him, dear. Didn't the three of us have a jolly visit Wednesday?"

I took the cup that was handed me and paused while my aunt drew another chair to the table. "I don't know. Maybe Jeremy's right..."

"What?" My guardian's eyes widened.

"Well, he doesn't have much in common with the farmers and shopkeepers of the village, does he?" I shrugged. "As you said, he's too cultured."

"I didn't say *too* cultured."

"Well, he is and you know it. He doesn't belong in this wasteland."

Aunt Julia's chest swelled to the size of a pillow. She always bridled at my attacks upon Braxton. "I wouldn't call our village a wasteland, dear. Ours is a pretty place. Peaceful and quiet—"

"It's a wasteland!"

"It's not the hurly-burly of London, I admit. But not everyone finds that sort of life attractive. We had several applicants for his position, you know."

"Several?"

"Yes, Victorine. Several!"

The grocer's son flashed me a conspiratorial smile. "Point is, he works too hard at tryin' to impress other folks. All that talk about art and books. In the end, people around here will come to resent it."

"Yes, they will." I nodded. "But that's because they're fools."

Jeremy slumped back in his chair, uncertain of the meaning of my reply. He'd imagined me his ally until that moment. "'Is that what you think of me, then? Am I a fool?"

"Not a fool." I dropped a lump of sugar into my peppermint tea and let the pungent aroma fill my lungs. "But your studies never do come first, do they?"

"I like school, well enough..."

"Yes, but you don't read much. That's true, isn't it?"

"Haven't time. What with work and lessons—"

"And all those hours you spend on the moor flying your kites?

What about then?"

Jeremy's face grew red. He might have given me a retort but Aunt Julia interceded.

"Hush now, the pair of you. I'd like a bit of peace today. Besides, Victorine, Jeremy is our guest."

"Our guest? He practically lives here."

"What a wicked thing to say, dear! You make it sound as if Jeremy isn't welcome..."

The grocer's son scraped back his chair and rose, glaring at me. "It's all right, Miss Ellsworth. Everyone knows your niece is full of opinions. Not that anyone cares."

"Don't be upset, Jeremy. Victorine doesn't mean—"

The back door slammed before my guardian's sentence could be finished.

Turning towards me with her hands on her hips, she gave me a stern look. "Victorine Ellsworth! I'm astonished. Why bait the poor boy like that, especially with his mother in her grave less than a year? He comes here for a bit of comfort and that's as it should be. That boy's been a great help to us and a good friend to you. You've no call to mock him."

I shrugged as if to make light of her accusations, but I admit I felt guilty. I had been too harsh, turning on him the way my mother used to turn on me. That wasn't my intent. He was a good friend. He didn't loathe me for my illness, nor was he jealous of my talents. I trusted him; but in truth, my trust had its limits. He was to me, like a pet, a large, gangling Labrador that made no judgments but also lacked in understanding. From a friend, I wanted more, much more.

Unlike me, Jeremy never plumbed beneath the surface of appearances, was never curious about the secret lives of other people, their innermost fears, passions, morbid desires. And if I goaded him in those directions, he would gaze at me with his wide, blue eyes, reflecting his confusion, rather than any comprehension. He was, in sum, too loving, too forgiving of my twisted inclinations.

After giving me a proper chiding, Aunt Julia sent me to my room to contemplate the error of my ways. I could not feel ill-used by her rebuke, but my penitence was short-lived. Much of the time, I spent daydreaming about our new cleric. If I gave any thought to Jeremy, it was to wonder why he had taken such a dislike to the man. That was not his way. As I have said, he was usually too generous in his thoughts. Confronted by his opinion, which was so distant from my own, I became curious as to the reason. Indeed, the more I thought on it, the more curious I became and vowed to seek Jeremy out the following Monday.

✪ ❀ ❀

When Jeremy saw me waiting for him in the High street, he looked surprised. Breaking from his gaggle of classmates, he jogged toward me, wary of my mood but caring nothing for the taunts the other boys hurled at his back.

My smile reassured him and the moment he was at my side, he apologized for his behavior on Saturday. "I don't know why I got angry. I know how smart you are. You've won so many school prizes. I'm proud of you, honest. But sometimes...well...I don't always know how things stand between us. I get confused."

We began walking past rows of shops while I considered how to answer him. His charge was true. We were growing apart, not because he was the son of a shopkeeper and I had my roots in the gentry. That difference was real but of no consequence. Had I cared for him the way I sensed he cared for me, the difference in our stations would have been no impediment. I'd have thrown caution aside.

No, the growing distance between us stemmed, as I have said, from the difference in our natures. But how could I tell him that? How could I trust a friend with so little imagination? He was content with his lot while I... I hated mine—my infirmity, the suffocating village in which I was buried. I even hated myself, at times. He could never understand my despair. He'd make light of my feelings or, if I could make him see, he'd be bound to hate my dark thoughts. There was no way to explain my vicissitudes so I apologized for my behavior, as well, and said that I was on edge because of my upcoming exams.

The lie satisfied his gullible nature. Seeing him satisfied served to increase my loneliness.

We were approaching his father's shop when he paused to put a hand on my shoulder. As if attempting to read my thoughts, he said. "You like this new vicar, don't you? He's not a lout, like me, is he?"

"I never called you a lout. You're putting words in my mouth."

Jeremy's smile displayed a row of teeth that were white and even. "Oh, I'd never put words in your mouth, Victorine. You got enough of those already."

When I didn't return his smile, he rubbed his hand across the back of his neck. "I don't know why I said that. It was stupid. No wonder you think I'm a fool..."

"I don't think you're a fool. Nor does anyone else."

"Your aunt says I might turn into one."

"She doesn't mean it the way you make it sound. Besides, don't take too much stock in what she says. She called me a beast after you left on Saturday..."

"She didn't! She couldn't. I'm the one who was bein' stupid."

"You should have stayed to tell her that. I spent the entire afternoon in tears."

"Because of me?"

"Who else?"

My companion stared at his boots. "Gosh. I dunno what to say. I feel rotten."

"Say that we're still friends and that you forgive me."

He took the hand I held out to him and peered at me with a solemn expression. "It's me who should be askin' for forgiveness. I really am a lout, you know."

When I made no reply, he went further with his apology. "Look, from now on I'll keep my thoughts to myself. If you like the vicar that should be good enough for me."

We were stopped beside a crate of apples outside his father's shop at the time. I could see Mr. Simones waiting inside for his son. I picked up one golden orb and pretended to examine it. "You mustn't make me out to be such a tyrant, Jeremy. I expect you to be honest. If something's put you off about the man, then you must tell me. I might agree. You trust me, don't you?"

The shadow cast across my companion's face was not only from the fallen lock of his hair. He seemed torn between his desire to answer truthfully, yet do no harm. "I...It's not that I don't trust you, Victorine. It's just that..."

His father's call seemed to come as a relief to him. He started to back away. "I can't talk now, Victorine. Maybe later. But I don't know nothin'. Honest."

Two

OVER THE NEXT several weeks of Biblical studies, I came to learn that Vicar Flemming was like me in ways I could not have imagined. He took a deep interest in the lives of other people, deeper than was required by his spiritual calling. He was a collector of personal diaries, most of which were obtained by haunting auctions or estate sales, and sometimes seized properties from bankruptcies. The most prized were those written in a hand that gave additional insight into the author's temperament: thin, wiry lines, denoting words scribbled in haste, or round sloping letters with a happy, upward slant. Notes tacked into the margins also made the manuscripts valuable, and though most of the chronicles revealed little more than the ebb and flow of ordinary lives—deaths, births, weddings—there was one that he kept under lock and key.

I learned of this peccadillo from Aunt Julia who'd found the vicar in the church office one day, so engrossed in his reading that she was almost upon him before he noticed her. He shot up the moment he saw her and, looking a bit sheepish, swept the manuscript into a drawer, which he then locked. She seemed to take umbrage at this unnecessary measure of security. "I can't imagine what could be so important about a musty old book," she sniffed over our tea later that same afternoon. "I'm sure I wouldn't want to read it if it were offered."

Naturally, learning of the book's existence and the precautions the vicar had taken to keep it secure presented both a mystery and a challenge. He had invited me to browse through his library on several occasions and while the selection was varied, much of the material was academic bearing on religious argument or history. Nothing had ever caught my eye that required that it be secreted away. So, what was the nature of this book that the vicar meant for his eyes only? I decided to find out.

My opportunity came on a mild afternoon in February. The vicar had gone to a conference in London, leaving my aunt in charge of the floral arrangements for Sunday's service. Together she and I carried armloads of hellebores to the church, the only perennial that was blooming as yet. I admired these little flowers, frothing in pink and white clusters above their lustrous leaves. They had no scent but their exuberant defiance of the snow, their seeming passion for life despite the hostile surroundings in which they found themselves, lifted my spirits.

The moment we arrived, Aunt Julia sent me to fetch flower vases. They were kept in the small kitchen which was used to set teas for meetings of the Church Council. Two doors away was the vicar's office. With no one to observe me, I thought it an excellent time to explore his premises in the hope that I would chance upon the mysterious volume that had been secreted away. With luck, I might find the drawer unlocked. In any case, there was time to search for a key, as Aunt Julia would be preoccupied for a time with sorting out her flowers. My absence would go unnoticed.

The door to the study was unlocked, as were most doors in our village, and as I entered I discovered the room was in disarray. So many books were stacked in precarious piles on the vicar's oak desk that the carved claws at its base seemed to strain under the weight. Papers scribbled with notes for a sermon were scattered on it like snow flakes, a few having come to rest on the floor. Such untidiness was uncharacteristic so I assumed that the vicar had left the premises in great haste. Further evidence of this fact came in the form of his pipe, which normally he kept with him. It lay on its side, spilling cold ashes in all directions in the center of the desk.

To my delight, I discovered that none of the drawers were locked; but upon opening one after the other, my disappointment became immeasurable. I found no evidence of a scurrilous manuscript, only writing materials—pens, ink bottles, blank paper—and a tobacco pouch that smelled like the rain drenched earth, all elements of an ordinary life.

After a few moments of surveying the contents of the room, I began to wonder if the vicar, clever man that he was, might have hidden his treasure in plain sight. Perhaps it was tucked away somewhere among the many rows of books that lined the walls of his study from floor to ceiling. As I considered the possibility, my spirits fell. To find one volume among so many seemed a daunting task, especially as I had neither the time nor any knowledge of the object's appearance. Was it leather-bound or a collection of sheaves? Was it large or small? Aunt Julia was the only person who'd had a glimpse of it and I saw no way of making her my collaborator. Indeed, she'd be scandalized to discover that I had intruded upon the vicar's privacy and for what purpose.

I confess that I, too, was surprised by my audacity. Yet, much of the blame I laid upon my aunt. Why present me with a mystery if I was not meant to solve it? Certainly, she was curious about the book. Nature may abhor a vacuum, but Aunt Julia abhorred a secret even more. She made a habit of ferreting out details of the lives of everyone in the village. Her mental inventory included not only the number of hats Mrs. Snively owned but the number of trips Mr. Cowley made to London in a year, or the quantity and types of bulbs Elliot Pounder ordered for his garden each planting season. She might deny an interest in the vicar's secret if I were to charge her with it, but if she thought I possessed any knowledge, she'd be relentless in her pursuit of it.

And I would have been happy to oblige if she, for her part, had obliged me with some hint of the book's appearance. I had no such information. To discover that, I would need her assistance. But how was I to obtain it? Some subterfuge was doubtlessly required, perhaps even one that might lead her to search the premises. Standing in the pale gray light of a half-opened window, I waited for an idea. When it came, the ruse was simplicity itself.

"Aunt Julia! Come quickly. Come at once!" My voice was high and shrill, like a bird's when it is startled from the nest.

Hearing it, Aunt Julia behaved predictably. Her footsteps clattered across the stone tiles of the chapel as she hurried toward the kitchen. Finding the space empty she commenced to the adjoining hall.

"Victorine, where are you?" Not waiting for my answer, she hurried to the study where, having flung open the door, she appeared in the vacancy like an apparition, pale and breathless.

"What is it dear? Is it a seizure? Are you having an attack?"

"You might think so, Auntie, from the fright I was given when I entered this room. I came because I heard something, a thumping, like the sound of a bird hitting a window. I wasn't sure what it was, but when I saw the condition of the room… Well, you can see for yourself. It looks as though someone has been rifling through the vicar's belongings."

Aunt Julia, paying little attention to my words, put her hand on my forehead. "You mustn't excite yourself, dear. Remember what Dr. Leach told you…"

"I'm fine, Auntie, really." In my annoyance, I swept her hand away. "I'm trying to tell you that I think there's been a theft. Look about you. See how all the desk drawers are open. Didn't you say the vicar kept a valuable book locked in one of them?"

"I-I don't know that it was valuable," my aunt sputtered.

"It must have been. See for yourself. The book is gone."

My guardian peered over the desk to satisfy herself that the book was not in evidence. "Perhaps he's taken it with him," she shrugged.

"Oh, but Auntie, dearest, look at this room. The vicar's so meticulous. He'd never leave his study in this condition, with things strewn about the place."

"He could have been in a hurry. I myself have sometimes..."

"But I tell you, I heard something, someone moving about in this room."

"It could have been the wind."

"There's no wind today. You remarked upon that yourself. I'm certain someone was here and left by the window when he heard me coming. Oh Auntie, at least help me look for the book. If we find it then I will be satisfied that you are right and that I have been imagining."

"But, Victorine, there are hundreds of books in this room..."

"A quick search, nothing more."

"I'm not sure I remember what it looks like, and we really ought to be attending to the flowers. They'll be wanting water soon."

"Please, Auntie."

I heard a sigh and knew my point had been won. "Oh, very well, a quick search, then. But if it's not here, that's no proof that anything's been stolen. As I say, the vicar may have taken it with him."

"Yes, yes. You're probably right, but just in case..."

I followed my aunt intently as her eyes scanned the row of books closest at hand. Her sighs and piping protests told me the search would be cursory and brief. I was almost without hope when I heard a chortling. "Ah, here it is!" Aunt Julia snatched a thin volume from among a row of books, rifled briefly through the pages then placed the object my hands.

"As I thought. Nothing's been stolen. Really, Victorine, you must learn to curb your imagination."

"Are you sure this is the book, Auntie?" I could hardly believe my good fortune. "The one the vicar had locked away?"

My guardian squared her shoulders. "I can assure you, there's nothing wrong with my eyesight. That *is* the book the vicar placed in the desk. I know it by its black-ribboned binding. Rather a crude assemblage. I doubt the piece is worth much. Now, I hope you're satisfied and we can return to our purpose."

My father's sister headed for the door, never doubting that I would return the manuscript to its proper place, being as she often described me, "a dutiful niece." But on this occasion she would be wrong. If the slim volume that I now possessed contained some secret, I felt certain it would draw me closer to the vicar. If so, I had to know what it was and so, instead of returning the object to its place on the shelf, I tucked it into the bodice of my gown.

❄ ❄ ❄

I delighted in the freedom of my room that night. The darkness rendered me safe from prying eyes. And if the moon provided enough light to create silhouettes on the landscape, these were meant more to mystify than to illuminate. In that silvered world, metaphor was real. A tree, a shrub did not *seem* to be a spirit: it was! At least, such was my mood as I withdrew the vicar's treasure from beneath my pillow where I had hidden it.

Holding the book in the half-light of my candle, my fingers explored the rough frontispiece while I savored the notion that in a few moments its mystery would be revealed. Did it contain a story, a lover's tryst, perhaps? The outpourings of a broken heart? Or was it a confession to some heinous act? A shiver ran through me as I turned the page and my eyes fell upon...

What blasphemy is this? My thoughts screamed out in anger. Here was no titillating account of an amorous adventure, no confession of murder. Here was a compilation of lists. Lists! Names, dates, a calendar of events for some wretched little village like my own. These sundries, together with a few boring notes scribbled into the margins seemed to be the sum and total of the book's contents.

I felt myself to be the victim of some hideous jest. Perhaps my aunt had conspired with the vicar to teach me a lesson meant to curb my curious nature. If so, Aunt Julia was the last person to lecture on that subject. Nor did it seem likely that my spiritual mentor would betray me with such a game. Still, how was I to understand the vicar's purpose in keeping so innocuous a document under lock and key?

I could think of no answer and came near to ripping the leaves from their stitching when a pressed lily, aged to transparency, stayed my hand,[18] drifting unexpectedly, as it did, from the pages and settling on my comforter. How many years it had been tucked away I could not say, but it must have been ages for its beauty was enhanced by its frailty.

Turning the pages with haste, I found the spot where the flower's image had been fossilized. It marked the beginning, I would discover, of a narrative that was at once melancholy and moving.

Three

I N LIFE THERE is no surcease from desire; yet desire must be resisted. To yield is to suffer endlessly in this world and the next. Once we succumb, we are little more than animals, driven by our passions and left to forage in a world where beauty and innocence are valued only in proportion to which they satisfy, nay, dull our appetites.

Once, in a peaceful farming community, there lived a mason's apprentice called, Nathan. Being considerably younger than his work mates, he was often the butt of their pranks. These he endured with humor, finding it easy to laugh at himself. This good nature won him much admiration and so he never lacked for company. Indeed, despite the scarcity of his years, he was a leader among men.

In that village was a factory where leather gloves were made. The owner was treated with respect, not only because he provided employment, but because he possessed a title—being distantly related to the royal family. Although he put little stock in such trappings for himself, he was scrupulous where they pertained to Elizabeth, his daughter and only child. As he was a widower, he lavished upon her all that money and position could provide. She was a beautiful girl and except for common sense, of which she had none, she seemed extraordinarily blessed.

That the mason's apprentice was enamored of Elizabeth, who had no notion of his existence, was clear to his companions. Who could be blind to his long, lingering gaze whenever she passed? Inevitably a round of good-natured ribaldry ensued. "Hey Nathan, when's the wedding?" Or, "Have ya bought the ring yet, lad?" These jibes the youth took well enough, though a rosy color would glow upon his cheeks as bright as any maiden's. At night, however, his dreams were of a different character—fraught with a passion so intense that his days were plagued by guilt.

In time he began to sicken, torn between his desire for Elizabeth and his feelings of unworthiness. He continued to work hard but without an outlet for his passion, his former humor left him. Over time, he found the good-natured taunting of his mates difficult to bear. He took solitary walks upon the beach to escape—a habit which did nothing to assuage his melancholy, but rather, inflamed it. And if his eyes retained their luster, they served no purpose but to stare into the distance.

His comrades wondered at the change, yet none could guess the reason. To be driven mad by love? Such depth of feeling was beyond their understanding. Witchcraft would have made a more convincing argument. Or an ague. And so they scratched their heads and left him to his solemnity, hoping time would affect a healing.

Sadly, they were wrong. Time was the acid that exacerbated his wound. A month passed, then two, leaving Nathan enthralled with no hope of respite. Elizabeth remained oblivious to his existence and hopelessly unattainable. Given this disparity in their stations, that one heart would break was predictable, but no one could foresee that it would be two.

The tragedy began on a day that seemed promising. Word came to the guild that a work crew was needed at the manor house. Nathan was among those hired and as the residence was Elizabeth Dernwood's, his companions took note of the fact by ruffling his hair and making lewd suggestions.

The boy endured these taunts with remarkable good will. After all, what lover bemoans a fate that ties him to his beloved? Each day was to be filled with the sight of her—Elizabeth walking along a corridor, among the flowers, or perhaps even acknowledging her admirer with a smile. That would be bliss. Or so Nathan thought, unmindful of the risks such attention might bring. No doubt he trembled upon entering the manor doors for the first time and finding a world so utterly foreign. Nothing in his life could have prepared him for what he saw. The paintings, tapestries and all the gleaming rows of gold and crystal bore witness to the folly of his passion for a person so high above his station. And yet, that hopelessness only goaded him.

That Elizabeth failed to acknowledge him at the outset was understandable. Nothing distinguished him from his fellow workers except a handsome profile. The boy took no umbrage. He was happy just to be near her. Besides, his nightly dreams continued to grant him certain liberties which, as they dissipated with the morning air, he grew to see as no disrespect to her but as a balm to him.

In time, however, these imaginings invaded his waking thoughts, as well. He could not gaze upon his beloved as she walked in sunlight and fail to recall how she had appeared to him on the previous night: naked, with her hair flowing across the pillow of his bed. That was how he longed to see her. And so, these images, intense and satisfying, began to gain mastery over him. The war between his conscience and his desire would have maddened many a man. Nathan was merely a boy.

In time, Elizabeth grew more and more conscious of his agitation but mistook it for shyness, an affliction common among the villagers. When she approached them, it was ever thus: that they should blush or giggle and stare at the ground. She was lonely, as a consequence of their behavior, but more, she longed to converse with someone near her age. That she refrained from doing so was evidence of her sensitivity and her desire to cause no discomfort.

When it became evident that his pallor was a permanent condition, she began to worry he might be ill or that he lacked proper sustenance. That she enjoyed so many advantages while he had few troubled her—for it must be noted that though she was ignorant about much in life, she was possessed of a loving and generous heart. Concerned as she was, it was natural that she should appeal to her father on behalf of the workers. He grumbled at first but in the end Elizabeth had her way, and each afternoon a table was set where the men were given a proper tea.

The masons looked kindly upon Elizabeth's intervention. Never before had a lady troubled herself on their behalf, and they strove to treat her presence among them as natural. That Nathan should be elbowed into her presence as much as possible was also a part of their plan. They did so out of mischief, to be sure; but they also felt empathy for their lovesick comrade. His station in society made it impossible that his feelings could ever be returned, but they hoped to foster a friendly acquaintanceship at least. To their satisfaction, the relationship did grow and flourish between the two young people. Before long, conversation flowed between them as easily as water through a mill; and though Nathan's grammar lacked refinement, Elizabeth understood him well enough and was grateful for his company.

How Elizabeth's father came to be aware of the attraction between them was not the result of personal observation but of common gossip. A village is a poor place for privacy. Without the diversion of other people's lives, one's sole amusement is to watch the rising and setting of the sun. To keep a secret, therefore, is unnatural. It must be told and remarked upon.

Sir Dernwood knew the ways of the village, accepted them and was as willing as any to bend an ear to someone else's secrets; but to hear his daughter's name joined with that of a mason's apprentice was more than he could bear. Perhaps, had there been more than one child in the Dernwood family, his temper would have been less severe. But there was no other. Elizabeth was sole heir to her father's obsession. That she should be linked by the barest thread of perception to one so far beneath her in station was not to be endured; and so her father sought the boy out at once and beat him senseless.

The man might have done worse but for the intervention of the other workers. There was no call, they said, to deal with the boy so cruelly; and making a stretcher for him, they carried the unconscious lad to his room above the Red Lion Inn.

For three days Nathan drifted in and out of wakefulness, ministered to by the barkeep and his wife. Friends came to visit, but they seemed to him no more than apparitions of a painful dream. Light fell like daggers upon his eyes and any movement was an insult to his senses. His only peace lay with the darkness to which his mind repeatedly returned.

When he saw how it was with Nathan, the doctor shook his head and rumor spread that the boy would soon die. But rumor too frequently relies upon exaggeration, which, in this case, happily proved to be the case. Given time, the vigor of his young body gained ascendance over his wounds. Nathan began to eat, a little broth at first, then gradually heartier fare that was consistent with his normal diet. Before the week was out, his wounds seemed nearly healed, though his hard thoughts remained implacable. The wrong that had been done to him festered. Not only was his livelihood threatened, but he had been denied access to his animus: that animating spirit which gave him the will to live and which he attributed to Elizabeth.

New fantasies visited him while he recuperated, plots, really, all with a common theme: the slow and torturous death of Sir Robert Dernwood. If there were any who imagined these poisonous thoughts would delay his recovery, they would be wrong. He grew more animated with each passing hour. Amazed, the doctor pronounced him nearly recovered, even allowed him to take short walks out-of-doors.

On warm days, he strolled the length of the Common, there to find himself greeted by smiling faces. The men and women of ordinary birth knew an injustice had been done to him. He had their sympathies. Some thought him a hero. But Nathan heeded none of their flattery. Could they but realize it, he was not truly among them. He dwelt in the parallel universe of his barbarous imaginings. Inevitably, on one of these excursions, Nathan encountered Elizabeth. Or rather, he sensed her. Perhaps the stricken looks on the faces of the villagers was a clue. Or perhaps there was some mysterious link between the two young people. Whatever the cause, he broke from his study of clouds and, looking across the village square, spied his beloved.

The girl stood gazing back at him. But the moment their eyes met, she broke off and hurried into a nearby shop without the slightest show of recognition. Nathan was devastated. Her father's cudgels were as kisses compared to her dismissal of him. Like one who had been dealt a fatal blow, he sank to the ground there to remain upon his knees until helped by a kindly passerby. The pain of his rejection was not physical, to be sure, but being of the mind, was far more devastating. He accused Elizabeth of all manner of deceits. Her interest in him had been no more than that of curiosity. His coarse manners and speech were no doubt an amusement to her. He could imagine how she and her father had laughed at him behind his back. He had been played a fool and he cursed them both, thinking it a thrift if they could be buried in the same grave.

In the days and weeks that followed, there was nothing in the girl's conduct to ameliorate his anger. The silence between them persisted. And if they met along some byway, she glided past as if he were a stranger. Poor Nathan. How could he know of Sir Dernwood's oath that any contact between the pair would result in the boy's further injury?

Ignorant of the cause for Elizabeth's neglect, Nathan's heart blackened. All tender sentiment was banished from him. Love, devotion, loyalty, these words were without meaning. In the future, he would be a creature carved from stone.

Without a scheme, his vow of evil was little more than invective; but by repetition it gained a life, provoking fantasies, which, when implemented, would succeed—if the destruction of a loved one can be called success. Nathan gave no thought to this question. He was too enthralled by malice.

One attribute more can be said to describe his state of mind—it was that he was patient. He knew that time was required to make the acquaintance of a servant girl from the manor and after that, still more time to gain her confidence—though the task proved easier than he imagined, given his good looks and winning manners. More to the point, village girls are a romantic lot, the least able to resist what they believe are entreaties of the heart; so this innocent whom Nathan had singled out, thinking herself to be Cupid's agent, finally agreed to carry his letters to her mistress. To his surprise, Elizabeth's replies were eager and effusive. Such ardor should have softened Nathan's heart or caused him to pause, at least. But he was blind to it and persuaded himself that she mocked him still. If anything, his thoughts grew more black.

In their exchanges, he began to press Elizabeth for an assignation. She refused, at first, mindful of her father's admonition. But against the claims of youth and the heart, reason has no armament. Finally, she agreed. The time, the place and the hour were set.

Before the bell tower had struck eleven, on that appointed evening, the Mistress of Dernwood slipped from the manor and hurried across the dunes, her cloak billowing, her eyes shining. Now and again she would pause, look back and listen, fearful that her father might be in pursuit. Sadly for her, he was not.

Gothic Spring

Finally, she found the object of her affection. He stood with his back to her gazing out to sea, the silhouette of a dark angel. Elizabeth paused a moment, still shy, unsure of herself; but the promptings of her heart grew too insistent. In the end, she ran forward and threw herself into the arms of her beloved.

What a joy to find him happy, though if she knew the cause she would have blanched in fear; for the smile that warmed her was no reward for her courage or the risk she had taken. Nathan saw none of that. His smile was for the vengeance he would reap upon her.

Certainly, his victim made his task easy. Childlike in his presence, she yielded to his embrace even as he grew insistent. Nor did she object to the kisses brushed along her throat. But when his lips fell hard upon hers, she pulled away, frightened by a rush of ecstasy that made her giddy. But Nathan continued to pursue her with sweet utterances. "I love you, Elizabeth, I love you." Words she longed to hear and which quieted her alarm as if they were an opiate.

Taking her into his arms once more, Nathan held her fast, caressing her with firm but gentle strokes until he felt her body go limp. Then by slow degrees, as she became all sighs and moans, he made himself known to her...

The moon was hiding its face in the western horizon when they made ready to part. Elizabeth would have lingered, despite the dawn, but Nathan made arguments touching upon her reputation and, at last, they went their separate ways—he with a step that was swift and sure; she with a measured one. Now and again the girl would pause and, with a melancholy longing, cast a backward glance in Nathan's direction. He, by contrast, kept his face turned toward the village.

In the days and nights that followed, Elizabeth's longing transmuted itself from bliss to fitful passion. Not one day but two, then three days passed with no word from her lover. Why was he silent? Was he ill? She felt certain that he must be and longed to fly to him, though she dared not for fear of her father. But when a week passed, then two more, with still no message, she dreaded that some darker force was at work.

Her first thought was to suspect the servant who carried their letters. Was she holding them back? If so, to what purpose? Perhaps the deluded creature wanted Nathan for herself? Certainly, he was handsome and carried himself well. He would make an enviable catch for a village girl; but when accused for her treachery, there followed such a cascade of tears and wailings that Elizabeth was convinced of her servant's innocence. There had to be some other explanation.

Had her father learned, somehow, of her assignation? Had he followed her that night, after all? If so, perhaps Sir Dernwood had carried out his threat against the mason's apprentice. Perhaps, even now, her beloved lay bleeding in a ditch with no one to attend him! Her duty was to fly to him! But where? How? Not knowing, she wrung her hands in utter despair.

At the height of this frenzy, word came to her of her darling boy: that he was well, robust even. The news brought no joy, but rather, made a trifling of her former misery, for it was said that he was seen carousing in the company of gypsies and women of the night and that he had taken up gambling, and drink, also. So changed was he, in fact, that the children of the village swore it was by witchcraft, though their parents felt otherwise and blamed Sir Dernwood for having beaten the poor boy senseless. In any case, all were saddened by the transfiguration. The women called him their fallen angel and prayed for his recovery.

Nightmares began to plague Elizabeth, as did fantasies, darker than her youth and privilege would have caused anyone to guess. Not that she doubted Nathan's love. She did not and, like the villagers, blamed Sir Dernwood for the transformation. But what was the remedy? She loved her father in spite of his threats. He had been her guardian, her protector, her entire life, and no doubt believed he was acting on her behalf even now. She could no more abandon him for his devotion than she could abandon the boy who loved her. Only one avenue of happiness existed, impossible though it may be—a peace must be affected between the two people she loved most.

Driven by this imperative, Elizabeth took to the streets. Once Nathan was found, she was certain, he would help her devise a plan to make the peace. Till then, nothing else mattered—not her position, not her pride, not even her appearance, which had grown wild enough to raise questions in the minds of even the most casual acquaintances. Certainly, old friends were stunned when she passed. They saw her large, staring eyes, her hair flying, her garments awry, and whispered, "There must be some history of insanity in the family."

When he learned she was looking for him, Nathan evaded her by making scouts of his cronies, the gypsies and thieves with whom he consorted. These lowlifes thought it an amusing game and with japes and sneers signaled for the youth to be away whenever she drew near. But upon one moonless night, as he walked alone, he was not so fortunate. The servant girl he had duped so ruthlessly emerged from the shadows to intercept him.

"Please, sir. My mistress is very poorly. You must come straight away."

"Poorly?" Nathan suspected a trick. "I'm sorry to hear it but why come to me? I'm no doctor."

"Please, sir. You must come. You must!" Gentle fingers trembled upon his arm. Tears sparkled in the lamplight. Nathan looked upon that sad face and felt ashamed.

"Take me where you will," he agreed. "I owe you that much."

When they reached the manor, he was led through the kitchen into the great hall where the grandfather clock was chiming midnight. In darkness they climbed to the upper floors, feeling their way through a maze of corridors until they stopped at a small oak door. Beneath it a crack of light shone. Nathan's guide gave a gentle rap and departed leaving him in the passageway. When the door opened, Elizabeth's face appeared. It was flushed with urgency.

"Thank God you've come!" she cried, pulling him into the light of her bedroom. "I was afraid my father had done you some wrong."

Nathan twirled upon his heels to prove that what she feared was not the case. He was well, in fact. Very well, indeed.

The Mistress of Dernwood placed her hand upon her heart as if to muffle its beating. "But you have been threatened, surely. Otherwise, why have you stayed away so long?"

"Stayed away?" He answered in a voice that reverberated with malice. "Given your father's beating and your snubbing, how was I to imagine that I would be welcome?"

"Oh, my dearest, I never meant to hurt you. I acted as I did to protect you from my father's wrath. I thought you understood."

The mason's apprentice made a sour face. "Indeed? Why should I know that? You never spoke!"

"And after our night together on the beach, you never wrote!"

This reply, so earnest, so fraught with logic, did nothing to assuage her lover's anger. Rather, it enflamed him more for, when he heard it, a flicker of doubt rose in his mind—doubt which he dared not entertain else he had misjudged her.

"This is some game you're playing to make a fool of me..."

"No, dearest, no!"

"But I'll not be tricked," he hurried on. "Your words are useless, Elizabeth. Useless! And you must stop following me about. If only you knew what people say behind your back. They call you Mad Elizabeth, Elizabeth the Demented, the Mistress of Dernwood Asylum..."

"Stop, please stop, my dearest. Your words are too cruel. If I have dishonored myself, I was blinded by my love for you!"

If this confession was meant to soften Nathan, it had no effect. He answered in a voice hard as granite. "Are you a truth teller, Elizabeth? I think not! You have lied even to get me here. I came because I was told you were poorly..."

"It's true! I have not slept. I cannot eat...."

"And so you sent for me? Why? To accuse me?"

"No! I swear that's not the reason. But be less angry. I begin to fear..."

"What do you expect from me if not anger, Elizabeth? First I am avoided, ignored by you and now hounded everywhere. What am I to make of these alterations? They are the acts of a mad woman."

"If I am mad, dearest, it is with good reason. I have longed to tell you, but now I am afraid, so afraid..." The girl clad in white covered her face with her hands and began to tremble. A fainter heart might have melted, seeing her so small and frail against the shadows, but the one who listened had steeled himself against pity.

"Do you imagine I'm taken in by this charade? Am I to believe you care for me so deeply? You? The Lady of Dernwood Manor in love with a mason's apprentice? I may be poor, Elizabeth, but I know my place well enough, especially after your father's beating. Though...." Here Nathan paused to deliver a stern look. "In your present condition, with your hair unkempt and those swollen eyes, I see little to distinguish us. You might easily pass as a vagrant."

The accusation, so cruel and yet near the truth, brought the object of Nathan's scorn to her knees. There she wept convulsively.

"Whatever I've become, it's you who have brought me to this pass. Call it madness, if you like, but I can think of nothing, no one but you, day and night. And now it seems the one I adore has rejected me. I am alone...so terribly alone!"

"What gibberish, Elizabeth! Get up. Get up, I say. If you go on like this, someone will hear us. Is that what you want? To be compromised?"

The Mistress of Dernwood Manor let out a wail sad enough to set the hounds at bay. "Oh dearest, dearest. I brought you here to tell you.... I am already compromised. I am with child!"

If a sentence of death had been pronounced upon the dark-eyed apprentice it could not have been more affecting. He staggered a moment, and then set his hand against the bedpost to steady himself. "Wh-what are you saying? A child? Are you certain?"

The question was a foolish one. A single glance at the abject creature lying at his feet and even the most devout cynic would have bowed to the truth. Nathan could not do otherwise and he was stunned. The bitter world he had so carefully built for so many days and weeks came crashing about his heels. He had been wrong. So wrong! Elizabeth was the dearest, sweetest creature ever to draw breath. For love of him, she had risked her wealth, her position and now her reputation. And what was her reward? To be ridiculed? Betrayed? Dishonored?

Shame, like the dark and murky waters of a bog, overwhelmed the trembling youth. What must he do? What could he say to her? In the entire world there was not enough remorse to amend the wrong he had done. Yet he must try...or tear out his eyes rather than gaze upon such misery.

"Elizabeth," he wept, kneeling down and taking her into his arms. "I love you. I love you." After that, words were no longer possible, for when their lips met, he smothered her with kisses.

They might have found their heaven, these lovers locked in an embrace, but at that exact moment, the bedroom door swung open and a man with a pistol emerged from the shadows. Elizabeth saw the metal's glint. "No, father! No!" she cried as with her body she moved to shield Nathan. But the pleading came too late. A burst had already sounded, one that was neither loud nor ominous but enough to summon Death.

Elizabeth collapsed in her lover's arms, a blow so stunning that he stared in disbelief.

Indeed, anyone happening upon the scene might likewise have been mystified. Except for the crimson stain trickling upon the Persian carpet, Elizabeth seemed to be dreaming. Certainly, her expression was tranquil. But if heaven showed itself in the girl, hell was mirrored in the faces of the two men who were joined by their mutual grief.

And now, in the world between heaven and hell, doors clicked open and slippered-feet padded along the hallway. Someone called for a taper. Other voices, too, were murmuring but, when a second shot rang out, they broke into cries of horror and dismay. Then a tumble of weeping figures broke into the bedroom and seeing that a life hung in the balance, they made wild gestures one to another, their dark pantomime being captured as shadows upon the cream-colored walls.

In the midst of this tumult lay Nathan and Elizabeth, their blood intermingling, though even as he clung to her, he could feel her limbs grow cold. How he begged her to wait for him! To tarry but a moment longer so they could make their journey together, for surely he must die... he wanted to die! But the Samaritans who bathed his wounds knew nothing of this desire and so, Life, in one so young, was helped to gain the upper hand. Nathan could feel its accursed stirrings even as he fell unconscious.

Four

Dawn was creeping into my room as I closed the pages of the diary. Wide-awake and exhilarated, I was also assailed by numerous questions. What had happened to Nathan and Sir Dernwood after so great a tragedy, and who had chronicled their story? As the homily implied, the purpose no doubt was to instruct, though I could see no real lesson in the story. I only felt its melancholy.

That I would never know the answer to these questions struck me as hard, a punishment, I supposed, for violating the vicar's sanctuary and making myself privy to his secret. But I knew I could not lay this history to rest until I had it out in the open with the vicar. The question was how to accomplish this purpose? Confessing that I had acted as a thief and a liar was a price I was unwilling to pay. I needed some other means to air my discovery and that conundrum occupied me for some time.

The afternoon was clear but crisp the March day when next I entered the vicar's office. He was deep into his work, preparing yet another sermon for yet another Sunday service. My interruption seemed welcome for he smiled and hurried forward with an outstretched hand. "Victorine, this is an unexpected pleasure. You are well, I see. Is your aunt with you?"

I told him no, that I was alone, and explained that I'd come for a new assignment, having finished the last. He looked both surprised and pleased, then made one or two suggestions to which I shook my head, asking if I might choose a reading on my own. He did not seem offended, even laughed, being well acquainted with my thirst for independence.

"By all means," he smiled, peering down at me. "I shall be fascinated to learn what interests you. A man of my years has little opportunity to acquaint himself with the tastes of a young lady."

"Oh, but you're not old, Vicar," I frowned. "Why, it can't have been many years since you were my age."

A slim finger wagged in my direction. "You needn't ply me with flattery, dear girl. I'm already putty in your hands. Choose whatever you please."

That said, the vicar returned to his desk and the flurry of papers he'd abandoned. For a suitable time, I made a pretense of browsing among the volumes stacked along the walls. Most of them were esoteric reference books, infrequently used, but some were dog-eared, indicating they held important wisdom for the vicar. These materials were of mild interest to me, as they provided insight into the man seeking the knowledge therein. But this exercise was a dalliance. My immediate purpose was to make the book, which I'd stolen and had concealed about me, appear to be found as a result of my perusing. With the vicar intent upon his writing, the task was easier than I would have imagined.

"What's this? Some sort of narrative, I think. Would it suit me?"

I half turned to face my mentor while he attempted to focus on the object at hand. His expression bore a look of concern when he recognized it; then he hurried forward, as if I had set the wall on fire.

"Not that one, Victorine. It's nothing of consequence. Try the Aquinas over there." His one hand waved me in the direction of a table, groaning under the weight of many books, while with the other he wrenched the manuscript from me, apparently for the sole purpose of tossing it into his desk drawer.

I admit to standing opened-mouthed. By his action, I was certain the story touched upon him in some way. But how? And to what degree? I decided to press him further.

"But you said I could choose whatever I liked. It's hardly fair to change your mind now. Besides, I know what it's about, having glanced through some of it."

By now the vicar had returned to his desk where he threw me a stern glance.

"How else was I to know if it would be of interest?" I shrugged. The answer failed to satisfy.

"You should have asked first."

"Why? Did I or did I not have your permission to choose whatever I liked?"

"I was talking about Scripture. That book has nothing to do with our studies. It shouldn't have been in the cupboard. I forgot it was in there."

"I don't see what the fuss is about. It's a love story, isn't it? I'm nearly sixteen. Surely I'm old enough for that." The vicar's pretense of not hearing made me more determined. "Shall we strike a bargain? Let me read what I want and I'll study two selections of your choosing. That's fair, isn't it?"

I bent over the desk where the vicar was seated so that he was obliged to reply. He threw down his pen, having made a pretense of returning to his work, and looked up. The square of his jaw led me to know he was as determined as I.

"As you say, you're nearly sixteen and capable of many things. One of them is to know that life doesn't always give us what we want. Whether you take one Aquinas or three, it doesn't change my mind in the least. Now be a good girl and chose something else. The subject is closed."

Wanting to see how far I could go, I stamped my foot. "I hate it when you treat me like a child. I'm not, you know. Neither am I naïve, nor an impressionable fool!"

The vicar remained unruffled. "No one's ever accused you of being a fool, surely. If my remark has given offense, I apologize. Nonetheless, my judgment stands. As you say, your selection may do you no harm; still, I am certain it will do you no good. I prefer that you make better use of your time."

"Must all my days be bent to some estimable purpose? What's wrong with whiling away an hour or two with a love story?"

"Did I say it was a love story? That was your surmise, I think."

"Well, it is, isn't it?"

"I very much fear that if I satisfy you on one point, I shall have to satisfy you on another. Next, you'll want to know whether it ends happily or not, and I shall have opened a Pandora's box."

"So I was right. It *is* a love story!"

Relenting, the vicar sighed and leaned back in his chair with his hands pressed hard against the edge of his desk. "My respect for your guardian grows by leaps and bounds. How does she cope, I wonder? Such resolve! Such energy! I'd sooner be pummeled by a storm... But yes, it is a love story. There, you have your answer. We'll speak of it no more. The room is awash in books. Choose another."

That said, his head, with its thick black hair, bent again to the task in front of him. A curtain had been drawn. The scene ended. Or so I was meant to believe. Poor vicar. How could he know that the stage was now set for a second act. I'd brought the existence of the manuscript to light and as time was on my side, the day would come when his patience would be tried further.

❋ ❋ ❋

The following Wednesday, he appeared at Windmill Cottage at his regular hour, this time with a peace offering, a collection of Shakespearean sonnets with my name inscribed on the frontispiece. Two or three of these were among his favorites, and he obliged me by reading them aloud in a well-modulated voice that did not lack for feeling. I was touched that he would do so, though my expression must have revealed that I was not as moved by the pieces as he. A brief period of instruction followed.

"The beauty of these sonnets is that they not only reveal Shakespeare's capacity for exquisite imagery and phrasing, but that they also tease the mind. Look here, at the one I read last. The body of the work seems sad. Beauty, it tells us, is no match against the ravages of time. Love is ephemeral. But, the couplet defies this truth. 'Yet do thy worst, old time: despite thy wrong. My love shall in my verse live ever young.' A turning point, you see. Time becomes love's servant, not its master."

"I see the paradox," I conceded, taking the book from him to read the poem for myself. "But yours is not the only interpretation. I have another."

The vicar raised his eyebrows.

"Isn't it possible that Shakespeare plays his poet for a fool? All things end, if Donne is to be believed—Death and Time itself. What becomes of the sonnet then, when there are no eyes to see? No ears to hear? I think Shakespeare mocks the arrogance of his besotted poet. He wants us to understand the folly of believing that Man can bestow immortality upon himself."

"My dear girl, what an astute observation!" The vicar slapped his thigh by way of exclamation. "Even if your reading contradicts Shakespeare's intent, it is a logical extension of his thought, and full of piety, I might add. Your aunt is to be credited for having nurtured such original thought."

"My aunt?" Now it was my turn to exclaim. "Mention Shakespeare to her, Vicar, and she'll assume you're referring to our chemist!"

A brief, involuntary smile illuminated the face of my companion. "A teacher, then? Miss Clemmons, perhaps?"

"She's not been my teacher for several years and to be honest, since I began studying at home, my contacts with anyone from Leland are slight. Various persons deliver my assignments each week, and if I have a question, which is rare, there's a brief instruction. Mostly though, I'm on my own. I'm not complaining, mind you. But if my thoughts strike you as unusual, the fault lies entirely with me."

"Originality is hardly a fault. It's a gift to be admired."

"Do you think so? I find it often puts me at odds with my fellow creatures. They either don't understand me, or if they do, they're shocked. In either case, it doesn't make for many pleasant conversations."

"Are you lonely, then?"

"Not lonely, Vicar. *Bored.* How could I be otherwise? Living in this tiny village where originality, as you call it, has no value. Where, every day is the same. People are the same. Only the weather changes."

"My dear girl, if only you could hear how well others speak of you..."

"What others? My aunt? Her associates? A few of my teachers, perhaps? I have no friends my own age."

"What about Jeremy? He's devoted to you. And there would be others, I'm certain, if your health allowed you more freedom. That may change in the future. Till then, consider how lucky you are to live in this bucolic village surrounded by peace."

"I don't want peace. I want *experience.* Surely, you can understand that. You've traveled, seen the world! What hope have I of doing likewise? My home is my prison."

"Oh, hardly that..."

"What then?"

"Your life is sheltered, that's true. But enviably so. I wish I could make you see."

"Take me to Paris. That way, at least I'd have some ground for comparison."

The vicar leaned into his wingback chair. His eyes drifted toward the east garden where a cherry tree was in bloom.

"Being young, I suppose it's natural to want to spread your wings. Certainly, I did. I was excited at first. But after a time, one begins to feel rootless, much like an exile. In the streets, people smile as they pass. But it means nothing, because, to them, you are nothing. A person needs roots, Victorine, as surely as does that cherry tree outside. Without roots, life becomes a never-ending drama in which one has no part to play. It's a lonely existence, I assure you. That's why Mrs. Flemming and I are happy to call this 'boring' little village of yours, our home."

Rather than contradict, as was my usual habit, I let the silence fall between us. Nothing he'd said had convinced me, but a faraway look in his eyes led me to believe he had more to say. "That love story you were curious about the other day," he began after a time. "I've decided to tell it to you—"

Clapping my hands in surprise, I received a stern warning. "Oh, it isn't going to be as wonderful as all that. You may become upset. Nonetheless, I want you to hear it. Promise me you will sit quietly and not interrupt. Will you do that?"

Nodding, I closed my eyes to indicate a rapt attention. After that, the entire story was poured into my ears and with such feeling that I felt myself transported to another time and place—though a small corner of me remained alert, sensitive to any alteration that would make the history less than true. I should be angry if the seduction scene was omitted, for example, or the ending softened in any way. It would mean I was being protected and thought of as a child. But to my joy, I was spared nothing. The compliment was so gratifying that when the vicar fell silent at last, I burst into tears.

"There now," my companion said, annoyed with himself. "You're upset, just as I feared. Your aunt will be cross with me."

"Oh, it isn't the story which was so affecting," I said, dabbing my eyes with the handkerchief that was offered. "It's the way you told it. So...*movingly.* You have a wonderful gift with words. They do whatever you like—jig, prance, pirouette."

Laughter greeted my remark. "High praise, indeed, coming from one whose agility with language makes me seem a poor apprentice."

"You're teasing me. And it's not true. Aunt Julia says you have a talent, and I've heard others say the same."

"Ah, then there's more to it than youthful exuberance? I'm flattered."

"Not so youthful, Vicar. Very soon, I shall be sixteen. Old enough for Shakespeare's Juliet to have married and gone to her grave."

A pair of dark eyes twinkled in my direction. "Nothing so drastic will befall you, I hope."

"In this drowsy little village? How could it?"

The vicar's expression became sober when he heard the acidity in my voice. "May I remind you that Nathan and Elizabeth lived in much the same setting; yet theirs was no less a tragedy than what befell Romeo and Juliet. Admit it. Their history brought tears to your eyes."

"It's true. I was moved. But is their story fact or fiction? Not many hearts could survive the humdrum of rural life and still be capable of passion. No one in Braxton, certainly."

"Do you include yourself in this condemnation, or are you an exception?"

The rebuke, though gently expressed, caught me by surprise. I felt stung by it but held my head high, all the same. "I suppose you'd think me vain if I told you that I was."

"No. Not vain. Young and inexperienced."

"You always hold my age against me. But tell me this. How am I to gain experience if I'm forever denied any, if some older and wiser mentor conspires with others to keep me ignorant?"

"You mean me, I suppose?"

"I mean whoever agrees that it's good for me to lead a sheltered existence."

"What would you have me do? Rescue you from a life of comfort and privilege? Arrange for you to live as a bohemian in some damp, Paris ghetto? You'd think that romantic, I suppose."

I was given no time to reply as here the vicar threw up one hand to prevent it. "No! Don't answer that. It's a road down which I've no wish to go. We've wasted too many words on the subject already." Turning to his Bible, he began to read aloud.

The remainder of the hour I spent tormenting myself for having tried the vicar's patience. Clearly he was put out, though the abrupt change in his mood did surprise me. Whatever I'd said to cause it, I knew it was the consequence of my habit of turning every conversation into a contest. I'd made myself tiresome and I could think of no way to make amends.

When the hall clock chimed four, my despair mounted, for the vicar rose and, without our usual exchange of pleasantries, announced that he would be unable to stay for tea. He'd remembered some errand or another, he said. I doubted the truth of that. But as I could think of no way to detain him, I watched, crestfallen, as he headed for the hall to fetch his cloak.

Aunt Julia, entering from the garden, was likewise disappointed. "What? Leaving so soon, Vicar? You usually make time for one of my scones."

Full of apologies, our visitor held firm to his purpose, though he felt obliged to back away from us by careful degrees, first from the threshold, then past the azaleas and rhododendrons and finally through the picket gate—an escape not entirely successful in that during the interval, he'd been made to promise to stay for tea the following week. Mollified, Aunt Julia closed the door, but as she laid out our supper she assaulted me with questions.

"Why do you suppose he sailed off so early this afternoon? It couldn't be on an errand for his wife. The shops won't close for another two hours. You must have said something to annoy him. That's it, isn't it?" Without waiting for a reply, she began scolding. "Honestly, Victorine! Sometimes you are too forthright for your own good. I warn you—you mustn't bully this new vicar the way you did the old one. He hasn't as much patience, is my guess."

The afternoon's experience had shown me that she was right and for once I felt properly chastised. Still, the time had not been spent in utter defeat. Truth be told, I'd gained an advantage. Nathan and Elizabeth were no longer subjects of a well-kept secret. Their history had been exposed, and as such, it could be talked about at a later date...even probed. That was something I intended to do, for the vicar's jealous guarding of them remained a mystery.

Mollified by the recognition of my accomplishment, my arms encircled Aunt Julia's ample waist. "I shall try to behave better," I promised. My hug was returned and amplified so that for a time, I rested in the warmth of her ample bosom.

The rest of the afternoon, the two of us occupied ourselves with making plans for my birthday party. It was agreed that I needed a new dress, and as neither my guardian nor I laid any claim to a talent with the needle, Mrs. Pardy would be drawn into service, as she usually was for such needs. Mrs. Pardy was our neighbor and my aunt's oldest and dearest friend.

I liked our little seamstress very much. She was short, plump and cheerful; and each time she came to us, she brought armloads of the most glorious catalogues that she had sent to her from London. These we would pour over for hours, our heads almost touching. Sometimes, her suggestion to add a flutter of lace or a row of buttons to the original design would appall my aunt, whose tastes bordered on the puritanical.

"God has given Victorine all the adornment she needs, Cordelia. I shouldn't want to encourage vanity."

Each time she heard the objection, this schoolmate of old would smile and nod in apparent sympathy, knowing that Miss Ellsworth the elder could always be brought round if Miss Ellsworth the younger set her mind to it. On the occasion of my sixteenth birthday, my mind was quite made up. The new frock was going to create a sensation!

"Do you love your wife?"

A week had passed since the vicar's hasty departure and I admit the days had drifted by slowly, like clouds in a windless sky. He arrived at the top of the hour and seemed in good spirits, though his formality was so out of keeping with our usual footing, that despite my aunt's warning against trying his patience, he set a mischief in me.

My question caused him to drop his Bible that had been marked and opened for the lesson the moment he sat down. He pretended not to understand me, so I repeated my question.

"I asked if you loved your wife. When you're together, you're so deliberate with one another, almost as if you were acting. It made me wonder."

He bent down to retrieve his book, which he then propped upon his knees as if to say there'd be no shilly-shallying that afternoon. "You've had few occasions upon which to form such an opinion, I should think."

I heard the edge in his voice—not sharp but brittle enough to serve as a warning. I shrugged in spite of the hole it left in the pit of my stomach.

"In the shops, I've seen you together. In the High Street, also."

"Hardly places for displays of affection. Besides, how do you want us to act? Billing and cooing after seven years of marriage? Behavior unsuitable, one would think, for a vicar and his wife."

"Then your feelings are less than they were when you first married?"

"Did I say that?"

"You said, 'after seven years'…"

"Yes, I *know* what I said. But that's not what I meant. In any case, your question is rather personal, don't you think?"

"You ask me personal questions."

"True. But as your spiritual advisor. It's not the same when you ask, is it?"

"If we're to be friends—"

"There are limits, even between friends."

"I don't see why. It's a simple question. Are we to talk of nothing except the Bible?"

"My dear girl—the reality is quite the reverse! We talk too little of the Bible. You have a way of diverting me which, if unchecked, could lead to your spiritual detriment."

"I'd rather you'd show more concern for my happiness, Vicar, as there are few enough temptations in Braxton to cause my downfall."

"There, I think you are wrong—"

"You imagine my soul is in peril then?"

"Come now! You're twisting my words. I meant that a study of the Scriptures lends itself to a happy life. I should have thought that obvious. And as for temptation, you needn't delude yourself. It can be found anywhere."

"Really? What tempts *you* in Braxton, Vicar? I should be glad to know."

I found myself being scrutinized as though I were an exotic bug.

"You're toying with me, aren't you? To keep me from the lesson? It'll do you no good, I'm afraid. I've been warned."

"Warned? By whom? Aunt Julia I suppose." My dour expression prompted him to lean forward, a smile drawn across his lips.

"'How now, pretty lady? God hath given you one face, and you make yourself another.'"

"At least the face is mine, in that I made it."

"I don't follow."

"You always hide behind Shakespeare rather than speak your mind. Why? Are you afraid of being honest with me?"

"That's not fair, Victorine. I am honest with you. Indeed, I'm quite surprised at the degree to which you draw me out."

"You think me a child, I suppose. Someone from whom you have nothing to fear."

"What do you mean by that?" His dark eyes flashed at me. "Why should I have anything to fear? From you or anyone?"

I attempted to answer but could not. Pallor invaded my complexion and I felt myself tremble. Seeing my reaction, the vicar took pity on me.

"Forgive me, my dear. I don't mean to sound harsh. But admit, you can be provocative upon occasion. Your youth is to blame. I should be mindful of that and more tolerant. At the same time, I must ask you to be aware that having no children of my own, I'm easily tripped by...how shall I call it? By too much impetuousness? I shall try to soften my responses in future. Now, as to my wife, she is an ideal companion. You've not made her acquaintance due to your confinement, but as you appear to be growing stronger, perhaps that will change. Once acquainted, you're bound to like one another. I've already told her a good deal about you."

"Really? What did you say?" I'd found my voice again and was eager to learn, by any device, the vicar's opinion of me.

"I told her how bright you are. How eager to learn. My 'star pupil,' that's what I call you. The fact that you're beautiful, she can see for herself."

"Beautiful? Do you think so?" I fairly leapt at the remark, another impetuosity that made him appear uncomfortable.

He turned the pages of his Bible without looking at me. "Surely, I'm not the first to have made that observation? I seem to remember hearing something about a former tutor. A Mr. Huddleston, was it?"

"Huddleston! Who told you about him? Not Aunt Julia? Some gossip from the village, I suppose. It's all nonsense. Every bit of it!"

"Then he didn't leave Braxton under a cloud? And you didn't cry? Or write endless poems of remembrance?"

"He's the one who wrote poems, if you can call them that. More like verses, really. I found them everywhere: at my desk, stuck into my books... The situation was intolerable. That's what I told Aunt Julia when she found them. Naturally, he had to go."

"Of course. And you were not sorry that he was sent packing?"

"If you'd known the man, you'd know the answer to that question."

The vicar looked up into my eyes at last, a pensive expression on his face. "Then I'm sorry for poor Mr. Huddleston. He seems to have 'loved not wisely, but too well.'"

We sat in silence for a moment; time enough for the faint scent of tobacco that hung about the vicar's clothing to invade my senses. The aroma always reminded me of my father. I thought of him then, and how I would sometimes be allowed to fill his pipe with the moist leaves from his humidor. Chocolate in color, they seemed good enough to eat.

Once, when I'd assumed he wasn't looking, I'd stuffed a fistful into my mouth—but spit them out at once, finding the taste bitter and musty. Father had only laughed. He'd been watching the entire time. I remembered how betrayed I'd felt that he'd kept his silence, willing to amuse himself at my expense.

"I suppose you think I'm heartless," I said, picking up the thread of our conversation. "I'm not. To be in love, truly, deeply in love, must be wonderful. Elizabeth Dernwood is to be envied for that. I should like to experience a passion as grand, one that I'd be willing to die for..."

"Please, Victorine!" A square hand flew up in front of me. "I despair that I ever told you that story, particularly if it's put romantic nonsense in your head. Die for love? A ridiculous notion!"

"And yet you admire Othello?"

"As drama, yes. Not as a model for life."

"But you've said many times that one is a reflection of the other."

"True, but you mistake the author's intention. In Othello's case, Shakespeare was writing about obsession, not love. Elizabeth would have done well to study his protagonist, or failing that, to have listened to her father. Either way, she might have lived long and happily."

"I doubt happily. Not without Nathan."

"Then she was doomed either way, for she would never find fulfillment with him. How could she? Cast out from society and left to eek out her days with a man who made her suffer? She was a fool to let her heart rule her head."

"As if love were rational! As if it were an item of clothing, easily cast off."

"Then, as I said, it were better that she had allowed herself to be guided by her father. If she'd been more obedient..."

"Pardon? I thought we were talking about a person. Not a dog."

"Oh, come now. Do you deny she had a duty to her father?"

"She had a duty to herself. To seek happiness."

"You talk as if her father were indifferent to her happiness when, in fact, he lavished every care upon her."

"Material comforts, yes. But he almost destroyed the one joy in her life. I don't see how you can take his part."

"Look at the consequences and you have my answer. He had a duty to protect his child. Surely that takes priority over youthful infatuation. If she had not deceived him..."

"Ah. It comes to that. The fault is hers."

"In part, though Nathan has the greater guilt."

"And I say it was her *father*. Her fear of what he'd do drove her to extremes."

"Oh, come now. You go too far."

"Do I? Is it inconceivable that a child might war with her parents if they conspire against her happiness?" I was trembling again, overwrought with emotion—a reaction that the vicar saw, and which caused him to temper his remarks.

"Why don't we walk for a bit. The air will bring color to your cheeks."

Obedient to his will, I followed him to the garden and, for a time, we stood beneath the cherry tree, both of us peering up through the branches, admiring the sun dappled blossoms. It seemed only yesterday that I had stood laughing with my father under a similar tree in the vicarage garden. The memory made me sad.

"Do you believe in ghosts, vicar? That dead people can come back to haunt us?"

My companion peered at me with lifted eyebrows. "What a strange question from one so young. What brings the notion to mind?"

"I was thinking of my father."

"Ah, you mean can memories haunt us? Yes. Assuredly they can. But memories of a father should be happy ones, not described as a haunting."

"I wasn't thinking of memories. I meant real ghosts. You believe in heavenly spirits. Why not ghosts?"

We walked a few paces deeper into the garden while the vicar ruminated. "I do believe in the Holy Spirit, of course. But as to the existence of ghosts, I'm inclined to take Horatio's view. '... I might not this believe without the sensible and true avouch of mine own eyes.'"

Disappointed by his answer, as I'd hoped for a more thoughtful discussion, I let my peevishness be known. "It's a wonder that anyone attempts to converse anymore. Shakespeare, it seems, has relieved us of the need for thoughts of our own."

The vicar bit his lower lip when he heard me and looked apologetic. "I've done it again, haven't I? Answered a question with a quote. I am sorry, as I very well know your opinion on that habit. Still, don't be annoyed. The day's too lovely for that—"

"Lovely? Is that the sensible and true avouch of your own eyes? It's going to rain!"

Looking up, the vicar could see the truth in what I'd said. A bank of black clouds was forming and threatening to blot out the sun. "I wish I'd thought to borrow a horse," he said wistfully, "as I'm expected at Benchley Farm later this afternoon."

"Yes. Then you could have galloped across the moor in a lather, the way I've seen you do in Ockely Wood."

He blinked in surprise. "Victorine Ellsworth! You've been spying on me."

The thought must have pleased him in some way, for he bent

down and planted a kiss upon my forehead, giving me no time to react before he strode off in the direction of Benchly Farm, whistling as he went, the way people do when they know they're being watched...which he was. Indeed, I remained standing where he'd left me, basking in the pleasure of that kiss, until he was a speck on the horizon. By then the sky had turned black in earnest and I knew I would be caught in a downpour. Nonetheless, as I turned toward the cottage, I was happier than I'd been in years.

I walked rapidly through the garden, so deep in thought that I fairly jumped when I discovered Jeremy was behind me.

"You shouldn't be out here with that man, Victorine," he said out of the blue. "He's not what you think. I saw him... Never mind. But he's not what you think."

Immediately I spun round, annoyed at being jolted from my reverie. "What are you talking about? You saw what? And what business is it of yours who I'm with, anyway?"

The youth, so much taller and stronger than I, took a step backwards, as if he thought I could do him harm. "I-I got a right to say what's on my mind, don't I?"

"Not if you're going to speak ill of the vicar. You promised you wouldn't. Or have you forgotten?"

"Th-that was before..."

"Before what?"

My challenge threw Jeremy into a quandary. For a moment he stood saying nothing, his eyes clouded with indecision. Then his shoulders drooped like a man who'd been whipped. "I-I'm sorry, Victorine. I was only tryin' to look after you."

By now a cruel rain was pummeling us both. I was cold and he looked so pathetic, with his hair plastered to his face, that I decided to forgive him. "Oh, come on, you fool. I'm famished, as you must be. Let's go to the kitchen."

I broke into a run with Jeremy hard on my heels.

Five

"My DEAR, GIRL, you look lovely. Absolutely lovely!" Mrs. Pardy had arrived early for my birthday party to see the results of her handiwork.

"It's a beautiful dress," I told her, my fingers smoothing the skirt of pink broadcloth. "It turned out prettier than the drawing."

Standing behind me, the seamstress gazed into the mirror at my reflection. "The color sets off your dark eyes and hair admirably. I couldn't ask for a better model."

Aunt Julia tilted her head and looked a bit uncertain. "Yes, but the neckline, Cordelia. Isn't it a little bare? Perhaps a scarf..."

"Oh no, Julia. Victorine has a lovely figure. We mustn't hide it."

A pair of crinkly eyes continued to survey my reflection. A coifed head tilted to one side. My guardian was about to offer a second suggestion. I thought it necessary to shift her attention. "How do you like the way Auntie's curled my hair, Mrs. Pardy? Isn't it lovely? I slept in rags the whole night. Rather like sleeping on nails, but worth it, don't you think? I feel like a princess."

"A princess, indeed," sighed the little seamstress. "You've made your niece quite the prettiest girl in the village, Julia."

The plump woman to whom the remark was addressed allowed herself a slight smile of satisfaction, though her words were as circumspect as ever. "Of course, looks aren't everything, Cordelia. We mustn't indulge in too much flattery for fear of turning the poor child's head."

"Oh no. Of course not, Julia. But Victorine is a sensible girl. And it is her birthday, after all."

Aunt Julia never looked kindly upon contradiction and being an inch taller than Mrs. Pardy, used her advantage to bear down upon her friend. "Having gone to a good deal of expense, that dress included, I'm well aware of the occasion, Cordelia; but I don't see it as an excuse for exaggerated compliments, such as you're prone to give."

Lips, which moments before were all smiles, began to tremble.

I felt sorry for the woman with thinning silver hair and ashamed of my aunt's bullying behavior, even though it was true that if Mrs. Pardy were ill or in want of money, the senior Miss Ellsworth was the first to remedy the situation. She had done so on several occasions, beginning with the death of Mr. Pardy, a scrivener who had died three years earlier and whose income was sorely missed.

Because of this difference in their financial positions, Mrs. Pardy was vulnerable to any rebuff and this last one hit her hard. Not only did her lips tremble but her whole body as well, which, draped as it was in a peach-colored dress a size too large for her — an unaccountable anomaly for a seamstress — made her seem all the more pitiful. I did a pirouette in front of them. Another distraction. "You've been generous to a fault, Auntie. And I do love this dress. Thank you, thank you. I may not be the prettiest girl in the village, but I am the happiest."

Throwing my arms about my aunt's neck, I gave her a loud kiss which made her giggle; then she stepped away to survey me for one last time, admitting, when she did, that I was a princess and that Cordelia had worked wonders with her needle.

The compliment brought a spot of joy to Mrs. Pardy's cheeks, even emboldened her to add yet another compliment.

"When I see her in that color, I think of the painting...what's the name of it? 'Pinky'! That's it. That's the one. It came to mind the moment I set eyes on her."

They were both standing, admiring me with their arms folded, when we heard footsteps along the gravel path. Aunt Julia trotted to the window and looked down.

"It's Jeremy," she said, "come to move some furniture. I need to make a space around the buffet or the guests will be bunched at one end of the table. Come down with me, Cordelia, won't you? I'd be glad for your advice."

"Of course, Julia. Of course. Anything to help."

The two women locked arms and descended the stairs, happy in one another's company, the squabble quite forgotten. What silence they left behind was soon interrupted with noises from below, the scraping of tables and chairs along the wooden floor.

Alone, I paced the length of my room, anxious for the guests to arrive. Except for Jeremy, only adults had been invited. As I have suggested, other boys were put off by my intelligence and as for the girls, they were consumed by jealousy, though, as I had mentioned earlier to the vicar, I'd had a true friend once.

Amy Spencer had sung like an angel and was in every way my complement, except for her fair hair, blue eyes and sweet, generous nature. Had she not died when she was nine, I often wondered how different my life would have been. Having a trustworthy companion with whom to share my confessions might have saved me from my darker inclinations and spared me the pain of isolation. In truth, her loss was such a devastation to me that for months I refused to believe she was gone. To myself, though not to others, I'd insisted that we still walked and talked together.

Whether mine was a delusion or a real haunting, I cannot say, but I drew comfort from this apparition, particularly as it came during a period when my seizures were severe enough to cause my parents to consider sending me to a sanatorium. It had been a very bleak period in my life.

The first knock at the door came precisely at two. Rather than hurry downstairs to greet the arrival, I left the welcoming to Aunt Julia. My intention was to descend the stairs only after the number of guests had swelled and I was certain that the vicar was among them. If habit were true to form, I would not have long to wait. Social events met with much favor in our village, and guests were inclined to attend early and remain late.

Miss Clemmons, Leland's third-form teacher, was one who could be counted on to appear at the top of the hour. Her booming voice carried up from the parlor, and though I could not hear him, I knew that Mr. Pounder was in tow. Like his companion, he was in his sixties and also a teacher, but served as the choirmaster at Chapman, the boy's school down the road from Leland. The pair was often seen in tandem and in their early days, it came as no surprise when they both trotted off to Manchester to do their teacher preparation.

Despite their inseparability, there was never a hint of a romance between them. Mr. Pounder was a bit too feminine and Miss Clemmons a bit too masculine for anyone to imagine them as lovers. Indeed, their idiosyncrasies set them so far apart that it was impossible to contemplate that they could live together in harmony.

Naturally, a generation of students had made endless jokes at the expense of these two teachers; but having matured and had children of their own, these former pupils had come to accommodate the arrangement, even made inquiries if one appeared in public without the other, and thought no more of their situation...except to remark that as the pair grew older, Miss Clemmons was more in need of a razor than her companion.

The vicar's voice rising from the hallway set my heart to racing. Here was the moment I'd waited for, anticipated...and now suddenly feared. How would the man I so admired react to my new dress, my upswept hair? Would he approve? Or would he frown and think me a peacock? I did not know, but there was no going back at this point. A final glance into my mirror and I was off, down the stairs at a hurried, nervous pace.

Mrs. Pardy, in the mantle of hostess, was quick to acknowledge me. "Ah, here she is, Vicar, our birthday girl! And doesn't she look wonderful? So grown up, don't you think?" She spun me round by the shoulders to give the full effect. The man in black was busy removing his cloak but he paused to gaze at me and, to my relief, registered his approval.

"Indeed, I'd say our Victorine is quite the picture."

"She looks like that painting, doesn't she? 'Pinky.' That's what Julia and I thought, at least."

The vicar came forward with his eyes shining. "How right you are, Mrs. Pardy. The very image of her." He took both my hands in his. "Happy birthday, dear girl. Your success is absolute! The gown is all the surprise that you promised."

"Surprise? What's this about a surprise?" Mrs. Flemming came forward, and seeing my transformation, drew in a sharp breath, as though she'd been pricked by a needle. Her words were complimentary enough but I noted that she was quick, almost eager, to turn the spotlight from me.

"This is your handiwork I suppose, Mrs. Pardy? I've been told you're a genius with a needle. Now I see that is no exaggeration. 'Pinky' pales by comparison."

The little seamstress quivered with pleasure. "Why, thank you Mrs. Flemming. I do try my best."

"Come now, you're too modest. A gown like this would cost a fortune in London. No doubt, your services are in great demand. But I was wondering...perhaps I might call upon you in the future... for a traveling outfit?"

The sun at its fullest could not have beamed more broadly upon Mrs. Pardy than it seemed to at that moment. "Of course! Of course!" the little creature clapped her hands. "I'd be delighted, Mrs. Flemming. A green coat, I think, with a bit of fur round the collar? We would want to compliment such magnificent hair!"

A spot of color rose upon an otherwise pale cheek. Apparently, the vicar's wife was not immune to flattery, though she protested well enough. "No, no! Nothing so extravagant as that. Gray was what I had in mind. More serviceable, don't you think?"

Mrs. Pardy shook her head with unaccustomed vehemence, then offered a compromise. "Gray isn't for you, Mrs. Flemming. Not with your delicate coloring. Consider blue, at least. One mustn't hide one's light under a bushel, you know."

Her creative thoughts flowing, the little seamstress took her new client by the arm and led her into the parlor, leaving the vicar and I entirely forgotten.

"I hope Mrs. Pardy has her way with my wife," the vicar confided once we were alone. "Blue would suit her better." As he spoke, he took a step backward and flattered me with a full inspection. "If anyone makes an argument for color, it's you. You look—"

"Ah! Here you are, Vicar. I thought I heard your voice." Aunt Julia came swishing through from the kitchen. "I've been waiting for you. We need to talk about booths for the bazaar." Without so much as a 'by your leave,' my aunt took hold of the vicar's arm and pulled him into the farther room, leaving me to sulk or to follow, as ever I chose.

Jeremy was the first person to catch my eye as I entered the parlor. He looked uncomfortable, hovering about the buffet, and so I was headed in his direction when Miss Clemmons threw out her arm to reel me in.

"Victorine! Look at you. You're an inch taller than when I last set eyes on you. And so grown up! I like what you've done with your hair. Doesn't she look beautiful, Elliot?" My former teacher craned her neck upwards to look at the man whose elbows rested upon the back of her chair.

Mr. Pounder nodded, adding that I reminded him of someone, but he couldn't think who.

"'Pinky!' There's the resemblance." Mrs. Pardy was a woman capable of listening to one conversation while carrying on another. "The dress helps, of course."

The music teacher nodded, looking at me with fresh eyes. "Yes. That's right. 'Pinky.' Just what I was about to say."

Satisfied that he had made his contribution, the man fell silent. Perhaps he found the hubbub that surrounded him daunting, like the hurly-burly of his classroom—'disciplinarian' was not a word that came to mind where Mr. Pounder was concerned. He had neither the stature nor the desire to bend youthful exuberance to his will. He taught with his nose in his music and refused to look up despite the occasional spit wad that came flying or any sound of scuffling from the back of the room. He lived for his music, pure and simple. Boys who shared his passion admired him. The rest used him as the butt of their endless jokes.

Miss Clemmons was used to these lapses in conversation. To compensate, she had developed the habit of asking a question and then providing the answer. "Are you feeling any better these days, my dear? Yes, of course you are. Any fool can see that..."

In some ways, such an exchange, if it could be called that, was relaxing. To keep up one's side of the visit required only an occasional nod or grunt. Nothing more. Since Miss Clemmons was conversing with me so well without my need to participate, I was free to cast my gaze about for sight of the vicar, which I obtained soon enough as he was standing with his back pressed against the china cabinet, a prisoner of one of Aunt Julia's monologues.

Certain he would welcome a rescue, I made my excuse to Miss Clemmons the moment I could and began elbowing my way toward him. I'd not gone far, however, when Mrs. Flemming called out my name. She was seated in one of two ladder-back chairs that stood in the shadows of a far wall. As the one beside her was empty, I could hardly refuse to join her.

"Jordan speaks so well of you," she said, pulling me down beside her. "I feel we must get to know each other better." Her blue eyes showed nothing but kindness in their expression, but I remained suspicious.

Up close, I had an opportunity to observe that she was prettier than I'd credited her. From a distance, her complexion might appear wan but in fact, it had a porcelain sheen. Her features were refined, her eyes lustrous, and though her teeth were small, they were almost artificially even. In terms of portraiture, she might have sat for Botticelli.

Her manners, too, were delicate. Occasionally, she spoke with a hand waving in the air, but in the main, she kept them both— small and well manicured—resting in her lap.

Her style of conversation was one most people found pleasing. Her habit was to ask questions, feigning an enormous interest to answers no matter how mundane. "You mean to say that both your daughters are left-handed? How amazing."

If asked, Aunt Julia might have argued that these questions were meant to put the listener at ease; but I was not so easily fooled, especially when she persisted with questions in areas where she was purported to have mastery—gardening for example. No, I knew that she was not only attempting to ingratiate herself with her husband's parishioners but also, through careful listening, taking their measurements so that she might exercise some influence over them.

She was enormously successful in this endeavor, and it hadn't taken her long to gain the confidence of even the most influential among us, my aunt included. In the past, my guardian would have felt it her duty to be vocal on church matters, but within weeks of the Flemming's arrival, all that had changed. Her opinions were aired only after she'd conferred with the vicar *and* the vicar's wife.

I admit to being a little in awe of the woman's power but perplexed as to why she felt compelled to live behind a mask. Still, believing her to be duplicitous, my remarks, during our short conversation together, bordered upon the inane.

"I'm afraid I don't share your longing for travel." Mrs. Flemming's eyes were fixed upon me and so she failed to observe that the vicar was making his way toward us. "I'm from a village myself and find that people everywhere are much the same. They laugh, they cry, fall madly in love. Scale is the only difference, and as to that, a smaller one offers great advantage. Details are sharper, hence one hones a sharper eye."

When the shadow of her husband fell across her, Mrs. Flemming looked up. "Ah, here's a world traveler. Let's ask his opinion. Victorine and I have been having a pleasant talk, Mr. Flemming. I confess I find her as engaging as you do."

"Yes, I've been observing you from afar. Like two bees in a hive. Whatever can the subject be? If it's music or poetry, my dear, I must warn you that Victorine's scholarship is formidable."

"And you know that mine is not." Mrs. Flemming laughed in a self-deprecating way. "No, we spoke of nothing so taxing as the arts. We were discussing her desire to travel, though if I'm to be honest, you also were part of our discourse."

"Me? What a boring topic. I'm glad I arrived to put a stop to it."

"Not at all, Mr. Flemming. Your pupil and I find you an admirable subject. Don't we, Victorine?" I lowered my eyes but did not answer. "She's too shy to speak," the wife went on, "but her glances give her away. I suspect mine were very like hers when you and I first met. You're an imposing figure, my dear. What could be more natural than for a young girl to admire you?

It's not as if she were the first."

Meant as a jest, I assumed, the remark struck me as innocent; but upon hearing it, the vicar altered visibly. His back stiffened and his lips bore a grimace, just as if he'd been struck from behind by a winter's blast. This show of irritation, so obvious to us both, urged his wife to explain. "I meant myself, of course. A-as a young girl."

To my surprise, the remark did little to mollify. Some etiquette had been breached which the vicar was unwilling to forgive. As if to dismiss her, he turned toward me, a thin smile drawn across his face in an effort to make light of the emotion which had overtaken him.

"I'm afraid Mrs. Flemming is playing with you, Victorine. She's prone to tease. But you mustn't gratify her by blushing."

"No, no, of course I meant no harm." The woman in gray laid a reassuring hand upon my arm. "Nothing untoward! But I so admire my husband that it's natural for me to assume the same of everyone else—"

"Eva, for heaven's sake."

"All right. All right. I'm sorry. I don't mean to make things worse. Perhaps it's best if I circulate. Come, Jordan. Take my place beside your pupil. Victorine's aunt has promised me a cutting from her rose bush. This, I think, would be a good time to remind her." A pair of cold lips planted a kiss upon my cheek. "Happy birthday, dearest girl. May you have a long life and a joyous one."

The vicar watched his wife disappear into the throng before taking the chair she'd vacated. "Don't judge her too harshly," he said in a tone more relaxed. "Mrs. Flemming means well, but she sometimes goes too far. Still, there are worse crosses to bear than a doting spouse, I suppose."

"Certainly there are," I managed to say, though my words were barely audible.

Sensing my discomfort, he changed the topic. "I didn't get a chance to tell you earlier how splendid you look. The dress, the hair...if we were to meet on the High Street, I might mistake you for a stranger, a remarkably beautiful one."

Hearing the compliment, the corners of my mouth turned up. In spite of myself, I was ready to forgive his behavior of moments before—though forgiveness wasn't really the word, for it struck me as natural that a man of so many talents would grow impatient with a woman who made a game of suppressing hers.

"Am I usually so plain, then?" I taunted the man beside me. My eyes were downcast as I spoke, not because of shyness, but from a desire to keep my delight hidden. Such modesty forced him to protest.

"Now you know that's not so. And you're a wicked girl to tease when I've already paid you many compliments. No, what I meant to say was that today you look especially grown up. So much so, in fact, that perhaps it's time for us to talk of making other arrangements for your spiritual education."

"What do you mean?" I felt myself grow tense. "What's wrong with our current arrangements?"

"Well, you must be getting bored with only me for company. I thought you might like to spread your wings, spend time with people nearer your age." A large hand went up to stifle any protest I might mount. "Now, I know what you've said in the past about having little in common with your peers, but how can you be so sure? A good deal of time has passed since you were in school. These former classmates are growing up, too. You might find you share more interests than you imagine. Mrs. Flemming has started a little Bible group—"

"No! Impossible!" I interrupted. "What if I became ill? It would be too horrid. I couldn't face it! I couldn't! We must leave things as they are. Besides, I don't find you boring in the least. I look forward to our conversations."

"Do you? I must say that mystifies me. To prefer the company of an old man to people your own age?"

"Why do you keep insisting that you're old? There's not a gray hair on your head. And, of course, I prefer your company. You have so much to talk about. You've traveled, you've seen exotic places. Why do you imagine I'd prefer the alternative? Listening to Jeremy go on about his kites or the gossip of silly girls! How could you even think of condemning me to that. You're teasing, surely. Besides, you mustn't disappoint Aunt Julia. She looks forward to your visits as much as I."

My last remark seemed to carry great weight. Far be it from the vicar to disappoint a prominent member of the church council. Besides, I think he took some personal delight in my protestation, for after I spoke he dropped one large hand upon his knee to indicate a decision had been made.

"In that case, I'll say no more of making other arrangements. I should hate to slight two such charming ladies. Anyway, to be honest, I, too, enjoy our visits. Especially"—here the vicar patted his waist—"your aunt's delicious cream cakes."

Our eyes meeting, we broke into laughter. The vicar was in high spirits again and I credited myself with that, although it was not long, as he stood gazing at me that he once more grew sober. "Mrs. Flemming was right in her observation, you know. Seeing you as you are now, 'Pinky' pales by comparison."

He was close enough for me to feel his breath upon my face, and my heart thumped like a wild bird. His earnest expression, those dark eyes... Dare I hope that what I saw in that look was more than admiration? A hint of affection, perhaps?

Under the circumstances, it was impossible to stifle my disappointment when Jeremy, like a portending cloud, cast his shadow over us.

"Brought you some sandwiches." He sounded surly enough as he thrust a Blue Willow plate under my nose. Triangles of cucumber and cheese stared up at me, clumped in an unappetizing mound to suggest they'd been assembled in haste.

The vicar refused to be put off by Jeremy's dour expression. He rose and greeted him affably. "Ah, here's proper company for you at last, my dear: a strapping young fellow who's not been able to take his eyes off you since you entered the room. Perhaps he wants to tell you about his latest kite."

Sensing the note of derision, Jeremy's jaw squared. "What do you mean? I thought she might be hungry, that's all."

"Of course. Of course. I meant nothing by the remark," the vicar responded. "Making idle conversation, that's all."

His words did nothing to assuage the tension. Jeremy continued to glare as if an offense had been given and so it was natural that the vicar would seek the means for his escape.

"Is that my wife waving to me? Yes, I think it is. I'm afraid I must go to her. If you'll both excuse me..."

A slight bow in my direction and the vicar beat a hasty retreat. He'd been routed by a surly boy whose face glowed with victory and who now stood watching the departure braced like a bulldog. This proprietary attitude annoyed me.

"Sit down, Jeremy, will you? I can't see anything with you in the way."

"You can't see *him*, you mean. You don't care a fig about anyone else."

"That's nonsense! And even so, you had no call to be rude to him. You're just in one of your moods. I warn you, if you go on being unpleasant, I'll leave and refuse to speak to you for the entire afternoon."

My threat had its wanted effect. Jeremy perched himself gingerly on the chair beside me, uncertain of how I would react.

"You look nice in that dress," he ventured after a period of silence had followed. "Is it new or somethin'?"

Not ready to bestow my forgiveness, I replied without glancing at him. "You've not seen it before, have you?"

"N-No."

"Then you have your answer."

Jeremy's chin slumped to its chest, his blonde hair falling over his eyes. "Look, I'm sorry about just now. A-and about the other day...in the garden. I shouldn't go stickin' my nose in your business. I know you like the vicar. I don't want you to get hurt, that's all..."

"You think that he's trying to hurt me?" My head snapped in Jeremy's direction. It startled him.

"Honest, Victorine. I didn't come over here to quarrel. I got somethin' for you. I wanted to give it to you." As he spoke, he took hold of the plate he'd given me, placed it on the floor and withdrew a small parcel from his pants pocket. "I hope you like it."

"What is it?" I looked doubtful. "Another frog I suppose."

"Can't you forget about that? We was kids then. This is somethin' I made."

"What?" I continued to look suspicious.

"Open it and see."

The box I was handed was no bigger than a half crown and no heavier than its wrapping. Afraid it might be fragile, I broke the seal with care, then lifted the lid. A layer of tissue paper unfolded and whispered to me. Something hard and shiny glinted below the surface. My curious fingers burrowed into the paper, and there I discovered a gift that made me gasp with delight.

"Oh, Jeremy, it's beautiful!" In my hand, I held a silver pendant of a gull with its wings outstretched. The eyes and feathers were delicately carved and the metal burnished at points to catch the light and create the illusion of flight. "I can't believe you did this for me. How clever of you."

"I seen how you watch them birds along the cliffs. So it come to me to give you wings of your own." The face peering into mine was aglow with pleasure. "Do you really like it?"

"Like it? I adore it! How did you manage? Where did you get the silver?"

"One of me mum's old buckles."

"Something of hers? Oh Jeremy, I don't know what to say."

"I made the mold and everythin'. Learned how from a book. That should please you, well enough. I do read, sometimes. When it's important."

"And this is the result—something so wonderful. Thank you, Jeremy. Thank you!" I threw my arms round him and was surprised to feel his body stiffen. "Such a dear, sweet gull! I'll wear it always. *Always!*"

Six

ON THE DAY of the church bazaar, I was free to wander among the rows of stalls set out on the Commons. My guardian, as an official of the event, had departed from the cottage early, leaving me with a few coins and the admonition not to catch a chill. The day was mild, so I had no fear of that and used my freedom to good advantage, browsing among displays of crockery, flowers and other sundries in the hope of spying the vicar.

The whole village had turned out for the occasion—some as merchants, some as prospective buyers, and some wanting no more than the chance to engage in friendly conversation. The manner of dress for these festivities was left to the individual. A few wore their Sunday best, but most were more practical. As sudden downpours were common this early in the season, many wore clogs or Wellingtons and carried their umbrellas at the ready. My aunt was one of those who took the cautious view and had insisted that I wear a winter cape. I did so to appease her, but underneath, and without her knowledge, I wore a gingham dress with a scooped neckline that I deemed was flattering.

As I walked, my eyes slid over an array of candlesticks, pewter mugs, and laces, none of which was of any interest to me. My attention was fixed upon the many faces drifting past—none of which, to my disappointment, belonged to the vicar. A third reconnoiter past the tea pavilion, held out more promise. Mrs. Flemming was standing at a dry goods stall, fingering what looked like a bolt of gray wool.

"Mrs. Pardy will be disappointed," I said, drawing up to her.

A guilty grin flashed across her face. "Oh dear, you've caught me out. Yes, I was considering the gray. So much more serviceable, don't you think?" When I said nothing, but stood gazing at her with eyebrows lifted, she understood that I did not agree and after some hesitation, returned the bolt to its place along the row of other fabrics. "Yes. Why not be a bit more adventurous? I feel the good effects of our acquaintanceship already," she said to me.

After that, she took hold of my arm and we strolled among the stalls, while she chatted amiably. "I hadn't expected to see you today. Your aunt said you had a cold, but you look perfectly well to me."

"A slight sniffle a few days ago. Nothing more. Auntie's given to exaggeration sometimes."

"I suppose your party brought it on. Too much stimulation can play havoc with one's constitution. But it was worth it, I hope. Such a lovely afternoon. And the food! Your aunt is a marvelous cook. Were I to live with her as you do, I'm afraid I should have to let out all my clothes. And speaking of clothes, you looked wonderful in your new gown. So grown up! Mr. Flemming remarked on it several times on the walk home."

"He didn't disapprove, did he?"

"Heavens, no! I never meant to give that impression. But he *was* taken aback, realizing he might soon lose his star pupil."

I stopped to face her directly. "Why should he fear that? Nothing's changed. I may be a year older but there's no hope of my ever escaping Braxton."

Her blue eyes stared at me, perplexed. "You speak with such certainty. What about your education? You're so very talented, by all report. Surely you'll want to go on to university..."

My response was unguarded. A nerve had been exposed and I shook my head, vehemently. "Auntie would never consider it. *Never*. So, you see, I am destined to live and die in this tiny, boring village."

The moment I spoke, I was angry with myself. To reveal a tension that existed between my guardian and I was never my intent. The truth had slipped out leaving me exposed and subject to the closest scrutiny. I watched with dismay as the whisper of a cat smile flitted across Mrs. Flemming's expression. All right then, she'd had her insight. Why deny it? My hope was that she'd keep her silence. Nothing should be said to the vicar to suggest I was unhappy with *his* mentoring. This hope I refused to put into words, however, for fear it might give her some power over me. I started to walk on, but Mrs. Flemming, who had hold of my arm, refused to budge.

"There's always the chance that someone will carry you off," she persisted.

"Carry me off?" I looked puzzled.

"Romantically, I mean. I was raised in a village small as this one, and happily so, for that's where I met Mr. Flemming. I confess, I wasn't exactly carried off. It wasn't a whirlwind courtship, at all. In fact, when the vicar first arrived, he was very circumspect, almost distant. I didn't let that put me off, though. For me, it was love at first sight and I made no effort to hide it. Such a young foolish girl. I must have made quite a nuisance of myself. But, in time, there were small signs that he took a similar interest in me. I suppose he was reticent because of the difference in our ages. But a decade counts as nothing when one is in love."

"So, that's how you met. I wondered."

"Yes. In a 'tiny, boring village.' His first assignment, I think, which was another reason why he may have been reticent. Still, I wore him down. We were finally married and not long after, we moved away. It's been ages since I've seen my beloved little village. I quite miss it, sometimes."

"I can't imagine ever missing Braxton. But how did you manage it? Getting him to propose?"

"Persistence. And, when I thought the time was right, I told him how I felt."

"You didn't!"

"I did!"

"But weren't you afraid he'd reject you? I'd die if that happened to me."

Mrs. Flemming gave my arm a pat. "I doubt that, Victorine. You strike me as being more resilient than most would suspect. In any case, mine wasn't the risk you suppose. I may have been the first to speak, but it wasn't until I was certain of the vicar's feelings."

"How did you know? I mean, if he'd said nothing..."

"He didn't have to, dear. A woman senses things. As will you when the time comes...." Her twinkling eyes laughed at me, content to keep their secret. "But there, I've exceeded my authority. Such conversations are best left between you and your aunt."

"Auntie? When she talks of marriage, it's always about duty. Never of love. It's natural, I expect, for someone who's never been courted."

"No? Never?" My companion looked surprised. "I thought... Oh, it doesn't matter. I promise, when the time comes, if you'll allow it, I shall lend a discreet ear."

She was peering out from under a gray felt hat as she spoke, scanning the horizon, a sign that her thoughts had already drifted. "Where is that wandering husband of mine? I'm desperate for a cup of tea and I suspect you are, as well. It's grown so *cold*. I think it will rain. Come on, let's find the vicar and get out of this weather."

Our search began with locked arms, but the moment I saw him, standing out from the crowd in his black attire, I broke free and plunged into the human tide with no more than a "There he is!" as a compass for his wife.

To be honest, I hadn't meant to be helpful. I wanted to be alone with the vicar, if only for a moment. He was engrossed in a slim, black book as I came up from behind.

"Anything interesting?"

He turned at the sound of my voice. "Victorine! No one was expecting you. Your aunt said you were feeling poorly. Or was that a ruse so that you could creep up on a person and give him a fright? Never mind. I forgive you as I'm happy to see you looking so well."

The genuine pleasure in his eyes with which greeted me made me feel giddy and, for want of something intelligent to say, I pressed him about the object in his hand.

"It's not a love story, if that's what you're wondering," he said, glancing down at it. "Nothing like. A book of manners is what it is...."

"Manners?"

"Yes, written in the eighteenth century. Books of this type were all the rage, then, because young ladies of the middle class were eager to enter into polite society without embarrassing themselves. These books gave them proper guidance. But I must say, it's unusual to find one in such good condition."

"Valuable is it?" The peddler who stood listening to our conversation broke in. "I guessed as much. I come by it from one of those fancy 'ouses down south. Colchester, if I remember rightly. Whatcha think it'd go for, Vicar?"

"Well, it might be worth anywhere from a few shillings to two pounds sterling." The prospective buyer examined the book's condition with an eye to making an offer.

The peddler rubbed one hand across the gray stubble of his chin and looked pleased. "If two pounds is your offer, Guv'nor, take it. It's yours."

The vicar looked up again. "I didn't say two pounds for certain. There's some damage, now that I look at it. See?" He pointed to the spine, which looked worn. "Two pounds would be a bit dear under the circumstance. A pound would be nearer the mark."

The peddler chuckled, rejecting the offer. I noticed that three of his teeth were missing and that the rest were the color of bark. So unkempt was he, that I couldn't take my eyes off him. His hands were dirty. His neck was dirty. And so was the red kerchief he'd tied around it. These wayfarers who made a circuit of the local fairs, buying, selling and sometimes thieving, were a disreputable lot. Their presence among us was endured in much the same way as flies that gather on a dung heap are endured. Never accepted by the communities they invaded, they lived as a race apart, if not an entire species.

What made them pariahs among us? Not their untidiness, certainly. In a farming community, like ours, many a hand was earth-stained. No, what made these drifters outcasts, I supposed, was their utter disregard for custom, most notably when it came to property. Other people's, that is—not their own. They would camp wherever they liked and poach the local wildlife shamelessly, as if it were their God-given right.

True, for all that, theirs was not an enviable life, the conditions under which they lived being appalling, disease-filled and dirt-ridden. Yet in exchange for the comforts of a conventional existence, they lived with a freedom which, when dealing with their betters, made them appear arrogant. In this regard, for their utter disdain of orthodox society, I envied them. They did not, it seemed to me, crawl upon the earth, as did most of their two-legged counterparts. In spirit, they were more like the creatures with wings.

Still fingering his treasure, the vicar began to bargain. "You realize, of course, this material is not to everyone's taste. It may be a while before you find another buyer. Tell you what? I'll offer another half crown. Will that suit you?"

The peddler scratched his head, considering. "Well now, if it's worth 'alf a crown more, it might be worth an 'ole one."

To this reply, the vicar shook his head and made a show of returning the book to the peddler's pile. "That may be so to someone else, but not to me."

A present sale being prized above a future one, the peddler put out a staying hand. "Now 'old on, Guv'nor. I meant no offense. But I'm a poor man, as you can see, with a wife and kids wandering somewhere here abouts. It's natural, with all them mouths to feed, to want the best price, isn't it? As to the book's value, I take your word on it." Here, the man chuckled a second time. "If you can't trust a vicar then who can you trust? 'Alf a crown more. It's agreed."

"Oh, Jordan! Not another old book?" Mrs. Flemming had

caught up with us and began tugging at her husband's sleeve, intent on leading him from temptation. "It's gone half past eleven. Victorine and I want our tea. Surely that can wait."

As it had started to rain, the vicar needed no further convincing. He dropped the requisite number of coins into the bookseller's hand and, thrusting his acquisition under one arm, he ran toward the tea pavilion, a large blue and white marquee, with the two of us in tow.

Others followed our example and within moments, the shelter was overrun, making it impossible to find a place to sit. Fortunately, Miss Clemmons, who'd arrived well before the cloudburst, saw our dilemma and waved us in her direction with a napkin. It served as a beacon, and after elbowing our way through the throng, we eventually reached her. She was seated with Mr. Pounder amidst a table of crumbs and empty crockery. Beside them was an extra chair buried under a mound of rain gear.

"The cream cakes are delicious," her companion said, by way of a greeting. He patted his round belly in evidence, admitting that he may have indulged a bit. "Still, what's the good of a fair if one can't spoil oneself a little?"

Miss Clemmons, whose circumference matched his own, nodded in agreement, which made her chin waggle like a blancmange. A few more niceties were exchanged before Leland's third-form teacher rose and offered us the table. "Elliot and I were just going for a walk," she said by way of explanation.

When he heard her, Mr. Pounder looked up, both dubious and surprised. "B-but it's raining, Anthie! I shouldn't like to get wet."

"That's what umbrellas are for, old darling." He was already being pulled from his chair by a hefty pair of arms.

Denied a choice, the music teacher rose, and with heavy footsteps, followed his friend out into the inclement weather, but not before looking back once or twice at the cozy seat he'd been forced to vacate.

We three who remained sank gratefully into the empty chairs, mine still warm from its former occupancy. Now that we'd found sanctuary, the human ebb and flow around us seemed less chaotic and more merry than it had moments before. Still, so much chatter and laughter confined under one awning was at times a bit deafening. We had to shout to be heard, and on those occasions, we, too, broke into laughter.

The excitement around us fueled my appetite. When tea arrived, I dived into one of Mr. Pounder's celebrated cream cakes with such enthusiasm that some of the confection squirted from the side. My hands were covered in a sugary cream that I impulsively licked. Mrs. Flemming, suffering the same untidy fate, did likewise. Observing one another, we broke into giggles like mischievous schoolgirls. The vicar, to the contrary, was a model of restraint, barely touching his plate so that he could keep his hands free to examine his new purchase. He did look up now and then, when greeted by his parishioners, but only long enough to utter the requisite pleasantries.

His wife, hungry for his attention, encouraged him to put his book aside, which he did; but it was not long before he was fingering the pages again and drifting back into it. Frustrated in her attempts, she turned her attention to me.

"You're in the fifth form, are you not, Victorine? Studying Grey's 'Elegy,' I suppose?" Her voice was flat, revealing that she wasn't the least bit interested in my studies, which was understandable for, at the moment, neither was I. That didn't keep me from correcting her, however.

"Grey's 'Elegy' is part of the curriculum for the fourth form, not the fifth."

A small hand flew up to her lips as she tittered with embarrassment. So many years had passed since she'd been a student, she explained, and even then, she'd not been an attentive one. Nonetheless, she persisted in her catechism, touching the arm of the vicar now and again to draw his attention.

"Coleridge then? It must be. The 'Ancient Mariner' and such?"

A puckish mischief overtook me, as I was growing bored with this charade. "'Our bodies why do we forbear?...We owe them thanks because they...Yielded their forces, sense, to us...Nor are dross to us, but allay.'" I sat back to look at her. "John Donne's 'The Ecstasy.' That is my proper course of study."

The Vicar's wife looked taken aback and cast a furtive glance in her husband's direction; but from him there was no reaction, except, perhaps, signs of suppressed laughter in that he grew pink about the ears.

"I-I'm amazed," the wife complained, faced with her husband's silence, "that such ideas are considered a proper study for a young lady. It's a bit explicit, isn't it? Or am I being old-fashioned? Have you been listening, Mr. Flemming? What do you think?"

The vicar looked up, hearing his name. "Oh, I don't know, my dear. When it comes to passion and desire, no one, I think, writes with Donne's eloquence. He was a man of the cloth, after all."

"Was he? Then what possessed him to express such ideas? That would be my question!"

Her husband drew in a deep breath, as though considering how to frame an answer that would satisfy, but not pander to, his wife's narrow virtue. "Banish Donne for his thoughts, and who will be next, my dear? Shakespeare? Chaucer? Perhaps you would censure God as well for there are passages in the Bible that..."

"You're teasing me, Mr. Flemming," came her robust reply. "You know right well, I mean to do no such thing. But it is fair to ask, isn't it, whether or not Mr. Donne isn't a bit too..." A pause followed while she searched for the proper word. "...too *advanced*, for a girl Victorine's age? Yes, that's what I intended to say."

"Apparently, those in charge of curriculum do not agree."

"Yes, but that's the question, isn't it? Who are these people? And what gives them the right to affront community standards? I mean, all that talk about bodies and senses and ecstasy."

Here the vicar puffed out his cheeks in disagreement. "My dear woman, I know of no lay institution that more adheres to community standards than the British school system! It's positively feudal in that regard. There's not a single modern work included in the course work, from the first form to the sixth. And while there's no greater admirer of the classics than myself, I think it wouldn't hurt to include a few modern poets just to let in a breath of fresh air."

"Who, for example?"

"Who? Why ask when you admit that you neither read, nor care about, poetry?" The vicar's hand flew up to stay her objection. "But putting that remark aside, my point is, that if a flaw exists in our system of education, it lies not in its failure to uphold community standards, but the reverse. It clings to them far too long. I'm sure Victorine agrees with me: today's studies are more apt to bore young people than corrupt them!" He thumped his large hand on the table to underscore his point.

It made the vicar's wife blink.

"I'm sure I'm not quarreling with you, Mr. Flemming, though you seem to think it. Your opinion was sought, that's all. Heavens! What must Victorine think to see you so agitated?"

Disdain, like a curtain, fell across the vicar's face. If he was to be denied forceful expression, if all that could or might be said on the subject had to be funneled through the high-strung sensibilities of the woman seated opposite him, then the discussion was at an end. His eyes drifted back to his reading. Mrs. Flemming was left to make whatever amends she thought necessary.

Understanding him well enough, she leaned forward to replenish my cup with more brown liquid. "My husband's right, of course," she said, somewhat revived by this simple act of nurturing. "It's silly for me to have opinions on issues I know little about. Everyone acknowledges that Mr. Donne is a great poet, so who am I to question? Still, there are others, aren't there? Others whom you're studying?"

Being embarrassed for the poor woman, I replied at once, without giving my answer much thought. "After the 'Ecstasy' there's 'Paradise Lost.'"

The moment I spoke, we both understood that, without meaning to, I'd hatched a joke, one that Mrs. Flemming seemed eager to share. "Did you hear that, Vicar? About ecstasy being followed by paradise lost? Staid though it may be, the curriculum is not without irony, at least."

If she expected her pleasantry to be returned, she was disappointed. The vicar looked dour, as he might appear catching a child stealing coins from the collection plate.

"'Paradise Lost' describes the fall of man, Mrs. Flemming. You must pardon me if I fail to see any merit in the irony to which you allude. Nor how or why it should amuse you."

These words, delivered slowly, pointedly, fell like drops of water upon a fire. Each utterance had the effect of dousing any joy his wife had derived from her word play. Indeed, it would be truthful to say that being stunned by the upbraiding, she sat like a statue carved from stone.

"B-but surely you see the humor?" she sputtered after a few moments had passed. "First comes the ecstasy and then...."

Vicar Flemming slid back his chair, rose and peered over his wife's head into the distance. "You must excuse me, I'm afraid," he interrupted, showing his disdain for the conversation at hand. "Victorine's aunt has entered the pavilion. I need a word with her." He bounced a few coins upon the table as he spoke, intending that we should indulge ourselves in a second pot of tea. Then he abandoned us, leaving his wife and me barely enough time to crane our necks round to watch him disappear.

What followed then was an interval of mutual discomfort, where one woman sat disconsolate and unable to speak while the other struggled for words that might be of comfort. Certainly, I pitied the woman whose red-rimmed eyes stared resolutely into her lap. I felt responsible, too. If I hadn't encouraged her with my smile; if I hadn't misspoken in the first place... Yet, it was foolish to chastise myself for a situation that was beyond my control, especially when here was corroboration of what I'd suspected from the beginning: that the vicar and his wife were completely unsuited to one another.

Still, her rejection touched me for I knew that pain well... I thought her treatment was unfair, and yet, I couldn't bring myself to blame the vicar. Impatience with a wife so much his inferior seemed inevitable.

Mercifully, the revelers swirling around us had seen nothing of her humiliation. In their happy nescience, several of them stopped to extend their greetings and were so generous with their compliments regarding her work in the village that before long the spirits of the injured wife rallied. After all, these good men and women were her parishioners as well as her husband's, and the warmth of their fellowship gave her reason to feel of value.

She was so buoyed, that I suspect she began to doubt the cause of her dejection. She was a good wife, after all. Or tried to be. And hadn't the vicar spoken well of her before the congregation? She was being far too self-critical when she knew that, for the past several days, her husband had been struggling with Sunday's sermon, a lesson on sloth, which he'd had difficulty writing. His impatience could be laid to that and nothing more.

Such thoughts as these I read in the returning brightness of her expression—the upturned lips, the moist eyes banished by a handkerchief. I knew of that inclination to make excuses for the person someone adores. I'd done as much myself, when it came to my father. I was not surprised, therefore, when Mrs. Flemming gathered up the coins left upon the table and tottered off, almost joyfully, to buy us each another cream cake.

In her absence, Jeremy made an appearance. I'd observed him earlier, working at his father's stall, and was surprised that he'd been given time to himself. Mr. Simones was a man who put business before leisure and held his son to the same standard. If the father needed no rest, why should his offspring? Besides, he viewed making a profit a far greater pleasure than indulging in the amusements that a fair or some other rural fete afforded. "A penny earned is a penny saved," was his oft-repeated phrase, one which could set his son's teeth on edge.

To say that the younger Simones showed none of his father's ambition was an understatement. In that regard, he was more like his mother. She had been a gentle person who, because her parents had died and left her well-off from an early age, had lived without financial concern—which made it possible for her to marry for love, even though the match was beneath her social station.

The income she brought to the union was sufficient money to maintain a comfortable home and a bit more, all of which she entrusted to her husband who used it to purchase his coveted green grocer's shop. To his credit, he made good use of his opportunity. And if the consequence was that he neglected his wife some of the time, it was on account of his determination to do justice to her faith in him. The result was that the family lived not lavishly but well.

His sole acknowledged failure was his inability to communicate with his son. Jeremy, though no scholar, lived in his head, in a dream world that inspired his kites and a host of other inventions. His father tolerated, perhaps secretly admired, these skills, but he could see no practical use for them. They were, he knew, attributes of the mother—a woman who was, herself, a dreamer, and glad to be unencumbered of financial concerns so that she could devote herself to her watercolors. All in all, the arrangement suited both husband and wife well. That was before a lingering and fatal illness overtook the latter and made chaos of a once happy home.

Thinking of Mrs. Simones, it struck me that she bore a remarkable resemblance to Mrs. Flemming. The similarity was not so much in their appearance, though both were tall and auburn-haired, but in their mannerisms. Each had the habit of tapping her chin with a finger while in thought, and resting a hand at the base of her neck during conversation.

These habits, so alike, caused me to wonder that no one had remarked upon them before. Aunt Julia, who prided herself upon her powers of observation, had failed to make the connection. So had Mrs. Pardy, who was consulting with the newcomer regarding the proposed travel outfit. Was I imagining the similarity? I felt that I was not and that I'd discovered the underlying reason for Jeremy's dislike of the vicar: he was jealous of the man.

"I saw you with Mrs. Flemming, just now," he said, lightly touching the back of her empty chair. "Nice lady, isn't she? Not like the vicar. I-I mean, she smiles more. Suppose she'll be back in a minute?"

I nodded that she would be. Disappointed, he remained standing, though his eyes flitted with a question to the second empty chair, which I pretended not to see.

"I-I just come for my tea. Got to get back to the stall in a minute."

He shifted from one foot to the other, a sign that he felt uneasy. "I see you're wearin' the pendant."

I reached up to touch it. "Yes. I never take it off, as a matter of fact. Not even when sleeping."

"I'm glad," he said, breaking into a grin. "When I was makin' it, I wasn't sure if you'd like it."

"I'd have to be blind not to! You've a talent, Jeremy. You really do."

"Thanks. That means a lot, comin' from you."

"I don't know why." I shrugged. "I'm not artistic in any way. Sometimes I doubt I have any talents at all."

Jeremy's mouth fell open. Without thinking, he sank into Mrs. Flemming's vacated chair. "That's not true. You got lots of talent. My gosh, you're the smartest person I know—"

"That's not a talent. I can't paint like your mother or design like you, or even lay out a pretty garden the way Aunt Julia does."

"Aw, what does that matter? You've got a talent for makin' people happy."

"Liar. Most of the time, I make you angry."

"No, you don't. Well...maybe sometimes. But what about your aunt? You make her happy, don't you?"

"What does that prove? We're flesh and blood. I haven't friends the way you have—"

"I'm your friend, aren't I?" Jeremy's blue eyes grew so wide that I had to take pity on him.

"Yes, but you don't count. We've been together since we were infants. We're practically brother and sister."

Jeremy shook his head. "I don't think of you that way. I-I think of you as...as..." A blush overtook him. He choked off his words while I stared at him expectantly. "...as a person I admire on account of your bein' such a good student."

"Being a good student!" I could barely contain my disappointment. "What does that matter? I'll never *do* anything, *go* anywhere. I read about the arts, the great cultural cities, but knowing I'll never see them only makes me miserable."

"Don't say that. You'll see 'em one day." Jeremy's face brightened. "I'll take you! When we're grown up. You can show me all the wonderful places you've learned about. I'll be your pupil!"

The devotion shining from his eyes made me lower my own. I had treated him with indifference, abused our friendship time and again, yet all he'd been guilty of, all he'd ever meant to do was to show that he cared for me. How was I to account for my perversity? The rub of it was, I think, that being such a good person, Jeremy made me feel ashamed.

This was not one of those times, however. I put out my hand to touch him lightly on the shoulder. "Thank you for trying to cheer me up, but we both know it won't make any difference. I'll never leave this place. Not ever!"

"'Course you will. You won't be a ward all of your life. When you're twenty-five, you can go where you like. That's when you come into your inheritance, don't you?"

"Yes, but by the time I'm twenty-five, you'll be married. I've seen the way girls look at you."

"Ah, that's crazy!"

"Anyway, my inheritance won't be enough. I'd need someone to look after me. And, who is there to do that besides Aunt Julia, a woman who hates to travel?"

"Didn't I say I'd be with you? That means I intend to take care of you. Me."

The reply was so heartfelt, I exclaimed in spite of my better judgment. "Why, young Mr. Simones! That sounds very like a proposal."

Too shy to look at me, Jeremy dropped his gaze so that his golden hair fell over his face. As I observed him, I wondered what I'd ever done to deserve his good opinion of me.

"Jeremy, how lovely to see you." Mrs. Flemming had returned with our tea and was delighted to discover that our number had grown to three again. "Do join us," she said to the boy, who had leapt to his feet at the sight of her. "The vicar's left us for another woman, I'm afraid. Victorine's aunt to be precise. So you see, there's room at the table."

Jeremy hesitated, waiting for a sign from me. When I gave him no encouragement, he told Mrs. Flemming that he couldn't stay, that he had to return to his father's stall.

The vicar's wife set a small tray down at the center of the table. "I'm sure a few minutes more won't hurt. I've been meaning to ask about the pendant you made for Victorine. It's so lovely. I wondered if you'd make one for me. Not a seagull, of course. A rose, perhaps. You'd be paid for your work, naturally."

The green grocer's son looked at once surprised and pleased. "I-I suppose I could...but you wouldn't have to pay me for it, except for the materials, maybe."

"Oh, but I insist! I couldn't accept it otherwise. Your time is worth something."

"Naw, I'd enjoy doin' it. A rose wouldn't take much silver, either. If you wanted a whale that would be different."

Mrs. Flemming tittered appreciatively. "A whale? Heavens no! I'm not at all drawn to the wild creatures of the sea."

Her eyes were planted on the face of the youth in front of her, but I had the niggling suspicion that this last remark was addressed to me—though what she meant by it, I was unable to fathom. Still, it put me on my guard, which was just as well, for once Jeremy left us, the conversation became personal.

"Nice lad." Mrs. Flemming sat pouring tea into our milk-white cups. She handed one to me. "He's fond you. Have you noticed?"

I made no reply.

"That seagull of yours—it must have taken him ages. He wouldn't go to all that bother for just anyone, I should think."

"He's agreed to make a pendant for you," I pointed out.

She paused, holding the teapot suspended in mid air. "Yes, but I'm afraid I made it difficult for him to refuse, catching him out of the blue, like that. And he'll be paid for his work. That makes the circumstances different. I hope he didn't mind my asking. He hurried off so soon, without our finalizing anything."

"He had to get back to the stall. He told you. But he was pleased when you asked. Anyone could see that. I imagine he's already working out a design in his head."

"Yes...well, you're probably right. You know him better than I do." She leaned forward to offer me the sugar, studying my expression as she did. "What are your feelings toward him, I wonder. Is there an understanding between you?"

The woman is a goose. I thought. What business was it of hers how things stood between Jeremy and me? I might have asked the same about her and the vicar, but of course, after today, the question was unnecessary. Perhaps that's why she was probing. Having herself been exposed, she wanted to do the same with me. I was determined that she would fail.

"We're friends, if that's what you mean."

"Friends? Then you don't return his affection?"

My cream cake went slithering across my plate as I stabbed into it. "There *is* no affection to return. Not the way you mean. We're like brother and sister, having grown up together."

"Yes, I was wondering about that." A finger tapping against her chin informed me that Mrs. Flemming was in thought. "How is it that you're so close? There are other children in the village for whom you might have formed a similar attachment. Why

Jeremy?"

"You must ask Auntie. She's the one who brought us together. She's Jeremy's godmother, you know."

"No, I didn't. But it makes perfect sense..." She half-murmured to herself, as if recalling some information to which I was not privy.

"What do you mean?" I asked. She pretended not to hear.

"I still think I'm right about Jeremy. He cares for you more than you suppose. People change, after all. You're not children anymore. You're both coming to an age...how shall I put it? When there are mutual attractions? Certainly, Mr. Donne has given you an inkling of what that means already." When I failed to respond to her little jest, she hurried on. "If I'm right about your friend, I hope you will be kind to him. A young man in love can be so vulnerable."

"No more than a young lady, I should think, and perhaps less, given that a young man has ways to compensate: politics, commerce, travel. Or, if he means to die of a broken heart, there's always the Foreign Legion."

"The Foreign Legion? To risk one's life in a faraway land? That's a form of compensation a young lady isn't likely to envy."

"Oh, I don't know. It might be exciting to be a soldier."

"Such ideas! Keeping the peace is a better occupation, I should think. If women were allowed a say in the affairs of state, I suspect the outcomes to international squabbles might be different."

"You'd defeat the enemy with tea and cream cakes, would you?"

"Why not? Christ didn't exhort us to smite one another, did He?"

"What about the crusades, then?"

"What about them? A lot of people died and the world's still three-quarters heathen."

"That's a funny attitude for a vicar's wife, I should think."

"Why? Because I propose other ways of converting people besides cutting off their heads?"

"What does the vicar say about your opinions?"

"He doesn't say anything because we've not discussed them."

"Why? Are you afraid?"

"Of course, I'm not afraid. But it isn't a wife's place to talk of such things. Her responsibility is to hold the family together—a responsibility not to be taken lightly and quite as satisfying as politics or commerce. More so, I think."

Her reply struck me as ingenuous. How was it possible to hold firm opinions on important matters yet feel obliged not to express them? And did she really expect me to believe that cooking, cleaning and airing out the linen cupboard compared to holding sway in the great halls of human endeavor? I threw down my napkin in disbelief.

"I cannot agree that domesticity should be put on such a high plane. If a husband is made happy, well and good, but what of the wife's happiness? Is her ambition of no account? You suggest that she's little more than a slave, obligated to serve her master well, yet never to be set free?"

Mrs. Flemming's dainty hands flew up in mock protest. "Oh I'd hardly equate a wife to a slave. Surely, the wife is more *valuable*." When I failed to acknowledge her little jest, her voice became apologetic. "My dear girl, you mustn't take me so seriously. I was teasing, honestly. I take your point, but I must ask you to consider mine. A woman derives much satisfaction by helping her husband. The trick is to accomplish this without drawing attention to herself and *away* from him. Society laughs at a man who lives in his wife's shadow. But if she is clever and smooths his progress without being visible, then as he rises in wealth or position, she rises, also. Is that not a form of power?"

"You do that for the vicar? You smooth his way?"

The woman dropped a lump of sugar into her tea. "If I admitted to that, I'd lack discretion, wouldn't I? But, I wasn't thinking of me. I don't pride myself on being clever. Mr. Flemming has enough sagacity for us both. I was thinking about you."

"Me? If marriage means that I must live in someone else's shadow, then the idea has no appeal at all."

"One day, when you fall in love, you won't think of it as living in someone's shadow."

"One day, *if* I fall in love, it will be with someone who requires no pretense from me."

Mrs. Flemming's eyes grew wide. "I-I didn't mean to imply—"

"That a woman must live in awe of her husband? That she must suppress her thoughts in favor of his?"

"Not at all. Of course she has thoughts and feelings of her own!"

"But she mustn't express them. Is that fair? Is it honest?"

Mrs. Flemming smiled and shook her head in amused derision. "Oh, to be so young and see so clearly."

I stared back at her, not bothered in the least by her ridicule.

Indeed, as I contemplated her marriage, one guided more by decorum than candor, I grew in awe of it. What, in fact, did her husband know of her? More to the point, what would become of them if, for some reason, the veil of discretion slipped and the vicar found her out?

As if reading my thoughts, Mrs. Flemming leaned forward. Nothing she'd said, she assured me, implied that a woman should deceive her husband. What she'd meant to convey was that a wife must not be at cross-purposes with him, or the influence she exerted could destroy them both.

"Influence? What influence could she have if her thoughts are to be kept to herself?"

Another titter. "My dear, you are too modest, especially when your own powers are considerable. The way you flutter your eyes? Or brush your brow with one hand as if feeling faint? When a man sees that, he becomes all protective."

"I assure you, I never meant to convey..."

"Oh, my dear, I'm not judging you. But you surely aren't ignorant of your effect! That's why I urge you to be kind to Jeremy. Where women are concerned, men are gullible and easily hurt. It's their pride, you see. Makes them like children, sometimes."

Her thoughts drifted and she fell silent until animated by a new train of thought. "Sometimes, when I'm in London, I like to visit the House of Commons, a place of pomp and ceremony, one would think. But it isn't always, is it? Sometimes, sitting in the gallery, I'm astounded at the almost schoolboy hi-jinx that these men get up to. They grow red in the face, shout and shake their fists at one another. If the affairs of state weren't in question, it could be amusing. You know what I mean..."

"No, I've never been to London, much less the House of Commons. I should like to. But it's not possible."

"Not possible? Why not? Braxton's not at the end of the world."

"Auntie thinks it would be too much for me. The journey, the excitement and all."

"Oh, but it's a glorious place! You'd enjoy it. Such lovely shops. And places to eat, people everywhere, walking or in carriages. The noise would amaze you. But that makes it all so exciting. The hustle and bustle. I remember my first visit with Mr. Flemming. I was like a child at Christmas. My eyes couldn't take it all in. And you know, I've been back several times but I still get a thrill. There's so much to see. And it's always changing."

She regarded me with a good deal of sympathy. "Oh, you must have the experience." She patted my arm. "Once, at least!"

I was about to tell her the idea was hopeless when, struck by a notion, her eyebrows flew up. "I wonder if your aunt would entrust you to me? The vicar and I will be off for London next week. It's a short stay. A matter of a few days, but time enough to show you the high points. I'd love for you to come. Shall I ask her?"

The offer was so generous and so unexpected that the tension between us melted into thin air. "Would you? Would you, really?" I clapped my hands. "That would be wonderful! She might listen to you."

Pleased with herself, Mrs. Flemming took hold of my hand. "Come then! Let's find your aunt and beard her."

Seven

THE WALLS OF the room are damp. Faded paper peels from the corners. Its pattern is obscured by the darkness, which, but for a slant of light, is all-pervading. One of my arms is tied to the spindles of a chair. The other hangs free. In the vast stillness I hear my heartbeat.

No doors, no windows are visible. Still I rise, having set myself free, and press my fingers along the hard, vertical surfaces, desperate for a means of escape. Nothing! Nothing! No scent nor sound from the world beyond. Where is this place? How did I come to be here? How long must I stay? Terrified, I sink to my knees and weep bitterly.

✪ ❀ ❀

"My dear child! My poor dear child. You're conscious, at last. I've been so worried. Speak to me. How do you feel?" Aunt Julia was leaning over me, laying a cold compress on my forehead.

The glare from my window, as I opened my eyes, was enough to force me to close them again. I turned my face toward the wall and Aunt Julia, alert to my discomfort, hastened to draw the curtains.

"I've been so worried," she said when she returned to my side. "The doctor's been here twice. You've had such a fever. I blame myself, of course. I should have known the fair was a bad idea. The weather this time of year's too uncertain. Never mind. Now that you're awake, you'll soon be better. I'll make you some hot broth, shall I? You've had nothing but water these past three days."

Too weak to answer, I shook my head, but "no" was not to be taken as a reply.

"You must eat something, dear. How do you expect to regain your strength?"

A plump hand touched my forehead. A satisfied grunt followed. "The fever's gone, just as Dr. Leach predicted. He'll be so pleased when he comes this afternoon. In the meantime, he's left some medicine..."

My bed sagged under her weight as Aunt Julia sat down. "You've had a narrow escape, you know. Running off like that! What were you thinking? If Constable Mills and Jeremy hadn't found you so quickly, one shudders at the prospect of what might have happened. Mrs. Flemming is partly to blame. Putting the notion of travel in your head. You were disappointed when I refused, naturally. But I couldn't agree. You know how too much excitement affects you. Mrs. Flemming wouldn't have coped. She sees that now, though at the time I didn't much care for the looks she gave me. Anyway, it's all behind us. You'll feel better with some hot broth down you."

These remarks were all the apology I was to receive. Soon after, my guardian left me to prepare a tray. In the silence that followed, I tried to piece together the lost fragments of my memory.

After Mrs. Flemming and I had left the tea pavilion, I recall that it was some time before we found my aunt in the exhibit tent. She was a judge for the embroidery competition, and we had to chase her round the tables to gain her attention. Almost at once, I knew our proposal would fail. Aunt Julia made a habit of pretending not to hear ideas that displeased her, and this was her manner as Mrs. Flemming pressed her about the trip. When the assault became too long and too persistent, my aunt dropped the tea towel she was examining and looked her tormentor straight in the eye, the way a cobra might do prior to striking.

"You must pardon me, Mrs. Flemming. I think I know what's best for my niece. Being new among us, you're unaware of how too much excitement affects her. I'll excuse your misguided enthusiasm but take my word for it, the idea is a poor one."

The tartness in her manner was sufficient warning to the vicar's wife, who realized that nothing was to be gained by alienating this pillar of the church. She apologized at once and even suggested that in our exhaustive search for my aunt, I may have become overtired.

To hear myself discussed in the third person — as though I were not present or I was too ignorant to understand my condition — was humiliating. I felt betrayed and stormed from the tent in a temper, not caring what impression I left behind. My last recollection was of myself, stumbling across the moor, my clothes weighted down by the rain.

✪ ❀ ❀

Whatever her failings, Aunt Julia was an attentive nurse. In a matter of days, I was restored enough to move from my bedroom down to the parlor; but then time weighed heavily upon me. Mrs. Pardy dropped by with a few magazines, which I was quick to devour, and there were notes from well-wishers to answer, Miss Clemmons among them. With the vicar away and my studies denied me, however, it was difficult to occupy an entire day.

On Saturday, Jeremy came round with our delivery. I confess, I had looked forward to his visit all week. Even talk of the weather would be a welcome diversion.

"I must look dreadful," I fretted as he entered from the kitchen and drew up a chair beside me. The afternoon was sunny and with the curtains drawn back, light fell even into the farthest corners of the room, so that I felt exposed. My guest, however, was kind enough to flatter me.

"You look beautiful. Almost your self again." His blond head swiveled around, taking in the beams that crossed the walls and ceilings. On a bright day like this one, they made the space seem like a prison. "How much longer are you gonna have to stay cooped up in here?" he asked sympathetically. "You should come out, if you can. The wildflowers are in bloom."

Jeremy knew how much I loved the moor in the spring, when its colors, its perfumes could overpower the senses. If ever the earth held a mirror to heaven, it was then; for to compare the play of colors—pinks, yellows, whites, blues—to a mere tapestry or carpet was to neglect their impact upon the spirit, as well as the sensibilities. The heart leaps into the throat and the breath expands almost into infinity. Seeing it on a day like this, I observed, would do more good than all the chicken soup Aunt Julia had poured down me.

Jeremy smiled when he heard my complaint. His mother had been a believer in chicken soup. When he was poorly, with a cold or some other childhood malady, she'd boil a pot of the brew until it was thick and steamy. Then she'd coax him to drink it down, concocting some adventure story or other in exchange, and refusing to reveal the ending until his bowl was empty. By such means she always had her way. Or thought she did, for Jeremy had not been completely honest with his mother. He quite liked her chicken soup. It's just that he liked her attention more. And so, to the degree that she tricked him, he returned the compliment, with the result that those days of convalescence had been happy ones for them both.

"Didn't help her, though. Did it? Chicken soup." Jeremy's eyes clouded as he spoke. He had vaulted from his childhood to his mother's final days, forcing me to remember as well: how agony had stalked her to the grave; how the family had grieved as if Death were to be a permanent resident in the house; how the community had bowed its head and spoke about the loss of a sweet lady. She had lived quietly among us and with such humility that, except for her many kindnesses that testified to her existence, she might have been a dream.

Naturally, Jeremy missed her. But, there being no balm to his past suffering, I thought it best to recall him to the present.

"Auntie's been in the kitchen ever so long. I'm famished for my tea. Aren't you?" My head turned toward the swinging door just as a mob-capped head poked through. "Come give me a hand, Jeremy. I've prepared too much for one tray. You must carry in the treacle tart."

The mention of treacle tart brought Jeremy to his feet, as he liked nothing better. Disappearing into the kitchen, he returned almost as quickly carrying the pastry with enough solemnity to satisfy the keeper of the crown jewels. Placing it carefully on the table beside me, he then saw to the hearth. The logs had burned down and so he laid on new ones, which sent the sparks flying.

Aunt Julia looked grateful as she entered, balancing an over-laden tray in front of her. "Thank you, dear boy. Soon we won't have any need for a fire, but I admit I quite like how it makes a room feel cozy."

Jeremy took a second look at the walls and windows, this time appearing more favorably disposed. "It's a nice room, really. Flower-patterned, and all. Just like your garden, Miss Ellsworth."

"Thank you, Jeremy. Not many your age take any notice of gardens. Or if they do, it's to steal the flowers. And that's not the half of it. Most of the time, they throw them away!"

"Not thinkin', that's all." Jeremy's remark was meant to console, but the effect was quite the opposite.

"Yes, well, they *should* think. I spend too many hours on my hands and knees for them to go pillaging about. Believe me, at my age, it's not easy to keep up with all there is to do. I could understand if they *wanted* the flowers. But no! Not three paces along the road, the blossoms are thrown to the ground and trampled on. I can't tell you how it annoys me."

"At least there's a picket fence..."

"Yes, but that doesn't keep the flowers entirely in or the vandals entirely out!"

"Maybe you should get a dog," our guest proposed.

"A dog! That's more work, isn't it? Besides, there's Victorine's allergies to consider."

"Aw, she's probably grown out of 'em." Jeremy looked in my direction and smiled. "Bet she'd like a dog. Wouldn't you, Victorine?"

"Now don't you go putting ideas in her head!" Aunt Julia waved a plump finger in the air. "She's enough of those already."

In a diverting gesture, she spun her head in my direction and offered me a scone with a dollop of red jam on it. "Try this, dear. It's not our usual brand of preserve, but it costs considerably less. Is it as good, I wonder?"

Her forehead creased with so much expectation that I found it hard to tell her the truth: that there was more sugar than fruit in the confection. Her face fell with the verdict, for though she was not as penurious as Jeremy's father, she liked to save a penny.

"Well, that's settled, then," she sighed, slapping one hand to her knee. "We go back to the Robert's. Can't have you refusing to eat to save a few coins. You're skin and bones already."

Jeremy rose to my defense when he heard her, saying he thought I'd never looked better. His opinion counted as nothing, however.

"You may be right, dear boy. But she's not apt to stay that way if she starves herself." That said, she dropped a plate full of sandwiches on my lap.

For the sake of peace, I nibbled at the edges of one of the triangles and watched as Jeremy received a similar treatment. Having no mother, he adored the fuss being made over him, and received his portion with both hands, making certain that no crumb should escape. Aunt Julia looked pleased, and having served us both, took an equally generous portion for herself, then sat back to regale us with a bit of harmless gossip.

One of her stories was directed at Mr. Pounder. It seems that he had taken it into his head to teach himself a few of the turning dances that were all the rage in London. He needed a partner, of course, and as Miss Clemmons had always hated dancing, he had asked Mrs. Pardy, who had been pleased to accept. But when his old friend got wind of the arrangement, she was said to have flown into a rage—so much so, that upon meeting the little seamstress in the High Street, she chastised her severely, a caterwaul that could be heard up and down the avenue and in all the nearby shops.

"I sorely wish that I'd been there," Aunt Julia sniggered. "They say that people had their noses pressed against the windows afraid to go out in the midst of so much yowling. Mercifully, someone thought to fetch Mr. Pounder and he came running. Poor man had to agree to teach them both how to dance before peace was restored. So now, if you can imagine it, there's Anthea taking lessons, just to spite Cordelia! What a dour threesome that must make."

Her laughter was infectious and Jeremy followed her example, though a bit sheepishly, as Mr. Pounder was a schoolmaster and his father had drummed it into his head that he must be respectful of his teachers.

Fueled by the success of this first story, Aunt Julia launched into a second. This one was about the early days of Dr. Leach, a man now in his late fifties, with a flowing gray beard, but who had been no more than twenty-five when he arrived in our village. Though shy and unsure of himself in those early days, he had exhibited the same passion to prevent suffering that drives him today. That being the case, he did not hesitate when called to a nearby farm to deliver a goat of its breached kid—our veterinarian being at the far end of the county. This was the first time he'd been asked to assist with the birth of an animal, but as I say, when suffering was involved, Dr. Leach could be counted upon. And, to his delight and surprise, he was successful in his attempt. By the time he emerged from the barn, both mother and kid were doing well. The farmer was overcome with gratitude for he'd called for the new medical man out of desperation and without much hope.

Needless to say, when it came time for the good doctor to be paid, there was no stinting and for his efforts he received—not the customary armload of eggs, butter and cheese—but a veritable cornucopia of food stuffs.

Being a widower with no children at home, he knew that such a quantity of perishables was likely to go unused, and so when he returned to his infirmary, not only did he dispense the customary medicines for his patients' afflictions, he also sent them home with a parcel of dairy products. This distribution went on the next day, as well, so that in no time, word had got round. By the third day, the good doctor's waiting room overflowed with patients as hale and hearty as he would wish them to be, but who weren't adverse to a pound of cheese.

Under these conditions, the supply of dairy soon ran out and business returned to its normal pace. For several days, however, the inhabitants of Braxton couldn't resist making light of the affair. The title of "good doctor" was corrupted to "goat doctor," though not to his face, of course. Yet, somehow, the physician got wind of the appellation and was determined to have the last word.

On a night when the Crown pub was its fullest, he put in an appearance and ordered a round of beers for everyone. This generosity elicited a cheer from the crowd but one of the regulars felt obliged to ask, "What are we celebrating, doctor? Have ya come into an inheritance? A wheel of Stilton, maybe?"

A spasm of laughter rocked the room. "Why no, Mathiam," came the grinning reply. "Something a bit grander than that. It's my new title we're celebrating. Of course that raises a question. If I'm the 'goat doctor,' what does that make my patients?" More laughter punctuated the room.

In our community, nothing becomes a man so much as his humor. The appreciation stems, in part, from an unvarnished understanding of the vagaries of life. The birth of twin calves is an occasion of joy; a sudden rain can spell disaster. Whereas art, theatre, music are distractions which a city affords, in rural life these "veils" are too much absent. That one lives on the razor's edge is an inescapable truth. To endure, one must have humor or risk going mad. Needless to say, the good doctor's performance in the pub that evening enhanced his reputation and he was admired even more than would have been thought possible.

Three quarters of an hour passed and we, beguiled by tales such as these, were surprised to discover that the once-bountiful tea tray was empty. Aunt Julia took pleasure at the sight of so much carnage and, though Jeremy and I swore that we could not swallow so much as a morsel more, she bustled into the kitchen to see what remained on her shelves. Our one hope was that the sight of her garden awash in sunlight would make her forget her mission and that she would abandon us.

Had we but known how swiftly silence would flow into the parlor and overwhelm us, we might have been more careful with our wishes. All the laughter and merriment vanished. The enchantress who had plied us with good food and good stories had so lulled us into a stupor that, in her absence, we could do nothing but stare into the fire as though we were strangers with no common history. To be alone and silent can be a great comfort. But in the presence of another, it chafes.

"You're very quiet," I said at last, to fill the space. "What are you thinking about? Your kites, I suppose."

The question held no interest for me; I merely hoped it would rekindle the conversation. Jeremy looked up at the mention of his kites, his eyes shining, a smile upon his lips, and as I had hoped, began talking of his latest design—which included not only a detailed description of its appearance but also a thorough discussion of the materials to be used, including the type of glue, together with concerns about the hazards of spring flying. I could feel my lids grow heavy.

"The sky's always churnin', you see. So the winds are good this time of year. 'Course it don't help if it rains, but I usually get the birds down in time. It's the hikers that are the nuisance. They see me and want to talk, not realizin' that flyin' takes concentration."

I propped up my head with one hand, trying to stay awake. "Maybe you should try flying in the woods. That way no one would see you."

Jeremy frowned, taking me seriously. "B-but there's all them trees, you see—"

"I'm teasing! Anyway, it's a bit of a cheek to imagine you should have the moor to yourself in the spring. You've got three other seasons, when it's too warm or too cold or too rainy for most hikers. Don't be so greedy."

"You're always there," Jeremy responded defensively.

"What if I am? Would you like me to stay away as well?"

"No! 'Course not. You're the heart and soul of the place. The moor belongs to you more'n it does me."

"It doesn't belong to either of us. Nor to anyone else. That's the point."

"Free like the birds, you mean?"

"Yes, like the birds."

"Then you don't mind that I'm there?"

"Why should I?"

"I just wondered. You seem standoffish sometimes."

"Out of respect for you. You just said flying takes concentration."

"Yeah, but I wouldn't mind if you interrupted. It'd be like when we were small. Remember how it was? We were always together, sharin' with one another. I wish we still did."

"We were explorers then. We know the moor like the back of our hands, now."

Jeremy shook his head. "I don't just mean the moor. There's other interests. I could teach you to fly. You'd like it once you got the hang of it. Why not try sometime? It'd be better than lazin' around here."

Lazin' around was a phrase that didn't strike me as either an accurate or flattering description of my recuperation, but I took no umbrage, being more surprised by Jeremy's offer. He'd never suggested teaching me before. I'd always assumed that he cherished for himself those rare moments that his father permitted. And yet, he seemed sincere.

"It'd do you worlds of good," he persisted. "Get your mind off bein' sick all the time."

Now he had gone too far!

"I don't care for the notion that my illness is in my head, thank you very much." Annoyed, I pulled on the counterpane from the back of the settee and covered myself in a manner to suggest I was building a barrier between us.

Jeremy looked alarmed. "I-I didn't mean it to sound that way. I just thought you'd enjoy yourself. The vicar gave it a try yesterday—"

I sat up in surprise. "The vicar? No one told me he'd returned. Not you. Not Auntie. We've been together a full hour. Why have you said nothing?"

He shrugged, appearing guilty. "Been home a couple of days. Figured you knew. He was walkin' back from Matthew Oralley's place. The old man's down with the croup. Poor Mrs. Flemmin' didn't look so good either. She might have been cryin'. Pale, she was."

"She's always pale." I waved my hand in the air, dismissing his observation, and returned to my original question. "I wonder why I've had no word? They might at least have sent a note..."

"Maybe they didn't know they was supposed to keep you informed of their comin's and goin's."

"Don't be smart alecky. It doesn't suit you. I mean, *I've* been ill. Why not pay me a visit? Especially as Windmill Cottage is on the way to Oralley's."

"You're not ill—you just ate your way through a tea tray!"

"I didn't eat as much as all *that*. Besides, how do *they* know? I was ill when they left."

"Maybe your aunt told 'em you was better."

"She'd never do that. According to her, I'm always too thin and in need of a rest."

"You're stronger than you look." My companion kicked at the fire, which sent sparks flying into the room. He was annoyed, by the look of him. I didn't know why, but I didn't care, either.

"Did he ask about me, at least?"

"He might of done..."

"Surely, you remember. It was only yesterday!"

"Yeah, I guess he did, but mostly we talked about kites."

"Well, what did he say? What did you tell him?"

Jeremy stood up. Placing his hands on his hips, he glared down at me. "We didn't have no big discussion about you, if that's what you imagine. I told you, it was mostly about kites. Come to think of it, Mrs. Flemmin' was the one who wanted to know how you was doin'. Not the vicar."

"I don't believe you!" My voice cracked with anger and surprise. "Why should she care?"

"'Cause she's a nice lady. That's why."

"How can you say that? She's the one responsible for what happened to me."

"What? Never heard such nonsense." Jeremy crossed his arms and frowned. "You're responsible. You done it to yourself."

That he would take her part against me was more than I could bear.

"You always take her side!" I exploded. "You don't even know what happened. You weren't there."

"Everyone knows what happened," he roared back. "The whole village! Throwin' a tantrum and runnin' off the way you did. It weren't right to scare people like that."

As if he feared losing control of himself, Jeremy rose, turning his back on me to face the fire. He clutched the mantel, trembling as he did. For the first time since the incident, I understood how much my disappearance had frightened him. He must have thought I was dead when he found me lying unconscious on the moor.

"I-I don't know why you're so angry," I said after a time. "Maybe you're right. I shouldn't have run off. But you don't know how I felt. How Mrs. Flemming betrayed me."

"Best leave her out of it, Victorine!" He swung round, his eyes flashing. "The fault's with *you*, not with her."

His complete abandonment of me came as such a shock that I had to blink back my tears. *How dare he speak to me like that!*

"You know what I think, Jeremy? I think you've got a crush on Mrs. Flemming and it's made you go all soppy."

His blond head tipped backwards. "That's a stupid thing to say. She's a nice lady, that's all. You shouldn't always be tearin' her down."

"Me? What about you? You're not the one to call the pot black. When's the last time you paid the vicar a compliment?"

My arrow struck home. If Jeremy was anything, he was fair. He crumpled onto the settee beside me, looking genuinely distressed. "Look, I'm sorry, Victorine. You're right. From your point of view, that is. But in his case, I got my reasons."

"Then tell me!" I snapped. "You know I hate secrets."

A pause followed while his sapphire eyes peered down at me. My childhood companion seemed to be struggling with a question. Whatever it was, he decided not to share it with me; or if he did, it wasn't what I expected. When he spoke again, it was of Mrs. Flemming.

"About a fortnight ago, on a Wednesday, when I delivered at the vicarage, I found Mrs. Flemmin' in her garden. She was bent over one of her rose bushes, watchin' this big, orange spider make its web there. Standin' beside her, the sun was so bright, I could see every detail. How it worked its legs. How the threads come out of its body. How it kept swingin' back and forth like a pendulum. Before I knew it, the web gleamed in the sunlight. Lovely it was, like a delicate lace doily.

"Mrs. Flemming remarked on how wonderful it was and I agreed, only I added that it didn't strike me as fair that a trap set for other creatures should be so beautiful. Mrs. Flemmin' took issue with that. She said the spider was doin' what God intended. The web was His mystery and whether we understood or not, it was part of His divine purpose. We shouldn't see anythin' wrong in it, she told me, and she looked so earnest it got me to thinkin.' I mean about what's good. What's bad. I haven't sorted it all out, yet, and I don't want to speak until I do. But you can see what I mean about her bein' a nice lady and why I want you to give her a chance."

"Goodness! You *have* got a crush on her."

"You think the story's silly, don't you? That don't matter. It means somethin' to me."

"I've an idea! Why not make her a spider pendant instead of a rose?" I said facetiously, my eyes open wide.

Jeremy was not amused. He leaned forward so that I was pinned against the settee. "If you could just hear yourself. So smug. Like you're the only one's got a right to breathe. And the vicar, of course. I forgot about him."

"You're jealous, that's all."

"Don't you wish! But even if I were, it's got nothin' to do with him. I'm complainin' about your haughty ways."

"Why should my ways offend you? I'm one of God's creatures, aren't I? You must take me as He made me."

"*If* He made you." Jeremy was bent so low that our foreheads were almost touching. For a moment neither of us flinched, our breaths mingling. Then suddenly, inexplicably, a melting softness came into his eyes and I knew—he wanted to kiss me!

At first, I didn't know what to do. Certainly, I'd imagined my first kiss many times, but never in this faded parlor and never with Jeremy. In my dreams, I'd always stood with a mysterious stranger in some glorious, almost mystical woods. The face of my companion, until recently, was cast in shadows; but of late, it had become distinct. The recognition brought no shame as the tryst was in my head. But this present situation was all too real and nothing like my dreams.

I should have pushed Jeremy away. Yet the pounding of my heart was far more intoxicating than any imagined passion. Add to that my curiosity, Jeremy's good looks and his fervent longing, all reasons enough for me to close my eyes and offer no resistance.

A moment passed. Then two. Why was he waiting? When I opened my eyes again, I had barely enough time to see Jeremy striding from the room.

Eight

I DID NOT SEE Jeremy for several days, in part because I took walks during school hours but also, I suspect, because he, likewise, was avoiding me. The loss of his company left a gap, particularly as Aunt Julia had asked the vicar to suspend his sessions until after my upcoming exams. She was afraid that too much study would affect my flagging health. I was annoyed with her for making this request without consulting me, but as there was nothing to be done to change her mind, I made it a daily habit to walk on the moor in the early afternoon, spending as much time as I could in the out-of-doors, and returning to Windmill Cottage just in time for tea. Aunt Julia fretted about these excursions but as she was often away, attending one committee meeting or another, she could do little to prevent them.

Given this period of isolation, it is understandable that I should be overcome with delight when, on a day that was breezy but sunny, the vicar and I met by chance on his walk to one of the nearby farms. As he was in no great hurry, we spent an hour in one another's company—it being the first time we had clapped eyes upon each other since his return from London. Our stroll together was so pleasant that its effect lasted well into evening, a glow upon which Aunt Julia remarked. As to the reason, I gave her no satisfaction.

If I was made happy by this first encounter, imagine my joy when the vicar and I met on a second and third occasion so that by the fourth chance meeting, I began to suspect they occurred by more than happenstance. Naturally, I was flattered to think he was making an effort to seek me out. I hoped it was a sign of a mutual attraction, and so I took great pains over my appearance when preparing for these outings.

Aunt Julia made note of this exercise and shook her head. "Put as much effort into staying warm, dear girl, as you do with those ribbons. The rabbits don't care how you look. It's the weather you must satisfy." Practical advice to be sure, but it fell upon deaf ears. Nor did she entirely discourage me. Many times, a flower from the garden would be pinned to my lapel. "'Sweets to the sweet'" Aunt Julia would say. Then she'd kiss my cheek and send me off, happy that I was happy.

The weather was mild but cloudy on the day I discovered Vicar Flemming strolling along the cliff's edge. Overhead, the gulls soared in numbers, for the incoming tide was pounding on their customary perches, the rocks below. Braced against the wind, the man in black walked with one hand clasped tightly to his hat while, with the other, he endeavored to control the cloak that was flapping behind him like a large wing.

"Ah, Victorine. We meet again," he smiled as I caught up with him. "I've just returned from the Benchleys. All is in order there, I'm happy to report. The old man is up and about and threatening to repair his roof again. I advised him to let his son do it this time, but he's reluctant to admit his age. I suspect he'll ignore my advice, to his detriment. You, on the other hand, seem to be benefiting from these frequent walks of yours. Mrs. Flemming will be glad to hear it. She mentioned the other day she was thinking of inviting you to tea. 'A break from all those dreary studies,' is how she put it."

"I should like to come," I replied smiling up into his dark eyes, "but please assure her that I don't find my studies dreary in the least."

My smile was returned and as we began to walk together, the vicar spoke indulgently of his wife. "She means well, but never having been a scholar herself, she finds it difficult to believe a person, particularly a young girl, could take pleasure in history, geography and the like. I, on the other hand, having the privilege to be one of your tutors, know the quickness of your mind. You could never be satisfied with anything less than a rigorous challenge."

"You mustn't flatter me so, Vicar. Auntie says flattery turns the head. You wouldn't want to spoil me."

My companion laughed. "I'm sure I could never do that. Besides, what I've said is true. It's not flattery in that case."

"Yes, but you said as much yesterday, too."

"Did I?" My remark brought my companion up short. He stopped and peered down at me, frowning a little, not out of annoyance, but the way one does when grappling with memory. "Was it yesterday that we met?"

"It was. And again two days prior."

"I had not realized." He took my arm and we began walking

again. The gesture was natural enough, without awkwardness or premeditation, the result of a mind still in thought; but it was the first time he had ever done so and I was forced to drop my gaze to prevent him from observing my blush.

"I suppose we're bound to meet with a degree of frequency," he went on, explaining the coincidence...to himself and to me. "You see, I've taken quite a fancy to the moor. The vista being almost limitless, the mind is allowed to explore with no visual impediment. I honestly believe I do some of my best thinking here, preparing sermons and the like. But you know, sometimes, when there's absolutely no one about, I'm inclined to feel as if I'm alone on the planet. Do you ever get that impression? Liberated, yet somehow anxious?"

"Yes, I know exactly what you mean. The lack of accountability. One could commit murder here and never get caught."

The vicar nodded, narrowing his eyes as he considered my suggestion. "A strange notion, that, for one so young; but you describe the sensation, exactly. Total freedom. With the decision whether to do ill or good left entirely to the individual. The spirit unbridled by social conditions. God sees everything, of course. We mustn't forget that."

A silence fell between us as we continued walking. Then the vicar, having taken time to consider the import of what I'd said, spoke again. "You put great store in the idea of freedom, don't you? I've no wish to imply that you lack obedience, but certainly there is a seditious undercurrent to your nature."

I opened my mouth, but his hand went up to forestall my reply. "I mean nothing critical by my observation. In fact, I admire your spirit. One or two others I know could do with your fire."

"Mrs. Flemming, for example?"

The vicar paused and gazed at me as if to assess whether or not I meant to be impertinent; but I gave him no satisfaction. My expression remained impassive. Let him make what he would of the remark. All I risked was to learn something of his opinion of me or of his wife.

"I never said so," he answered at last. The reply was so neutral, so equivocal that I was neither chastised by it nor was Mrs. Flemming defended. Hearing him, I became emboldened.

"I hate the word obedience, if you must know. Why should I or anyone be servile if we're all equal in God's eyes?"

"A child has a duty to one's parents—"

"Yes, but I'm not a child. I've a right to my opinion, surely."

My companion laughed, amused but without derision. "I can't imagine anyone denying you that, Victorine. But holding an opinion is different from being free to act upon it. At one time or another, we must all bow to someone else's intention. Obedience has little to do with age, although a child is apt to imagine that his parents are free while he is not. But that is the child's illusion. In important ways, his parents are less free than he. They, too, have obligations: to him, to each other, their community and most importantly, to God. Indeed, I'd go so far as to say that the older one grows, the less free one becomes. Still, you mustn't imagine that it chafes to bear one's burdens. Often, our greatest rewards come from doing our duty."

"You sound very much like Mrs. Flemming and my auntie."

"Well, there you are. I can think of no two women who could offer you better advice. And no two women, I believe it safe to say, whom the good people of Braxton hold in higher regard."

"As if I cared for the opinions of the good people of Braxton. I hate it here. No freedom, no privacy... How is one expected to breathe in so small a space?"

"And so you come to the moor?"

"Exactly. Here, I walk in the presence of my pure self."

"*Pure* self? By that you mean your essence, I imagine. And what have you learned, in these walks with your pure self? That you are free to commit murder? Doesn't the notion frighten you a little? That you could even have such thoughts?"

"As you said, the difference lies between thinking and doing."

"Clever girl. And a brave one, I might add. Not many have sufficient courage to confront the beast within. But be careful. Innocence could lead you astray. And, I take back what I said before. Thinking *is* a form of doing. God sees and knows all, I remind you. Especially what's in your heart."

"Of course, He does. He made me, didn't He?"

"Yes, but you needn't imply that He's responsible for our dark thoughts. Those are a gift of the devil. That traitor is the beast within and we must grapple with him, wrestle him to the ground, and not be fooled into imagining his promptings are those of a higher spirit. My advice is that you look more kindly upon the strictures of society, Victorine. Unbridled freedom, though you may think otherwise, is the way of savages."

"And is their way so bad?"

I stood looking up at him as the vicar eyed me curiously. Was I teasing or had I answered in earnest? To satisfy him, I told him what Mrs. Flemming had said about the spider being part of God's divine mystery. "It would follow then, wouldn't it, that savagery, too, reflects God's Will?"

I expected him to be shocked, or confounded, at least, having used his wife's words against him. But he was neither of these. Instead, his mood changed and he looked amused.

"You would abandon society, then? Have us all out here, running with the rabbits?"

"Only those who deserve the privilege."

"A secret society, eh?"

"A select one."

The man at my side laughed heartily. "Does your aunt know of these libertine ideas? I suspect not. Am I right?"

"You're disappointed in me, aren't you?"

"No. I prefer to think this is a phase. Part of growing up. When one is gifted like yourself, challenging ideas is as natural as breath. I wish some of my parishioners would venture beyond what they've been told. There's a danger, too, in untested faith."

"Why Vicar," I said, as I peered up from under my bonnet. "I suspect you of being a libertine, as well."

"At some point I may have been. I haven't conformed to everyone's expectations, certainly."

"Oh? Whose for example?"

"Ah! That would be a list too long to mention. Besides, it's you I want to talk about. I'm anxious to learn how preparations for the exams are going. Are you getting the assistance you need?"

"I don't find my subjects difficult, if that's what you mean."

"How about mathematics? Young ladies often find it a struggle, I'm told."

"Oh, but you mustn't believe what you've been told, Vicar. At least, not without questioning it."

Hearing his words thrown back at him, he staggered in mock surprise, a hand pressed against his heart. "'A touch, a touch; I do confess't.'"

"Not Shakespeare again? Are there no other authors worthy of being quoted?"

His ragged eyebrows lifted. "Whom would you recommend, Miss Ellsworth? I should be pleased to know."

"Webster," I replied without hesitating. "He writes as well as Shakespeare and his Bosola equals Iago when it comes to sheer villainy."

"*The Duchess of Malfi*? It's true. Bosola's dissembling brings the poor woman to as wretched an end as Desdemona. I'm surprised you admire the play."

"Why? Because she's murdered? Events don't have to end well to please me." I spoke cavalierly, I admit, being safe in the company of the vicar on a mild spring day. During the midnight of one of my blacker moods, these words would have stuck in my throat. I was playing the fool and knew it, but was quite unprepared for the shadow that fell across my mentor's face. Murmuring as if to himself, he noted that if it were possible to take pleasure from bad endings, then Life was certain to satisfy.

It seemed an odd sentiment for a man of the cloth and I wondered about it as we continued to walk in silence. Except for the glimpse of their courtship, which Mrs. Flemming had given me, I knew little about my mentor except that he was well traveled and had served as vicar in a number of parishes. The many times I'd tried to draw him out had met with little success. Like his wife, he was a master at turning a question back upon the inquisitor. This ploy convinced me that he was hiding a secret, some tragedy that had once clouded his life. What it could be, I could not imagine.

Perhaps his fascination for Elizabeth Dernwood's history provided some clue. That he'd been secretive about the diary suggested more than a fascination. Was there information in that account he wished to hide? Had he known her? Perhaps been her spiritual mentor? Or was there a greater emotional connection? I've often been accused of having an overzealous imagination, but in the vicar's case I felt certain these speculations were not far a' field.

Imagine my despair when, without a word spoken, we came to the edge of the moor. There our single path diverged and became two: one returned me to Windmill Cottage; the other led to the village which was the vicar's destination.

Conscious that we had come to a parting of the ways, he took my hand in his large one and held it...rather longer than I would have expected. My own hand trembled and as it did, those dark, hooded eyes peered down at me as if to ask a question. What it was, I could not fathom, but I felt it was a serious one as his mood remained unchanged and there was no trace of a smile, such as one might expect when friendly acquaintances are about to take leave of one another. Perhaps I was over imagining, but as my hand grew warm in his, I became embarrassed and mumbled something about having enjoyed the afternoon and hoping that nothing I'd said had given offense.

He dropped my hand and looked surprised when he heard me. "Not at all, dear girl. I enjoy our skirmishes. Mrs. Flemming accuses me of putting ideas in your head, but I think it's the reverse. You keep me on my toes, certainly."

"She knows we've been together, then?"

"On the moor? No. As a matter of fact, I haven't mentioned But she's aware that we have conversations. Your aunt is cognizant of our meetings, I suppose?"

"No, I've said nothing either. I was afraid... I mean, I wasn't entirely sure..."

"Afraid of what? Sure of what?"

His face became tinged with red, like a man holding his breath. "There's nothing to hide, after all. It isn't as if we've been seeking one another out."

I made no reply and avoided his gaze, a clear sign that I did not believe him. When he saw my reaction, his voice rose a decibel. "My dear girl! Unless *you* have made some effort to study my movements, these meetings, I can assure you, are by chance! If you think otherwise, then it's well your guardian has no notion of them for I can assure you, if what you imagine were to become common gossip, the entire village would object to such assignations. I hope you see that. You do, don't you?"

I could feel myself growing warm all over. Whatever I believed, whatever I felt to be the truth, it had been stupid of me to succumb to my vanity. I'd been too eager to expose what I felt was a mutual attraction and risked the goodwill of the one person in the world I admired. At that moment, had the wind lifted then plunged me headlong over the cliffs, I would have considered myself blessed. But no such rescue was afforded me. I stood exposed to the air with neither a shrub nor rabbit warren to hide my shame. Tears streamed down my cheeks and like some babbling fool, I repeated the words, "I'm sorry. I'm sorry."

The pain was so unbearable that all I could think of was that I needed to put distance between the person I adored and myself. I ran away, heedlessly, mindlessly, my face braced against the wind, never daring to look back, never dreaming that so worthless a creature as myself would be pursued. But, I was. I was! A hand clasped me by the shoulder and held me. I looked up and through my tears saw that the vicar's eyes were brimming, too.

Nine

"TELL YOU, JULIA, it was a shock. Unheard of! That's why I came at once. I knew you'd want to know."

Entering the parlor late one afternoon, I found Miss Clemmons seated on the edge of the settee, staring into the wide-eyed expression of my guardian. They rose and hurried to my side the moment they saw me.

"My dear! My dear! Such news! The exam results are in. You've passed every subject with *record scores*. Oh, you've brought such honor to the school!" Miss Clemmons clasped her hands to her bosom in exaltation. "The staff room is abuzz, I promise you. Anyone who's had the slightest responsibility for your education is taking credit. I admit to feeling some satisfaction, myself. But it is *your* achievement. We all know that." She bent closer to my ear to reveal a secret. "I shouldn't tell you this, but I've heard a certificate from London's to be awarded on Speech Day!"

I stared at her blankly.

"Yes!" she went on. "You've been singled out for special recognition from the Queen. I can't tell you how proud we all are."

My third-form teacher gave my cheek a pat. "There! I've told you everything. Now, I must go. The news hasn't reached the boy's school yet. Elliot knows nothing of your achievement. But I'm dying to see his face. He'll be positively green with envy."

Still talking, she headed for the hall with my guardian in tow. "There's word of a full scholarship, Julia, which means Victorine could be off to university next year. I hope you don't intend to remain as stubborn as you've been in the past about her leaving."

Too much in a hurry to notice the effect of her utterances, my third-form teacher sailed over the threshold and up the garden path, unmindful of my aunt's sour expression or the way the cottage door was slammed behind her. Having managed a last word with one old friend, Miss Clemmons was in pursuit of another. Mr. Pounder, at least, would make a fuss over her, as though she—and she alone—was responsible for my success.

Aunt Julia came bristling back into the parlor. "It's all very well for Anthea to put out ideas. She's not the one with responsibilities..."

Remembering my presence, she addressed me. "It's no good glowering, Victorine. We've been through all this before. Money isn't the issue. I've your health to consider. Who'd look after you so far from home? If you wish to continue your studies, we'll find tutors here, just as we've always done. But leave Braxton? It's quite impossible!"

To avoid an argument, she headed for the kitchen. "I don't know what the world's coming to. All this talk about an education... In my day, a young lady needed virtue, not a degree."

When it dawned on her that I'd said nothing since hearing the announcement, she paused for a second and looked at me curiously. "All this news, it comes as a bit of a shock, doesn't it, dear? Are you all right? Why don't I put on the kettle and cut into the pound cake I made this morning? We should celebrate your good news, after all."

She disappeared behind the swinging door without waiting for a reply, and I was glad for it, as I needed time to consider what I'd been told. Had knowledge of my achievement arrived a month earlier, I confess, I would have danced upon the ceiling. A month earlier, my right to enter university would have been defended. But in the time it takes to shatter glass, the construct of my life had altered, and any desire I might have had to escape Braxton had vanished. Why rush headlong into the world when all that I longed for or cared about had become centered in this one, small village? Let it be as my aunt would wish: that I should live content in Braxton until the end of my days.

The miracle of this change could be laid to the vicar. That day on the moor when we'd parted, after so much misunderstanding and so many tears, had proved to be my happiest. Once he'd caught up with me, he'd held me and uttered assurances which, by themselves, would have revived my battered spirit. He'd never meant to hurt me. I was dear to him. A treasure! Then came the words I'd wanted to hear but dared not imagine.

He'd told me he loved me.

✪ ✳ ✳

Thanks to Miss Clemmons, news of my achievement spread throughout the village. Mrs. Pardy paid a visit, assuming that a dress for the awards ceremony would be required. Her assumption came as a surprise to my guardian.

"What's wrong with the pink frock you made for her birthday?" she bridled. "It's only been worn once!"

Her comment received a disapproving frown. "You said it yourself, Julia. That dress is a bit bare. Not at all suitable for Speech Day."

Forced to eat her words, my guardian allowed that a new frock should be ordered—one that buttoned all the way to the collar. As no stipulation was made as to color, a soft lilac was recommended—a shade that, according to the little seamstress, was all the rage in Paris. When I readily agreed, a bargain was struck which brought satisfaction all around.

Soon congratulations on my achievement poured in from all corners of the county. Even Jeremy brought flowers. He was delivering them for his father, he said, but that was a partial truth. He'd come to make amends for having left me on the settee with my eyes closed. If he supposed I was still angry, our hour together left him in no doubt of my good will. As such, he could be heard whistling as he peddled his way back to his father's shop that afternoon.

Why wouldn't I be kind to him? Much had changed since we'd last been together. I was happy, and I wanted him to be happy, as well.

Of all the communications delivered to Windmill Cottage in the days that followed, the one of greatest interest arrived in a cream-colored envelope. Addressed in a large, Spenserian hand, I admired it at once, for if I had one failing as a student, it was in my penmanship. The patience to master the demands of so ornate an alphabet was a quality I lacked. I wondered who'd sent it and turned the missive over and over again before opening it, trying to guess. To my astonishment, the note was from Mrs. Flemming, an invitation to tea on the following Friday.

This first surprise was compounded by a second. No mention was made of my aunt, who liked nothing better than to be entertained at the vicarage. The omission set her to grumbling, and I confess being uneasy myself, even though the vicar had signaled that an invitation was in the offing. Had I a clear conscience, I'd have welcomed a private tête-à-tête. But mine was not a clear conscience, not with my remembrance of the vicar's kiss still burnished upon my lips.

Had he done or said something to make his wife suspicious?

Perhaps he'd been too generous in his praise of me? Too persistent in his references? Being ignorant, I counted the days till our meeting with a mixture of dread and curiosity.

✪ ❊ ❊

The sky on the appointed afternoon wore a long gray overcoat. A steady rain beat down, as well, turning our camellias brown and scattering petals, thick as a carpet, upon the ground. Likewise, the daffodils bent earthward, their yellow trumpets speckled with mud so that they looked diseased.

My own fate was no better. Venturing forth, I was ill-treated by the elements and reached the vicarage in a dreadful state. My hood was blown back and my hair plastered to my head so that rivulets of water cascaded over my nose and chin. The effect must have been very like a drowning. Certainly, Mrs. Flemming looked aghast when she opened the door.

"Come in, dear. Come in. I'm surprised you braved such terrible weather. Or that your aunt permitted it."

Once drawn into the hall, I was helped out of my rain gear, including my Wellingtons—which took effort on both our parts. Then, with my outer garments left dripping on their pegs, I was led into the guest parlor. The fire-lit room had warmed the walls to the color of honey and was welcoming.

"Auntie doesn't know I've come," I said after being encouraged to stand before the fire. "I slipped out while she was in the kitchen."

As to that, Mrs. Flemming made no comment but invited me to sink into a large, chintz-covered chair, which I did, being satiated with the heat from the drowsy fire. Then she left me and went in search of a towel so that I could dry my hair.

During her absence, I had a look around—something I was eager to do, as I'd not been inside the vicarage since she and her husband had arrived. Much had changed since then.

Vicar Soames, out of respect for my father, had always maintained the premises as it had been while I lived there— except for the area rebuilt after the fire, of course. Now, with the arrival of Mrs. Flemming, it was impossible to recognize the place. Loomed carpets had supplanted the braided ones and the love seat, formerly upholstered in a sturdy brown bunting, was smothered in damask.

Gone, too, was all trace of scholarly endeavor. The mantle,

which used to groan under the weight of stacks and stacks of books, had been cleared to make room for prancing figurines: porcelain milk maidens, shepherds and the like. Crocheted doilies, too, were in evidence, as were shawls, one thrown over a chair, another blanketing the piano. And everywhere, vases burgeoned with freshly cut flowers. In sum, what had served as my father's study had been given a feminine character. I cannot say that it suited the room or me.Mrs. Flemming returned with a thick towel, as promised, and I set to work repairing the damage wrought by the weather. As I did so, she disappeared a second time, only to return with a tea trolley laden with crockery that rattled as it was pushed into the room.

Content that she'd provided for my immediate needs, my hostess sat in the chair opposite me, a match to the one I occupied, and began pouring tea. Her gestures were graceful, and I noted that the hands wielding the sugar tongs were not only slim and well manicured, but today were adorned with several rings, a vanity that surprised me.

At first, our conversation bordered on the mundane. We talked of the weather, of the changes made to the decor and, of course, I received one or two perfunctory compliments on my scholastic achievement. As these topics provided little challenge, I could sit nodding and smiling at the woman opposite me while a separate monologue played in my head. As always, the enormous differences between the vicar and his wife opened before me like a chasm. They shared so little by way of background, interests, or disposition. Why on earth had he ever proposed?

She had a pretty face, yes. A trim figure, certainly. But why condemn himself to a life without intelligent discourse? Mrs. Flemming, it seemed to me, fell into that category of people whom the vicar eschewed as never having ventured beyond what they'd been told. To live with her struck me as tantamount to being buried alive!

And yet, there were little anomalies—like the rings, or a glance that was too penetrating, or a question asked in innocence but with an edge to it—that taunted me to consider whether or not I had a complete view of her.

Hers was a nature easily pleased, that much I knew. Not that she was blind to evil. She was never that. But what she made of it astounded me. Like her observation concerning the spider. She was inclined to blame God for everything so that a failed harvest, or the death of a spouse was, inevitably, His will and a test of faith.

Satan, apparently, had been banished entirely, a rather childlike simplicity. And, at times, she was a child! In the vicar's presence, for example, when she allowed her views to be overshadowed by his.

That she would behave in so self-effacing a manner may have pleased him but it disquieted me, for I suspected her of being more skilled than she cared to admit. Certainly, she managed her social duties admirably and in such a way that as many people sought her out for advice as they did her husband. Aunt Julia said her humility put people at ease. But I doubted her use of that gift. Like a crab fork, she was apt to pry secrets from the unmindful—a well-practiced art which made me wary, as I'd no wish for her to make a study of me.

I was pondering these anomalies when the expression on my hostess's face made me aware that I'd been asked a question.

"I was talking about men, dear. Do you find them difficult to fathom? I did when I was a girl. In fact, I still do. They go about their business in ways so different from women. Communication seems impossible sometimes. But of course, one must try. Otherwise there'd be no hope of resolving differences."

In my mind's eye, I was shaking my head in order to make some sense of her line of questioning. I remembered talk of flowers and crochet patterns... When had the conversation taken this dramatic turn?

"You must pardon me, Mrs. Flemming. I know little about the ways of men. My father died when I was a child."

"Yes, I heard about the tragedy. To lose both parents in a fire like that. How awful for you. Still, your achievements do honor to their memory. They'd have been very proud of you, had they lived."

A pause followed out of respect for my circumstance, then my hostess went on. "But you're not entirely sheltered from the male population. You're close to my husband, are you not?"

"He is my teacher."

"Yes, but you discuss subjects besides your Biblical lessons, don't you?"

My hesitation must have been palpable for it brought a light touch to my forearm. "You needn't be circumspect with me, dear. Jordan shares everything. Well, not everything," came the correction. "As your spiritual advisor, he keeps your confidences; you may be sure of that. No, what I mean is, he's fond of you and you feel the same, I think. Am I right?"

"I-I like him well enough."

"Oh surely, it's more than that! From what my husband tells me—"

"I'm sorry, Mrs. Flemming," I interrupted crossly, "I've no idea what Jordan's been saying!"

The moment I spoke, I realized my mistake. Her pale blue eyes flew open like shutters.

"*Jordan*? My husband doesn't encourage familiarity, does he?"

My cheeks grew warm. "N-no, of course not! You called him that and I... I must ask your pardon."

Mrs. Flemming leaned back in her chair. "No harm done, my dear. You were endeavoring to shock me, I suppose. Young people do that, I'm told. Perhaps I deserve it. I mean, if you thought I was becoming too personal. But I do so want us to be friends. Is it possible, do you think?"

If I had answered truly, I would have said that I'd as soon kiss an adder; but candor was out of the question and so I nodded without saying anything. My reward was a thin smile from the woman in gray.

"I'm afraid I must apologize for having confused you," she went on, brushing a few crumbs from her lap. "Mr. Flemming says I'm too indirect. But I find it difficult to speak bluntly on personal matters. I see now that my approach was in error. I should have spoken plainly. Truth is, I was trying to sound you out on Jeremy's behalf."

As the grocer's son was farthest from my thoughts, I couldn't help registering surprise. "Jeremy? What about him?"

"Oh my dear, he's so fond of you. I wonder if you know how much? Or, if you share his feelings to any degree?" Her eyes, which moments before had viewed me with suspicion, looked pleading.

"We're friends. That's all." I shrugged.

"Nothing more?"

"What more could there be? He's a boy."

A pale hand waved away my remark. "A few months younger than yourself. That's all. Oh I know, at your age the gap seems enormous. But as the years pass, it will count as nothing. There's a decade between the vicar and myself."

"I still don't see..."

"He's so unhappy, Victorine. Something about the way you last parted. He thinks you're angry. But you mustn't be, whatever the cause. Best friends do quarrel. Even lovers. If you care for a person, let the bad feelings pass and hold on to what's best in the relationship. This advice will serve you well throughout your life, I promise you. Oh, forgive him, please do!"

As I sat listening, I was of different minds. That Jeremy had confided in the vicar's wife came as unwelcome news, but it offered an advantage, as well. Since he and I had already settled our difference, something she did not know, apparently, I was free to react in one of two ways. I could tell the truth and put an end to this discussion, or gull her into believing she might be able to affect a reconciliation. The former course was the more honorable, but the latter pleased me more as I felt she deserved to be duped. Besides, flattery of the kind that allowed her to imagine she could influence me was bound to work in my favor.

"Oh, you needn't think we were gossiping." Misreading my frown, the vicar's wife was eager to reassure me. "Jeremy has nothing but praise for you. That's why he's so disconsolate. He'd never want to lose your good opinion."

"You've been asked to speak for him, then?"

"No, no! The idea's entirely my own. Two young people out of sorts with one another saddens me. I was hoping to set it right. That's why I asked you here. Now I'm afraid I've made a muddle of it. I can only promise that whatever he's done, he's sorry and hopes you can forgive him." She paused to assess my reaction.

"To tell the truth," I began slowly, "I find Jeremy very puzzling of late. He's grown so moody. I never know what's going to set him off. Perhaps you *could* offer some advice..."

"Oh yes, dear. Do let me try!" Mrs. Flemming leaned forward with the enthusiasm of a dog wagging its tail.

"Are you sure? I wouldn't want to trouble you."

"That's what I'm here for, dear. It's no trouble at all. Besides, we've agreed to be friends, haven't we? Then we must feel free to share our thoughts."

"Yes, but you and your husband are so close. It's not like Jeremy and me at all."

A row of even, white teeth showed themselves as she laughed. "It's not as if we fit hand and glove, dear girl. My husband and I are very different people. We had to learn to grow together."

"But you seem so happy."

"Happiness doesn't mean being alike. Heaven forbid! In fact, I'd say that people too much the same are in danger of boring one another. Although, I do admit that where there are differences in a marriage, the wife usually makes the greater accommodation."

"But why? That doesn't seem fair."

More laughter followed. "Leave fairness to the courts, child! It has no place in a marriage. Relationships are far too complicated for the simple rules of law."

"But why must the woman accommodate? Where is it written?"

"In our natures, I suppose. We are nurturers, after all, tending to the fires, so to speak, while our husbands make their way in the world. And as the world is a large and sometimes cruel place, it's hardly fair to make demands at home, as well."

"But you work in the parish. You sit on committees, help with charities. How is that different from the vicar's work?"

"How is the leaf different from the tree? I'm a helpmate, Victorine, but the burden of success or failure lies with Mr. Flemming. That's why I make every effort to see that conditions at home are to his liking."

"And you find that fulfilling?"

"Immensely. Except for being in service to God, a woman has no higher calling. To attend to one's husband and one's children..." She suddenly stared down at her hands. "The vicar and I have not been blessed in that regard. That's why it's important that I not fail him otherwise."

In the half-light of the fire, I could see her eyes glisten with the threat of tears. I admit to feeling embarrassed by them, but I also understood her passion, and that hunger made me feel closer to her than I had thought possible.

"You probably doubt what I'm saying," she said looking up again, having mastered herself. "But you're young, yet. When the time comes, you'll see that for a woman there's no greater recompense than a good marriage, the security and respectability it affords."

I would have liked to hide my surprise at her description of wedlock, but I could not. Here was a woman who'd come near to tears over thoughts of an unborn child, but when it came to marriage, her words evinced not a shred of emotion. Security? Respectability? What about love?

"Aunt Julia never married," I objected. "She's secure. Respectable. And what about Miss Clemmons?"

"Admirable women, both of them," came the swift reply, though it lacked conviction. "But as wives and mothers, we have the unique opportunity to..."

"Serve others. Yes, you've said that. But Auntie works hard

for the well-being of this community, as does Miss Clemmons. Besides, has a woman no duty to herself?"

"A duty to oneself? I don't know what that means. We aren't living in a void, Victorine. Whatever we are, whatever we become, it's due to our place in society. That shapes us and defines our responsibilities. If you were a boy, this conversation would take a different direction. But as you're not, my wish is that you see the benefits of your feminine heritage. A good wife works for her husband's success and that of her children—"

"Are we to achieve nothing that is our own?"

My explosion caused her eyebrows to lift in astonishment. "You mistake me entirely. Why make it sound as if service to the family is a sacrifice? It isn't. A woman doesn't live through others, as you seem to suggest, but *for* them—which is the highest form of spiritual reward. One day, I hope you'll come to see this."

Her turn of phrase, I confess, was a pretty one and would have served her well had she been a poet. But as argument it remained unconvincing.

"Tell me. Tell me honestly. Have you no dreams?"

A pause followed and, as I suspected, she preferred to evade my question. "I begin to understand why my husband spends so much time in your company. What a probing mind you have. Quite a challenge for him. One which he enjoys, no doubt."

"What about you? Do you enjoy challenges?"

The woman, barren of child, brushed back a lock of my hair and looked me straight in the eye. "No, I prefer that my life go smoothly."

Ten

OR THREE DAYS I lay in a darkened room, exhausted by a migraine that would not abate. Drops prescribed by Dr. Leach were useless and I often wept in pain. No one was allowed to disturb me, not even the vicar, though I heard his voice in the hallway on several occasions, making inquiries as to my condition. No doubt he felt a responsibility for my illness as it followed hard upon my tea at the vicarage.

I wish I could affirm that my condition was due solely to the dreadful state of my arrival home, the storm not having abated during the entire time of my absence. But it was not. Something about my interview with Mrs. Flemming troubled me, and I attributed my illness as much to my ruminations as to the drenched condition in which my aunt found me.

Questions lurked in the back of my mind, thoughts from which I could find no release. Did Mrs. Flemming suspect our relationship, the vicar's and mine, or had I imagined her suspicious glances? All that talk about being a dutiful wife. Was it to put me off? A warning? Certainly, her remark that the vicar spent a good deal of time with me seemed pointed. Each remembered incident, a tone, a look, a tilting of her head, caused my thoughts to fester. At times I almost welcomed her suspicions. Why not have it out in the open? Let the vicar choose between us.

At other times, when I considered the scandal, I became a coward—particularly as he and I had not had a moment together since our parting on the moor. I wondered if his feelings had changed—if he regretted his kiss.

Nothing could be resolved until we were together again. Each day in solitude became an agony for me. I had to get stronger so that I could see him again. To that purpose, I became a model patient, much to my aunt's surprise.

But even with the best of care, my progress was slow. The Leland prize ceremony came and went without my being there. Jeremy accepted my award for me and visited the cottage a few days later to bring me my parchment certificate, together with a book of Robert Browning's poems signed by all the teachers from the school. He was my first visitor and I was delighted to see him, even though the flowers he brought me were carried downstairs to the parlor for fear their perfume might induce another migraine.

I felt the precaution was unnecessary as that morning I'd eaten a full breakfast and felt well enough to sit up in bed. Still, my guardian must have given Jeremy a stern warning or perhaps it was the cautious way she tiptoed into my room that left an impression on him. In either case, he sat in the chair next to my bed hardly daring to look at me, as if the weight of his glance might set off another attack.

"It was a nice ceremony," he said in a voice low enough to count as a whisper. "Everyone from the village was there. Well, almost everyone. Anyway, I never seen so many people in one place, except at the fair, maybe. When your certificate signed by the queen was announced, the hall exploded with applause. It gave me a start, I can tell you. I can't recall seein' so many pairs of eyes starin' at me. My dad made me memorize a speech on your behalf. But it went clean out of my head. Couldn't remember the first word let alone the first line. I took the award and said 'thanks,' that's all. Sorry, Victorine. You know I'm not one for words."

To put him at ease, I told him that events of that kind always dragged on too long and that his brevity had probably relieved people.

He perked up after that and talked more readily.

"They had cake and punch afterwards. A lot of people asked about you. I told them you was doin' better. Mrs. Flemming sends her congratulations and hopes you'll be up soon. The vicar was there, too, of course."

"Did he say anything? Give you a message?"

"Naw. He nodded after what his wife said, that's all."

Jeremy saw my disappointment and hastened to explain. "There weren't much time to talk. People kept comin' up to him. Mrs. Flemmin' and I went outside after a while. She said she needed some air."

"Why? Wasn't she feeling well?"

"She was fine as far as I know. But she looked pale."

"She *always* looks pale. What did you talk about while you were outside?"

"Nothin' much."

"No spiders, then?"

My guest laughed. "It's no good my tellin' you anythin'. It's bound to come back at me."

I admired Jeremy for not taking himself seriously. With his blond good looks, he could have done otherwise. Even as children, when we played at fantasy worlds on the vicarage lawn, he was amiable. He would have preferred games that pitched us headlong in the grass or had us swinging from the trees, but he acceded to the gentler amusements that pleased me, unless I bullied him. Then he would stomp off and stay away long enough for me feel the weight of his absence; but he'd always return with a flower or with candy from his father's shop.

"She asked about the pendant again," he said, picking up the thread of our conversation. "Not a sea gull, of course. A rose is what she's partial to."

"You're going to do it, then?"

"Don't see why not, if she gets me the silver. Why? Do you think I shouldn't?"

"I don't care." I shrugged. "Only, why go to such trouble for someone you hardly know?"

"I know her well enough. I told you, we talk."

"So I hear," I said, taking the opportunity to mention a sore point. "I wish you wouldn't make me the subject of your idle gossip."

"Gossip? Me?"

"You needn't play the innocent. You told Mrs. Flemming we'd had an argument, didn't you? You blamed it on me, and now she thinks you're heartbroken. What nonsense! If anyone had the right to be offended, it was me. But I didn't complain to anyone, did I? No. I forgave you. That's what I did."

"Y-you got it wrong," Jeremy pleaded. "I never complained."

"Then Mrs. Flemming is lying? Is that what you expect me to believe?"

"No, 'course not!"

"Well then, she must have been telling the truth."

"She misunderstood, that's all. I didn't blame ya. She asked what was wrong and I told her. I said we'd had a fight and that it hadn't been our first, neither."

"And whose fault is that?"

"I'm partly to blame, I suppose..."

"You *suppose*?"

"It's not like you've not done your share, Victorine. You have. Trouble is, you don't see how you've changed."

"Changed? I haven't changed. You're imagining."

"Since the vicar come here—"

"There you go again. Blaming the vicar. Now he's responsible for our fights. They've got nothing to do with your behavior, I suppose. You know what I think, Jeremy? I think you're jealous of him."

"That's stupid. I'm not jealous of that old man."

"He's not old!"

"Too old for you!"

"What's that supposed to mean?"

"It means you've been turning yourself inside out just to please him. That's what it means. You should see yourself like I do. Ever since he come here you've been puttin' on airs."

"You mean we talk about things you don't understand. That's what makes you jealous, doesn't it?"

"I told you, I'm not jealous. I think he's a—"

"Gentleman? Is that the word you're looking for?"

"Believe me, Victorine, he's no gentleman. He's as common as any laborer, only he's found a way to put a gloss on. All his talk about art and books—that's how he pulls the wool over your eyes."

"But you see through him, I suppose."

"Better'n you do! That's for sure."

"And none of this has anything to do with his wife, does it?"

"What d'you mean?"

"Any fool can see you're infatuated with her. Why, I don't know. Her charm eludes me. Maybe it's because she resembles your mother. Have you ever thought of that?"

The grocer's son swallowed hard before he could answer. I'd handed him a bitter pill and it didn't go down well. The veins in his temples stood out, and I knew that he was angry, really angry.

"You must be out of your head still, you know that? Mrs. Flemming's nothin' like my mum. You're sayin' that to get at me. It shows you've changed, Victorine. Why would you say a thing like that? Why would you try and hurt me?"

Aunt Julia was coming in with a tea tray as Jeremy flung himself toward the door, just missing her by a hair's breadth. He was halfway down the stairs before she thought to call out to him.

"Jeremy! What's happened? What's the matter?"

There was no reply. A moment later, the front door slammed and the wheels of his bicycle could be heard traveling at full speed up the garden path.

"Whatever's got into that boy?" she said, laying the tray on a table beside me. "He lit out of here as if his pants were on fire. I suppose the pair of you have been arguing again. Why can't you two get along anymore? You used to play together so sweetly as children. Angels, that's what you were. Not like now when you fight all the time."

She looked tired as she eased herself into the chair Jeremy had vacated. Wisps of hair dangled across her neck and forehead, yet she'd made no effort to tidy herself. "I'll sit with you a while since he's gone. I don't mind being off my feet, I can tell you. It's been hard work in the garden. I trimmed back the azaleas and staked out several rows of beans. My knees hurt me so these days. I'm not as young as I once was."

Her confession was a moment of rare candor. Aunt Julia never liked to talk about her age, but that day I could see that she felt the weight of her years.

"Poor Auntie," I said, patting one of the offending knees. "I wish I could help."

She gave my hand a pat in return and smiled a bit. "I know you do, my dear, and soon you will. I'm sure of it. The color's returning to your cheeks. Before long you'll be able to enjoy the fresh air."

"Oh, I hope so, Auntie. I seem to have been in this bed for ages. Is it nice out today?"

She began pouring our tea, making sure to put three lumps of sugar in my cup. "Yes, it's lovely. Summer's almost here. Of course that means the weeds are thriving as well as my plants. Why is it, do you suppose, that weeds grow so much faster than the flowers? My columbines should be so sprightly! Poor things! They're getting too much sun where they are. I'll have to move them in the fall."

Even as she handed me the plate of biscuits, I could see that she was replanting the columbines in her mind's eye, deciding whether to place them under the rhododendrons or one of the spreading trees. It seemed a good time to suggest that as the weather was good, I might spend an hour in the garden.

My idea met with a stern rebuff.

"Not today, dear. It's far too soon. Perhaps by the end of the week."

Seeing my disappointment, she stepped to the window and proposed to let in some light.

"Not too hard on the eyes, is it?" she asked as a shaft of amber fell across the wooden floor.

"A bit more, Auntie, please. I can't see anything yet."

A second tug on the cord opened a gap wide enough for me to see the tops of the trees. Their blossoms had already faded. Now they stood like elegant dowagers in gowns of dappled green.

I found much to admire in those subtle modulations, so unlike the riot of spring. They refreshed me like a glass of cool water.

"The seasons pass so quickly," came my aunt's sigh from a darkened corner of the room. "One set of chores is barely done before others are required. I hope this summer won't be as short as the last."

We both took a moment to remember an autumn that seemed to follow hard upon the footsteps of spring. A chill wind had blown from March until September, and one seldom ventured out without a jumper. Even the daisies had to be staked to keep them from bending to the ground.

There might have been more talk of the weather, except that the certificate Jeremy had left behind caught my aunt's eye. She took it up to read, her cheeks glowing with pride.

"We must hang this in the parlor," she said when she'd finished. "I want everyone to know how special you are."

"Jeremy thinks I've had too much attention already," I warned as I pushed back my comforter to let my legs feel the sun. "He says I've started to put on airs."

"He said that?" I was gratified by my aunt's indignation. "The boy must be jealous! So that's what the pair of you was on about. I don't understand. It isn't like Jeremy to go off like that. He's usually even-tempered, like his father. Arthur Simones would never utter a harsh word to anyone. Why, even with his wife dying, he held himself in. Heaven knows he didn't need to. People would have understood if he'd allowed himself to flare up once or twice. I suppose that's his mother's mark that's affecting Jeremy. Now there was a troubled soul! 'Artistic temperament' some called it. I say it was moodiness plain and simple."

"She tried to kill herself, didn't she, Auntie?"

"We don't know that, Victorine. Not for sure." My guardian shook her head, unwilling to acknowledge the unthinkable. "Anyway, you mustn't say so openly. She was ill, remember? Oh, I did feel sorry for her. I really did. She was in so much pain. It must have been hard on the boy, seeing his mother go like that. We must make allowances, Victorine. In a way, Jeremy's as vulnerable as you, my dear. His mother's been gone barely a year, so he can't have recovered. Not fully. Who knows? Perhaps he never will."

Eleven

ITH THE WEATHER turned warm, I was able to resume my walks. School was out, so Jeremy and I met on occasion. We had found a way to bridge the rift between us, though as we grew older each breach was more difficult to mend. Pride had a firm grip on us both. Most of the time we kept a respectful distance from one another. The arrangement suited me, as I hoped the vicar and I might fall into our former pattern of chance meetings upon the moor.

For a time, nothing came of my desire. Then, on a day when the heather was in bloom, I saw him—the man to whom all my thoughts bended. He appeared to be heading in the direction of Benchley farm and paled when he saw me. The reaction was one I'd feared, but it was not long before he regained himself and came toward me with a familiar greeting.

"Victorine, how good to see you. You've escaped your prison, I see. Fully recovered, I hope?"

I nodded to assure him that I was, then matched my pace to his without waiting for an invitation. We talked idly for a time, as people do when they have unfinished business between them. The vicar told me of Miss Clemmons's decision to mount a summer production of "Romeo and Juliet" and that auditions were set for the following week.

"Why don't you try for a part? You'd make a wonderful Juliet." He was clinging to his hat as he spoke for the wind was threatening to whisk it away. "A number of people are involved. I, myself, have been asked to help with props."

He glanced in the direction of Benchley farm as though anxious to be away, but I remained doggedly at his side, upholding my part of the conversation and even offering to help as his assistant for the duration of the play.

The vicar took out his pocket watch to observe the time, mumbling something about there not being enough work for two, then tried to remove himself by saying that Mrs. Benchley expected him for tea and that he was late.

He might have made good his escape had I not been desperate for some assurance of his feelings for me. He should have expected it, knowing my candor and the fact that the last time we parted it was as lovers. Given his current behavior, how could I do otherwise than accuse him of being distant?

He was so taken aback when he heard me that his lips literally curled, revealing his teeth.

"You mistake me, my dear. If I seem distant, I'm only thinking of my duties. A great many parishioners have need of me at the moment."

"As do I! Yet you've made so little effort to see me. Why? Am I not one of your parishioners?"

"My dear girl, I did try. *Twice* I came to your door. But each time your aunt sent me packing. She said you were too ill for visitors, though I feared the reason was that you'd no wish to see *me*."

"How could you think that after...after what happened..."

His hands flew up like birds. "Yes, yes. I know. That's *why* I wanted to see you. To talk to you. I was afraid you might have misinterpreted—"

"Misinterpreted? What do you mean? Did you not hold me? Did we not kiss?"

"I ask you to forget what happened that day. It was a mistake, entirely. I blame myself, of course. I should have been on my guard, but you looked so pitiful, weeping as you did. I wanted to console you just as I would any desolate child—"

"Jordan—"

"Please don't call me that. It's unseemly."

"What then? What must I call you, for I'm not a child and you well know it!"

"Yes. I'm afraid that's where I miscalculated."

"Nor did you kiss me as if I were one!"

The man in black agonized under my intense gaze, not knowing how to mollify me. I could almost hear the thoughts running through his head. "Should I be firm with her? Continue to deny? Try reason?"

Whatever path he chose, I was ready for him, for I would not be ignored, humored, or convinced that I was imagining. He had sworn his love for me. The words were true, the passion real. If a quarrel ensued, so be it. Like the aftermath of a storm, an exchange of anger might clear the air.

What I was unprepared for was a truth that was dishonest.

"I admit to this much, if it will satisfy you: I *was* moved by your beauty. For an instant, my emotions may have overpowered me. If so, I should have found the means to apologize long ago. Instead, I took the coward's way and allowed myself to be put off by your aunt. Perhaps, I hoped that with the passage of time you'd recognize my indiscretion yet think no worse of me. I've been a fool. I see that now and I ask your pardon. I ask it with all my heart. But you do see, don't you, that I was motivated by pity?"

My heart was pounding in my throat when I answered him, feeling at once frightened and betrayed.

"It wasn't pity. *It wasn't!* You said you loved me. You said it again and again. How could you speak those words and not mean them?"

"Victorine..." He tried to lay a hand on my shoulder but I pushed it away.

"Don't touch me," I cried.

"Please! Listen to me. If I said those words—"

"You did!"

"Yes, but I wasn't talking about the kind of love that passes between a man and woman. I was talking about that which passes between friends."

"I don't believe you. You're lying now or you were lying then. You can't have it both ways. Which of us is being deceived, I wonder. Me? Or you?"

The bitterness in my voice alarmed him. He took hold of my hands and refused to let go.

"Victorine, get a grip on yourself. Listen to me! Can't you see the danger? If you persist in this fantasy and someone should believe it, think of the consequences. You'd lose your precious freedom and I'd have to resign!"

He shook me, gently, as if to wake me from a stupor. "Come now. You know what I'm saying is true. You've been down this road before, though you may not think I know it. What was that teacher's name? Huddleston? Have you forgotten?"

"I never loved him. I didn't encourage him."

"Yes, but you know how propriety was served. I doubt the poor man was ever allowed to teach again. Do you want the same fate for me? Am I to be sacrificed for your infatuation? Is that what you want? To see me leave Braxton?"

I struggled to hold back my tears but failed.

"No! I couldn't bear to live without you. I couldn't!"

The vicar now let go of my hands, looking embarrassed.

"Come now. No more of such foolish talk."

"It's true. It's true! You've changed my life. Given it hope. I could no more exist in your absence than I could do without air. If you were sent away, I'd follow. Perhaps in another place we could be happy. You could show me Paris, Rome, all the wonderful sights you've described—"

"And how would I live, a defrocked vicar? What society would take me in?"

"I have money, or will have when I'm twenty-five."

"But you're sixteen. And have you forgotten that I have a wife? What should we do with her? Throw her over the cliffs?"

"You're making fun of me. It's not fair. Anyway, why should she matter? She doesn't love you, not as I do, at least."

"I see," said the vicar, looking bemused. "And on that basis, you propose that I wander about penniless with a girl young enough to be my daughter."

"A difference in years means nothing when two people are in love."

"But *we* aren't in love. At best, yours is an infatuation..."

"No, no. It isn't. I love you. I tell you, I love you!" My attempt to fling my arms around his neck was deflected. He stepped back in shock.

"Stop it, Victorine. Someone will *see* us."

"I don't care!"

"Yes, but I do! What's come over you? Is this some remnant of your illness? Surely, your fever has returned, for I can find no other way to account for your conduct. You must curb this behavior, at once. Such boldness is an embarrassment and unbecoming of a woman."

"At least I'm no longer accused of being a child," came my rejoinder.

The vicar appeared to be anything but amused. He stood looking down at me as if uncertain what to do.

"I'm very late. I really must go. Will you be alright?"

He offered me his handkerchief, which I refused. "You mustn't be unhappy, Victorine. I'm not angry. In a way, I'm flattered. You know how much I admire you—"

"Don't say that! I don't want to be admired."

"Well you are, in any case. You've no control over that, I'm afraid."

"So you're saying you don't love me? It was all a mistake?"

"I'm saying I care. Isn't that enough?"

"No!"

"Then I shall never forgive myself for disappointing you. I'm sorry. Truly sorry. Perhaps, if things were otherwise—"

"What things?" I looked into his eyes, searching for a sign of hope. "Tell me. I'll do anything you ask. Anything. Only don't pretend you've no feelings for me. I know it's not true."

I took his hand and placed it over my heart so that he could feel it beating. "I swear that I love you and will always be true and will never, ever betray you."

"Victorine, please..."

"Don't try to silence me. Why shouldn't you know what is in my heart? You're my confessor. Should I hide from you? Should I lie?" When he kept his hand where I held it, I found the courage to say all that was in me.

"I love you, Jordan. You're my life, my sole reason for being. I ask nothing in return, only that you acknowledge me. Say that you love me. Say it once and I shall go away from you and never speak of this moment again. To know. Just to know will be enough to last me a lifetime."

"This talk is madness. I have a *wife*."

By now my tears were flowing freely. "Love me, Jordan. Love me, *please*."

As I fell into his arms, I heard his whispered confession.

"May God forgive me...I do."

 Twelve

The first night's performance of "Romeo and Juliet" played to an overflow crowd. Ticket sales had been so brisk that a second performance had to be scheduled for the following weekend. The buzz from the audience in the Leland refectory sent the actors into a tizzy. A few began pacing behind the makeshift curtain in an effort to recall their lines.

"Don't worry. It'll all turn out," crooned Miss Clemmons from the adjoining hall. She was weaving among the dressers and make-up people as they fussed with last minute adjustments to some of the characters.

Mrs. Pardy was among those requiring consolation as some of the beads from Juliet's dress had come loose, and she was struggling to stitch them on again with the actress in full costume. "I'll never make it in time, Anthea. You'll have to delay the curtain."

The production mistress smiled benignly as she passed. "A few beads won't be missed, Cordelia. The gown looks splendid without them." That said, she hissed through the curtain for the overture to begin, and under the direction of Mr. Pounder, a few reedy notes rose from the Chapman Boys Band. The houselights went down and silence fell on both sides of the curtain.

Mrs. Pardy rushed to the wings to stand beside me, struggling to close her workbasket without the benefit of light. "Oh dear!" she cried as a cascade of beads pattered to the floor. "What must I do?" Without waiting for a reply, she fell to her knees to retrieve them. The decision was a lamentable one for she blocked the path of the on-coming chorus. Two actors tripped over her on their way to the stage and the rest, aided by the beads, glided into the footlights like novice skaters. Miss Clemmons, standing behind me, slapped her head in dismay. A slight ripple of laughter rose from the audience, but quieted as soon as the plot got underway.

From my vantage point as assistant prop mistress, I could see and hear the performance clearly. The play I knew by heart so I winced at the impromptu renderings that occurred when one actor or another forgot his lines. Few in the audience seemed to notice these gaffs, however. At first I was annoyed by such ignorance, but later I would be glad for it.

When the actor playing Tybalt lost his sword prior to his dueling scene, I was forced to improvise. Among the props I found a small dagger. This I tied to a length of wood and fashioned into an instrument that looked more like a pike than a sword. It was the best I could do in so short a time. Happily, the audience found no fault with the substitution. They met Tybalt's death with a rapt and stony silence. The crisis averted, I was free to watch the performance and bask in the vicar's presence.

Since the first rehearsal, he and I had spent blocks of time together, more than would have been prudent in our previous relationship. Add to that, news of an extended performance, and no one, not even Miss Clemmons, could have been happier than I. Jordan's behavior continued to be a mystery, however. He no longer denied his feelings for me, but his reserve remained. As we were seldom alone, what with the play and his schedule, there was no opportunity to probe him further. The moor was no safe haven. Not in summer. Too many hikers and naturalists were about. And there was always Jeremy to consider. For the time being, I had to be content with contact which was piecemeal and, but for the want of privacy, I was.

The audience's enthusiasm on opening night was gratifying. They laughed when a word or gesture encouraged them to do so; applauded when Tybalt and Benvolia came to blows; and sighed when Romeo kissed Juliet in the ballroom scene. By the time the first act curtain was rung down, the performance was already deemed a success. Miss Clemmons, intoxicated by the grease paint, rallied her troops as though they were an army and cautioned them to be in their places when the curtain rose again. All the while, her turquoise turban could be seen bobbing in and out of the shadows like a nervous bird.

Despite her fastidiousness, the second act had to be delayed. The problem was not behind the curtain but in front of it. Mrs. Snibley had worn one of her large, ridiculous hats and despite a chorus of catcalls from those unfortunate enough to be seated behind her, she refused to remove it. Finally, the vicar was called upon to calm the troubled waters and did so by coaxing the affronted lady into an aisle seat where her mountain of tulle and feathers would pose no problem.

For his efforts, he received a round of applause from the patrons. After that, the house lights faded again and events went smoothly until the intermission; then the playgoers swarmed around the refreshment table, nearly overturning it. Jeremy, who'd been serving as usher, was drafted to assist in the selling of tea and biscuits. With his help, the line went faster and at the end of intermission, people returned to their seats looking well-satisfied—all, that is, except Mrs. Snibley, who continued to sulk.

During the second half of the performance, the vicar whispered that he and Mrs. Flemming had arranged for a small gathering at the Crown Pub at the end of the evening. Aunt Julia had been informed and had already accepted the invitation, providing I felt up to it.

Wild horses couldn't keep me away, I assured him. In truth, the prospect of a nighttime revelry was so appealing that near the end of the play, when Juliet swallowed poison—a scene that left not a dry eye in the audience—I inwardly cheered.

After the performance, Jordan and I, being responsible for inventory, were left behind while Mrs. Flemming proceeded with her guests to the pub to await us there. Regrettably, Aunt Julia stayed behind, as well, fancying that she could be of use. At first, I thought her offer was annoying, but considering all that needed to be done, I was soon glad for an extra pair of hands. Even so, the church clock was striking ten when the three of us stepped from the Leland refectory into the warm night air.

The stillness surrounding us came as a shock after all the hubbub that had gone before. The people had vanished and there was neither a footstep nor light to be heard or seen anywhere. A trace of twilight still lingered in the west, but we hurried along in spite of its beauty, eager for good company and good food and aware that the pub closed at eleven o'clock.

A round of cheers greeted us as we entered the establishment. Many of the playgoers, along with the regulars, had crowded into the well-lit room, its brass hangings burnished by the hearth fire. All the patrons were in high spirits and not yet ready to go home to their beds.

Mr. Higgenbothem, the proprietor—a portly man in his sixties with a balding head—leaned across the bar as we passed. "I've added a few pork pies to the sandwiches and cider," he told the vicar. "Compliments of the 'ouse."

He was thanked for his kindness, then a red curtain was drawn back and we were led into the private room. The vicar's wife came forward as we entered. She was wearing a blue gown that exposed her long neck and a bit of shoulder. The style suited her but was so marked a departure from her ordinary costume that one surmised Mrs. Pardy had been at work.

Her hair, too, was arranged in a becoming fashion, not tied back, but piled high upon her head and allowed to fall in ringlets. She seemed taller and more regal as a result.

My appearance by comparison was drab, as Aunt Julia had insisted I wear a serviceable broadcloth to the performances. It may have been my imagination, but I thought I noted a flicker of satisfaction in my rival's eye as she noted our disparity.

"Ah," she gave the vicar a peck on the cheek, then proffered a welcoming smile on my guardian and me. "We've been waiting for you and talking about the play, of course. What a triumph. An absolute triumph!"

Miss Clemmons, overhearing the praise, joined us. "You're too kind, Mrs. Flemming. But of course, theatricals are the work of several hands. Your husband made a vital contribution. Especially, this evening. Imagine Elvira Snibley making such a fuss over that ridiculous hat."

Her remark was allowed to die without comment, which the schoolteacher noted, and so she turned her attention to me.

"Ah! Here's Victorine. Thank you, too, my dear, for all your good offices." She took hold of my hand and gave it a pat, then let it go as she addressed her next remark to my guardian.

"You know, Julia, your niece has a flair for the theatre. So intuitive! She made numerous improvements to our direction. If we don't make a teacher of her, she might consider the theatre — preferably in front of the curtain rather than behind it. Such a wonderful profile!"

On guard against excessive flattery when it concerned me, my aunt bristled.

"You put too many ideas in the child's head, Anthea. It's unfair when you know they can only lead to disappointment."

"Disappointment? I know nothing of the kind. You have a gifted ward. By now you must be used to the idea. Anyway, young people should be encouraged to have dreams."

"In Victorine's case, they would be false dreams. If you had a child of your own to raise you'd know to be more careful with your encouragements."

Never one to take admonishment kindly, Miss Clemmons extended to her full height—which, with her turban, was considerable.

"With thirty years of teaching behind me, Julia, I've had a hand in raising hundreds of children. I can safely say that in all that time not one of them has been harmed by my 'encouragements.' A far greater danger, in my opinion, is crippling them with obsessive fears."

My guardian's cheeks went red when she heard the remark, not the color of blood that is too pale for comparison, but a crimson seldom seen except in the imagination.

"Obsessive fears! Is that what you call my efforts to protect this frail child? I've never heard such nonsense. Though I shouldn't be surprised. You often voice opinions on subjects you know nothing about."

"I've known Victorine since she was a child, which, by the way, she is no longer. That gives me the right to an opinion, and I say that being overprotective creates, rather than prevents, difficulties. Give her air, Julia! Allow the girl to explore. We women have few enough opportunities in this world. Don't make a coward of her with your fears."

The chin of the woman to whom these remarks were addressed began to tremble. I sensed that at any moment she might break into tears. An act of diplomacy was required and that's when the vicar stepped forward.

"Speaking for my wife and myself, Miss Ellsworth—and for Miss Clemmons, too, I'm sure—your dedication to your niece's welfare is exemplary. You can be proud of that. On the other hand, this good lady is correct in observing that Victorine is becoming a young woman. Her future must be considered. No doubt, you've already begun to do so, but I have one or two ideas I've been meaning to suggest. Perhaps now is the perfect time?"

His voice trailed off as he took hold of my guardian's arm, intending to lead her out of harm's way. Aware of his kindness, she hesitated only a moment. Far be it from her to embarrass herself or her hostess, Mrs. Flemming, who stood looking aghast at the two older women. But she was not mollified. She continued to glare back over her shoulder as she withdrew, in the hope of delivering a withering glance to Miss Clemmons. The schoolteacher, quite capable of defending herself, returned each glare with interest, and the volley continued until the milling guests broke their line of vision. One had to conclude then that the skirmish had ended in a draw.

Eventually, the mistress of Leland's third form drifted toward the buffet table where Mr. Pounder was standing with a pork pie in one hand and a glass of cider in the other. Somehow, he was still able to wag a finger at Robert Cowley and was doing so with vigor. The latter was a robust man in his late sixties with a florid complexion and a pair of ragged eyebrows that made him seem more somber than he was. He'd long been head of the church council but recently had been appointed a local magistrate. The honor was one for which he was now paying as Mr. Pounder's harangue was no doubt his account of a long-standing feud with his neighbor, a local poultry farmer. Unfortunately, the problem at hand was one which neither Mr. Cowley nor the full weight of English law could remedy, as the neighbor had rightly observed in his defense:

"A rooster crows at dawn and that's the way of 'em. Pounder should have thought of that afore 'e ups and moves next to me."

Left to ourselves, Mrs. Flemming suggested that we find a place where we could talk—a task made difficult since the room was crowded even with our modest gathering. One spot remained unoccupied, a tired settee off to one corner. Its exposed horsehair made it appear menacing, but as no other chairs were free, we lowered ourselves on it, the way one might settle into a hot bath. It creaked a bit but held us, and so, teacups in hand, we began our polite conversation.

"I've organized a picnic for Saturday. The young people's group. Everyone will be there, your former classmates and one or two guests from out of town. I'd like you to join us if you feel up to it. Jeremy will be present, of course. He's offered to help with the refreshments. And there'll be singing and games to play. It should be a jolly time."

Nothing struck me as more abhorrent than the company of people my own age—adolescents who stood in clumps, segregated according to their sexes and wearing pained expressions, or whispering and giggling to one another. I told her I had to study.

When she heard the excuse, my hostess looked surprised. To spend the summer at one's books was a waste of good weather, according to her. She even had the temerity to add that there was a danger in too much work over too little play, and proposed speaking to my aunt.

"Oh, you mustn't blame her," I protested. "I'm already a disappointment on that account. She'd rather I spent more time in the garden than I do with my Thuycidies."

"You could never be a disappointment," said Mrs. Flemming, patting my hand as Miss Clemmons had done. "But I am curious. Is it Thuycidies that you love so much, or have you no interest in gardening? If so, I must try to persuade you. My little patch affords me the greatest of pleasures. The time I spend there is precious. Such beauty. Such peace. A young lady could do worse than become a student of nature."

"You may call a garden 'nature,' but I don't. To me it's a pale copy. Flowers are pleasant enough, I'll grant you. But it's sad to see them confined to tight rows or wrapped about a trellis. Quite unnatural, really."

"Oh, I don't see it that way at all. A well-tended garden is the highest expression of nature's potential. The abundance that comes from careful nurturing is evidence of what can be achieved. Sometimes I think of myself as Nature's handmaiden, especially when I'm rewarded with a bounty of new blooms. Outside the garden is where chaos is most likely to occur. No, I think you're wrong, Victorine. Nature thrives best where there's order."

"How can you look upon those tortured espaliers and topiaries, which people seem to cherish, and not see them as freaks of the natural? All that binding and twining! There's your chaos, not what goes on beyond the garden walls. Freedom seems to be what you fear. But nature requires wildness in order to create and to flourish. If you doubt that, compare the beauty of a spring moor to your pansies jammed along a footpath."

My companion conceded with a laugh. "Mr. Flemming is right. You have a unique point of view and a clever way to express it. Perhaps the pen should be your calling, if not the stage."

"Has your husband spoken to you of my ideas?"

"Frequently and with great admiration. Indeed, were you a bit older, I might be jealous."

She fixed her pale blue eyes on me and within them I detected the merest trace of a shadow.

"But as you say, I am quite young..."

"Oh, not so young as you make it sound. A bud, perhaps, on the verge of opening but capable of breaking many a man's heart. I've told you that already. Do you believe me, I wonder."

She must have taken my silence as a rebuff for she moved on. "I presume you're done with Donne in your studies? What writer occupies you now? Someone less exotic, I hope."

The names Keats and Shelley seemed as unacceptable to her as the previous poet had been. She frowned and turned up her nose as if at an unpleasant odor.

"'Ode to a Grecian Urn,' isn't is? Lovers frozen in time 'forever panting and forever young'? Such a hopeless situation. Frankly, I always thought that verse a bit silly. I suppose you don't agree."

"Not entirely. The poem's about immortality, not about love. My favorite work is '*La Belle Dame sans Merci*,' however."

"Ah yes. The beautiful maiden who steals men's souls. I suppose it would be."

Stung by the smugness in her remark, I took what revenge I could by quoting more of Keats. I extolled his vision, extemporized upon his genius and was so deliberately long-winded upon a subject that bored her that her once arrogant expression faded beneath its canopy of copper curls.

Her hand flew up as if it were a flag of truce. "Yes, yes. I've no doubt of his merits. You've convinced me. I am your convert. But do you not find all this vision and revision a bit remote? What has Arcady to do with England? Far better to be a student of the real world than one of fiction, that's my opinion."

"Then you would never visit Xanadu?"

"Coleridge?"

I nodded.

"Why Xanadu when there's Paris? That's what I should like to ask Mr. Coleridge. He took opium, didn't he?"

I nodded a second time. "For his rheumatism."

"Extravagant ends for an extravagant mind. A hot bath would have done as much. Which makes my point: genius does little to assure intelligent choices. Common sense is needed for that. Had I a daughter, my advice would be to study those around her. It's people who make the world a heaven or hell."

"One can always escape to Xanadu," I smiled, feeling smug in return.

"A temporary remedy," came the rebuff. "It's wiser to grapple with experience as it exists than to waste energy imagining it to be otherwise. Human voices will always intrude upon our reveries. We can't escape that. Take the exchange just now between your aunt and Miss Clemmons. They were quarreling over you, but were you really the cause? One had the feeling there was more to it, that they were pecking at old wounds. Miss Clemmons practically accused your aunt of being a coward. Why? What did she mean by it? I don't suppose you can enlighten me in any way, can you?"

The question was put matter-of-factly, but the effect was like a key being turned in a lock. I saw at once that the course of our tête-à-tête was not happenstance but had been orchestrated for the purpose of satisfying Mrs. Flemming's curiosity about the two older women. My guess was that she wished to make a study of them in the hope of gaining a new means of access. Next she would surely offer to be of help in mending any feud that might exist between them. She was, to my way of thinking, like the pyromaniac who volunteers to put out a fire merely to get closer to the flames.

"I wouldn't make too much of their quarrels." I shrugged. "Nothing ever comes of them. The only clash of import in Braxton this night was between the Capulets and Montagues."

"I pray that you're right"—my hostess smiled back at me—"though Braxton is as capable of high passion as is Shakespeare's Verona. How did the man come by his ideas, if not by observing life around him, in Stratford and its environs?"

"He was well read: Chaucer, Boccaccio. Some of his ideas came from them."

"The plots, yes, but not his understanding of character. Human nature isn't easily garnered from books. No, I believe Shakespeare had a keen eye and that's what served him best."

"You're entitled to your opinion, certainly."

"Oh come now, Victorine. You needn't stick your nose up in the air. I can make a case, if you'll be open to it. Ask yourself why tonight's play so affected the audience. They're not particularly well read. Yet they wept for Romeo and Juliet, a couple which never lived. Why? Because Shakespeare knew that all the world's a stage, even Braxton. Poverty, disease, death and yes, even lost love—we country folk know these 'actors' well. It must be so, or Shakespeare's art would have no power over us."

"Then you have loved and lost?" I asked peevishly, though I knew there was merit in what she'd said.

"Indeed, I have," came the reply. "As have you."

My hand flew to my bosom as though my heart had been exposed and was about to reveal my attachment to the vicar. "Me? You're mistaken, Mrs. Flemming. There's been no one in my life. No one at all!"

"No? Not a mother? A father?" Her eyebrows lifted. The innocence of her remark, unexpected as it was, left me feeling like a fool. My reaction had been too vehement. I was bound to have aroused a suspicion, or a curiosity, at least. And yet, I could not entirely acquit myself of a sense of impending danger. It seemed impossible that a woman who prided herself on her powers of observation should remain ignorant of my affection for her husband. I began to wonder if her question was as guileless as it seemed. She'd toyed with me before, at the bazaar and at the vicarage. Possibly, this was another instance.

"My parents died six years ago, as you well know," I stumbled. "I didn't realize you were thinking of them."

"No? Then who were you thinking of, I wonder? Someone. Your protest was too adamant, otherwise."

Her gaze sought mine in an effort to read my thoughts. Annoyed, I evaded her and stared elsewhere—at the picture of a farmhouse that hung crooked on its nail, its colors muted by months, if not years, of dust.

"I hope I haven't offended you," she said after a sufficient period of silence had passed. "I was merely teasing."

"Teasing? Then you must pardon me, Mrs. Flemming. I find the memory of my lost parents is still affecting."

"Of course it is. I-I didn't mean—"

"In any case, Aunt Julia's been good to me, as good as any parent could be."

As if speaking her name was a form of conjuring, my guardian appeared, standing in front of us, wearing her cloth hat and gripping the handle of her purse tightly.

"It's nearly eleven, Victorine. You've had a long day and there's been so much excitement. Oughtn't we to go home?"

Home! Why was my relative always driven to that place like a moth to a flame? I wanted to stay at the party where there was light and laughter. At Windmill Cottage nothing awaited us but the shadows of a dying fire and after that, a cold bed.

"We mustn't go yet, Auntie," I pleaded, looking up at her. "I've had little to eat and I'm not tired. Not in the least. Besides, Mrs. Flemming and I are having an interesting conversation. Why don't you join us?"

The vicar's wife broke into an encouraging smile. "Please do, Miss Ellsworth. Your niece and I have been debating a number of questions and would be glad for your opinion."

Aunt Julia, never reticent to express her views, craned her neck from right to left in search of a chair. Constable Mills saw her dilemma and came forward with his, explaining it was time to make his rounds. She thanked him for his courtesy; after which, she backed her large frame on to the narrow chair, carefully, the way a duck might settle upon its nest. A few moments more were spent smoothing out her dress and only after making a lap for her purse did she look up, her eyes shimmering with anticipation.

Mrs. Flemming took some pains to hide the smile that had

played upon her lips during this performance and, fortunately, my guardian had observed nothing. I, on the other hand, took umbrage at her amusement and thought it typical of the disdain with which a married woman often views a maiden lady.

"I'm trying to convince your niece that there's as much drama in the daily life of Braxton as can be found anywhere upon the stage." The vicar's wife was speaking in tones that were now unctuous. "Being young, she doesn't believe me and thinks our village a dull place where nothing happens. You're a woman of experience. What's your opinion, I wonder?"

Aunt Julia nodded her ample chin at her hostess. "I agree with you, Mrs. Flemming. Most emphatically. I often say to Victorine that she has only to open her eyes to see theatre around her. Why, had I the talent, what tales I could write. Amusing tales. Sad tales. And now and again, a mystery, like: Who Stole Emily Patton's Churn?"

"A churn's been stolen? I hadn't heard."

"Oh, it was before your time, Mrs. Flemming. Three years ago, at least. But it was the talk of the village when it happened."

"Indeed? And what became of the churn? Was it ever found?"

Aunt Julia made a second attempt to get comfortable in her chair before going on with her story.

"Well you see, there was this churn that used to sit outside the creamery. It wasn't good for anything. It'd been broken for ages so Emily used it as a flowerpot. Filled it with annuals each spring. Quite an eyesore, I can tell you. She has no sense of color, that one. The combinations she used to come up with would make a blind man squint. One year, she mixed hollyhocks with marigolds. Can you believe it? Well, anyway, one night the churn went missing. Just disappeared! Someone took offense to all that red being mixed with orange—that was my thought...but don't quote me, please."

Mrs. Flemming nodded her head of copper curls in agreement.

"Of course, how a person could move a heavy object like that without attracting attention is a further mystery. A cart or a wheelbarrow had to be used."

Mrs. Flemming looked as if she might offer a suggestion but the storyteller had found her stride and hurried on.

"Now, I don't want to be quoted as there's no proof, absolutely none, but some think—I find it hard to believe myself—that Noah Minton was the culprit."

"Noah Minton!" This time an interruption could not be

prevented. The vicar's wife exploded like saltpeter. "That shy little man who tends Mrs. Snibley's garden? Why would he want a tub of hollyhocks mixed with marigolds?"

"Oh, he wasn't a gardener, then," explained my aunt, well pleased with the response. "He worked for Earnest Patton at the creamery and some say he was sweet on Emily."

"I thought she'd been married to Earnest Patton for some time."

"Nearly twenty-five years."

"Surely then, you can't mean..."

"I'm only saying what some people thought. Noah spent a lot of time up at the house, doing chores for the wife, instead of working in the creamery for the husband. Earnest had to have noticed. Anyway, one day he up and fires Noah."

"For no reason?"

"Oh, he had a reason. An excuse, really. It came about when a load of manure was overturned near the cow barn. With the animals trapped inside, Earnest sent for Noah. Noah refused to come, of course, as it was Sunday; he's always been fierce about keeping the Sabbath. That should have come as no surprise to Earnest. Everyone knows of Noah's fastidiousness, but he was fired just the same. Some say Earnest dumped the manure deliberately so he could send the poor man packing."

"What was Noah's reaction? Was there a quarrel? Fisticuffs?"

"Not as far as I know. Anyway, Elvira came forward as soon as she heard the story and told Noah he could come to work for her. She's not a poor woman, by any means, and with her arthritis getting worse, she needed a gardener. Noah didn't know much about flowers at the time, but I suspect he's come to prefer them to cow barns."

"That was fortunate for him, but I wonder what Mrs. Patton thought about the fuss."

"She didn't talk about it, if that's what you mean. In fact, for the longest time she didn't mingle after church. She must have been embarrassed by all the gossip, even though no one knows if there was a word of truth to it."

"Yes, I understand what it feels like to be stung by accusations." Mrs. Flemming paused a moment and looked reflective before going on. "But I don't understand about the churn. Why would Mr. Minton be suspected? He'd no grudge against Mrs. Patton. Her husband's the one who fired him."

Aunt Julia's eyes twinkled. "Maybe he wanted something that

belonged to the wife."

"A keepsake, you mean?"

"If you can call a big old churn that, yes. Though where he hid the monstrosity is anyone's guess."

"So its disappearance is *still* a mystery?"

"Indeed, yes. To this very day."

Mrs. Flemming looked as pleased as if she'd been awarded first prize at the fair for her roses. "There! You see, Victorine? Drama. Pure drama."

"Oh, surely not," I scoffed. "You can't compare Romeo and Juliet to the plight of Noah Minton and Emily Patton? Their stories are as different as chalk and cheese!"

"A difference in degree, to be sure. But you must admit it has all the elements of tragedy: a jealous husband, an attractive wife, and an unrequited lover. And as the story is true, that makes it all the more poignant. I'm right there, aren't I, Miss Ellsworth?"

"Quite right, Mrs. Flemming!" My aunt nodded with sufficient energy to make her broach dance. "As you say, there's as much and more to be learned from observation than can be found in any book. I'm so glad you agree with me. Perhaps my niece will listen to you. Nowadays I have no influence over her, I'm sure."

"You're too modest, Miss Ellsworth. Her accomplishments are a tribute to your influence."

"That's kind of you to say, Mrs. Flemming. I have tried."

A period ensued where the two women tossed compliments to one another as if it were a competition. Stronger constitutions might have endured but mine was not so iron cast. Inevitably my eyes drifted across the room in the hope of being rescued. The vicar stood with his back to me, talking to Mrs. Pardy, whose anguished expression made it clear that she was recounting her bead crisis of the first act. Seeing him so thoroughly occupied was a disappointment to me, and Mrs. Flemming seemed to read my thoughts.

"Have no doubts, Victorine, if my husband were here, he would take your part in our discussion. Half his life is spent between the covers of a book. It's impossible to bring him to supper sometimes. Why this fascination for the written lives of others I'm sure I don't know, particularly when his own reads like a novel."

"Does it indeed?" quacked my aunt like a hungry goose. "I've often wondered. He's unlike most clergymen, isn't he? I mean to say, what with his knowledge of art and being well-traveled, he's quite a man of the world, really."

"That has been said of him, though not always as a compliment," his wife admitted. "It worked to his detriment where my father was concerned. He thought our new vicar—for that's how Mr. Flemming came to us—was too imposing a figure. He and the other gentry of our village were used to clergymen of a more modest and temperate nature, not one with an impassioned spirit and a certain degree of standoffishness."

"Yes, but you see, that's what I like about him. His impassioned spirit," my guardian confided. "Reminds me of my own dear brother. And like your husband, that dedication could make him seem austere at times, what you describe as standoffish. But of course, there was another side to him, as well. When it came to Victorine, he would laugh as heartily as any man, especially when she climbed upon his lap and wanted to be amused. Yes, there was always time for her... But, like your husband, James had a dedication to the scriptures. I can't say that he found any answers to life's mysteries but I suspect he enjoyed the hunt as much as the discovery. Victorine shares his single-mindedness, I fear."

A warm, plump hand covered mine to show no criticism was intended by that last remark.

"Then you know how difficult it can be to draw such men out of themselves," Mrs. Flemming went on. "That's where I feel I can be of help to my husband. When he grows too serious, I try to divert him. The path to heaven can't be all rocks and thorns, I tell him. Sinners we may be, but a smile doesn't lead into perdition."

"What does he say when he hears that?"

"He indulges me, but before long he is his dark self again." She fingered the neckline of her blue gown as she laughed, obviously unsure of how her remark would be taken.

My aunt, being more interested in a personal history she knew little about, let the inference go unheeded. "It's well that he chose a woman who compliments his nature," was her sole concession. "But I should like to be satisfied on one point. If your father disapproved of the vicar, how was a marriage ever arranged? It must have been difficult."

"More difficult than you can imagine, Miss Ellsworth, particularly as my father was not the only impediment. The vicar, too, took some convincing. Except for attending to his pastoral duties, he kept to himself much of the time, like a man scarred by a private tragedy. Of course, his reclusiveness made him all the more interesting. What young lady can resist a dark stranger with an air of mystery clinging about him? I could not, nor could many of the women of our village. I had my share of competition, I can tell you."

"I've no doubt of that for a moment. Many a country girl has lost her head under similar circumstances," my aunt agreed. "But he's greatly changed now, isn't he? One often sees him out and about. Windmill Cottage has received him on many occasions, far more than his predecessor, Vicar Soames."

When she heard that, Mrs. Flemming's eyes narrowed and her lips pursed like someone who had bitten into a rotten apple. "It's true. He seems to have given his heart to the parish; so much so that I sometimes accuse him of becoming a stranger to me."

"The price you must pay, dear lady, for having succeeded in drawing him out."

"Yes. Ironic isn't it? One doesn't always foresee the consequences of one's desires."

"You're not sorry for your effect, surely," remarked my aunt, looking a little surprised.

"No, of course not. But I am embarrassed when I think of how I went about it: how I plotted our chance meetings and volunteered for one activity after another just to be near him. It was shameless of me, really. But at the time, I was too smitten to care."

"You were young and in love. Such behavior is to be expected."

"There's that, of course. But how am I to account for my conduct toward my father? I knew his objections, yet I acted against his wishes, even kept the courtship a secret for the longest time."

"You deceived your parents? That was serious."

"Not my mother. She knew of the engagement, but the vicar and I were afraid that if father found out, he'd use his influence to keep us apart."

"Oh, surely not! The man couldn't be that vindictive. Love's no crime, after all."

Aunt Julia continued to remonstrate on behalf of the young lovers while my thoughts turned elsewhere. The similarities between Mrs. Flemming's history with the vicar and my own struck me as odd. Had the woman lived in my head, the verisimilitude could not have been more exact. I, too, had sought to draw him out; kept secret assignations and lived in fear of our separation. How was I to account for these coincidences?

One could argue that where clandestine relationships were necessary, certain behaviors bore a common thread; but there was another possibility which might equally be true: that the artless ramblings of the vicar's wife had an ulterior purpose.

"But your courtship must have ended happily..." Aunt Julia broke into my thoughts with a voice that clanged like a school bell. "Or was there a falling out between you and your father?"

"No, he was brought around, thanks to my mother's handling of him. She adored the vicar and used her influence on his behalf. In the end, father had no choice, really. It was either embrace Jordan as son-in-law or suffer the perpetual harangues of those nearest and dearest to him. I was glad when he consented, but I cannot say that the day he gave me away in marriage was the happiest in his life."

Remembering the event, Mrs. Flemming sat a moment with her eyes peering over the top of my aunt's head; then a slow, sly grin crept across her face. "The same might be said of the remaining single women in our village."

Ignoring the smile, Aunt Julia went to the heart of the matter.

"Yes, I suppose many a young heart fluttered when the vicar said 'I do.' I must say, had I been in your parent's position, I'd have been glad for so admirable a son-in-law. His vocation commends him, of course. But not only that, there's something so attractive... No. Mesmerizing's the word. Whether it's the rich timbre of his voice or the intensity of his gaze that's responsible, I'm sure I don't know; but there is an air of authority about him. A man might find that intimidating, but a presence like his builds confidence in a woman. She's drawn to him, the way one is drawn to shelter in a storm."

A slight nod from the woman in blue acknowledged the truth of what had been said. "I, too, have given thought to the quality you describe, and I agree as to its effect. People are drawn to him, women almost without exception."

"In your case, that proved to be a blessing, didn't it? Without your mother's help, your heart might have been broken."

"Yes. She did her best for me, believing Jordan would make me happy..."

Another break followed as Mrs. Flemming retreated into the past, her expression wistful, her eyes glazed. "We were close, you see. More like sisters. That's why I miss her so much."

"Miss her? But why should you? Surely it's time your parents paid a visit? You're settled now and there's plenty of room at the vicarage, drafty old barn that it is. Let them see what you've done with the place. Braxton would turn itself inside out to make them feel welcome, you may be sure of that."

"Would that I could invite them," came the reply, punctuated with a sigh. "But they were lost to influenza, three years ago."

"What? Both of them? My dear, I'm so sorry to hear it. The vicar, I knew, was an orphan. He told us that a patron saw to his education. But I'd no idea you were similarly afflicted. Have you no living relatives? No brothers? No sisters?"

"An aunt lives in Cambridge, but I seldom hear from her. She and my father never got on well."

"What a shame. A family is so important." After a period of looking suitably downcast, my guardian's face brightened. "But why not invite her here? There's no impediment is there, what with your father having passed on? Once she's been reacquainted with you, she'll regret not having extended an invitation herself. Of that you may be certain."

Mrs. Flemming looked up to discover that my aunt's eyes were glittering with encouragement.

"Do you think so? It wouldn't seem too forward, an invitation coming out of the blue, so to speak?"

"Oh my dear, it's never too late to make a friend. In this case, blood being thicker than water, she's probably been longing to see you. You've done her no wrong, after all. Your father's the one she quarreled with. Do write. A person needs the comfort of a family. It's a cold world otherwise. What I'd do without my own dear niece, I'm sure I don't know."

My hand was given a squeeze as Aunt Julia, overcome by a surge of emotion, searched for her hanky.

"I have meant to communicate," Mrs. Flemming explained, sounding a trifle apologetic. "It's just that for so long the vicar and I have lived like nomads."

"Yes, it must have been a great inconvenience for you. But I assured your husband at the time of his interview that our climate would pose no difficulties. Robust though it is, it's very good for the constitution. Time has proven me right, I think. I can't imagine that you ever looked better."

Rather than appear pleased by the compliment, Mrs. Flemming seemed nonplussed. A frown clouded her expression and she made no immediate reply but paused to weigh her words as if they were links in a chain she might be obliged to carry.

"My husband told you I've been ill, Miss Ellsworth? Is that his account of our peregrinations?"

"Oh you needn't feel embarrassed," came the warm reply. "Braxton is noted for its waters as well as its healthy climate.

You're not the first to come here to recuperate—and to succeed, I might add."

Mrs. Flemming continued to look both cautious and confused but thanked my aunt for her encouragement and admitted that she had found a degree of peace in our village. "In fact," she went on to say, "if the vicar and I do settle here, it's my hope that we can..."

Stopping herself in mid sentence, the vicar's wife blushed a little. "You must excuse me, dear lady. My husband knows nothing of my plans, as yet. I'm obliged to speak to him first."

"We understand," said my aunt, who knew better than to press for information but was not above coaxing. "You must do what you think is right; though I must say that Victorine and I are very good at keeping confidences. We might even be of help with this plan of yours, if we knew what it was."

The offer was met with a tentative smile. "How kind of you, Miss Ellsworth. I've not had anyone to confide in for some time. Not since my mother died. There's my husband, of course. I've no wish to imply I'm unable to speak with him, but a woman needs another woman's point of view, sometimes. Does that sound strange?"

My aunt reached out to touch lightly upon her blue gown. "Not in the least. A woman has one way of thinking; a man, another. Nothing could be more natural than to seek the advice of one's own gender. You may speak freely with us, my dear, as among friends."

Mrs. Flemming's eyes drifted in the direction of her husband. He continued to stand with his back to us, listening to Robert Cowley who had replaced Mrs. Pardy, and was looking relieved to have made good his escape from the music teacher. Unable to catch the vicar's eye, his wife fell into a quandary, and as if conferring with herself, let words drop from her lips that were soft as petals. Aunt Julia leaned forward to catch as many as she could.

"What's that you say, Mrs. Flemming? I didn't quite hear."

The woman's pale blue eyes turned again in our direction. The look was one of surprise, as if newly awakened.

"'Mrs. Flemming?' The appellation sounds strange after an evening of candor. Can you not address me by my Christian name? If we are really to be friends..."

My guardian interrupted by wiggling happily in her chair. "Say no more, Mrs. Flemming. Eva! Nothing could please me better than for the two of us to be on a first name basis. I was about to make that very proposal myself."

Mrs. Flemming looked pleased. A smile returned to those full lips as she let out a sigh. "Good! I'm so glad to be done with formality. I feel as if all the doors and windows have been thrown open and I can breathe at last."

"Yes, it's a joy to follow one's heart. From now on, Eva dear, we shall be to one another like the roots of the trees, steadfast and nurturing."

The two women locked hands and looked jubilant, like a pair of schoolgirls who'd exchanged diaries. The scene was poignant enough to have been composed by a painter, though I was more baffled by it than moved. This swift progression from acquaintanceship to friendship struck me as odd, particularly as I'd witnessed Mrs. Flemming's earlier air of condescension toward my guardian.

To be fair, I did consider whether or not her original conceit was a device: a way of rejecting before being rejected. I'd been guilty of that tactic myself. But that evening, so many aspects of her character had shown themselves that it was difficult to believe they were all genuine. If so, then cloud shadows scuttling across a barren landscape had more coherence. Surely, some of these anomalies had to be a form of a disguise. But to what purpose?

"Your niece may have already told you that I long for a child?"

Mrs. Flemming paused, letting the question—that was raised without a hint of rancor or betrayal—sink in. Would that my aunt had been so charitable. Her eyes flew from Mrs. Flemming's to mine, and if a bird had thumped into a pane of glass, she could not have looked more surprised.

"Victorine has said nothing," she answered starchly. "The child's circumspect, as I've said. Too circumspect, perhaps."

Fortunately, in any contest between contentiousness and curiosity, the latter was bound to win, particularly when prospective motherhood was the question; and so her eyes left mine and she turned again to Mrs. Flemming.

"I have wondered about the absence of a family. Had I married I should have wanted dozens of offspring. Well, six or seven, at least. But," she sighed, "plain creature that I am, that was not to be."

"Oh, but you're not plain at all, Julia. You're a handsome woman by any standards. And with so large a heart—"

My aunt raised a hand in objection. "Kind of you to say, Eva;

but the truth is, my gentlemen callers were few. While others found their happiness, I grew old, old and useless. At least, that's how I viewed myself, as did others, I'm sure. There was my brother, of course, and his wife, Edwina, to do for. But it wasn't like having children of my own. Then, six years ago they passed away in a terrible fire, and this dear little waif with round eyes came to live with me, so ill and so frightened she could hardly speak. My heart went out to her at once. Not that I didn't love her before. I did. But now she needed me and that's when I began to count the happiest days of my life. I can't tell you what a comfort she's been ever since."

Aunt Julia reached over and gave my hand another affectionate squeeze. "You're as dear to me as if you were my own."

Mrs. Flemming, visibly moved by what she'd heard, uttered her next words, not so much as a comment, but as if it were a prayer. "I do hope it may be the same with me. If only..."

"What is it, Eva, dear? You've a strange look on your face, both wistful and happy at the same time. Dare I guess your secret? You can tell us. Are you with child?"

The head of copper curls shook slowly. "No. God has chosen not to grant me that wish... But I am thinking of adoption."

My aunt's plump hands flew skyward almost before the last word was spoken. "Adoption? Really, Eva? How wonderful! How perfectly wonderful. What do you say to that, Victorine?" An equally plump face beamed in my direction. "You're to have a successor at the vicarage!"

Thirteen

NOTHING SUITED EVA so well as the season in which she died. A chill autumn had gripped the village so that only the hardiest or the most desperate souls made sorties through the early snow. I was among these, as prolonged confinement affected my mind and my health adversely. Aunt Julia turned a blind eye to these wanderings, knowing their therapeutic effect, provided I was warmly dressed.

To be honest, fall and winter were my favorite seasons, as no one, not even Jeremy, ventured onto the moor much. I could be queen of all I surveyed. At such times, the vast circle of the horizon seemed to welcome me. Snow blanketed the paths, giving a freshness to each outing, as if new trails were to be blazed. Nothing stirred except the wind and the surf below the cliffs. One could hear them like whispers from a derelict cathedral—haunting, mysterious.

My solitude provoked strange ideas. The wind and the sea became animate beings, divulging secrets that could only be heard by my attuned ear. Other senses grew more acute, as well. Sights and scents previously unknown to me were revealed. Indeed, the world was transforming itself as surely as if I had strayed into another dimension. Why I should be the recipient of such revelations, I never questioned. My heightened powers made me feel worthy, almost omnipotent; and I knew that the Providence which would doom Eva Flemming was about to reward me.

The feeling was particularly strong that crisp October evening when I was chased home by an incoming storm—a tumult so invigorating that I burst into the parlor with my cloak still hanging damp about me. To my surprise, my sudden appearance seemed to dismay my guardian. She collapsed into her chair and began to moan as if a knife had been thrust into her.

"Whatever is the matter, Auntie?" I rushed forward and took her hand, noting that her skin was cold to the touch and the color of whey.

"Victorine, it's so dreadful...so horrible. I don't know how to tell you except to say it outright. Eva Flemming has died."

Unsure of how I should react, I waited for more details. None were forthcoming. Aunt Julia was too grief-stricken. Apparently, she'd been crying for some time. In her lap lay a handkerchief already damp and so knotted by nervous fingers that it was no longer serviceable. A fresh wave of tears forced her to bury her face in her hands.

Not since my parent's funeral had I seen her so inconsolable. On that day, she had squeezed my fingers with a force that had made me cry out in pain. The sound had drifted above the heads of the congregation, startling them into silence, and not until the officiating vicar had called for the singing of hymns had they stirred again.

On the occasion of Eva's death, I knew better how to comport myself. I held the figure who was crumpled in the chair for a long time, waiting for her cramped gasps to lengthen into sighs; after which, I withdrew into the kitchen to prepare that elixir against all evils: a strong pot of tea.

In my absence, Aunt Julia made some effort to restore her appearance. She had swept the strands of her hair into place and by the time I returned, had replaced her damp hanky for a fresh one.

"Poor man," she sighed as I set a cup of steaming, brown liquid before her. "I don't know how the vicar will bear the loss. If his wife had been ill...but an accident...it's so *unexpected*."

I sat back to learn more of that which by now was common gossip, but Aunt Julia could add little, except to say that the vicar was under Dr. Leach's care and the only other person with a detailed knowledge of events was Jeremy,, who was being sequestered at his home pending the investigation.

The mention of his name in connection with the affair set off an alarm bell. What did he know—or think he knew—about the accident? My hand was shaking as I poured Aunt Julia a second cup of tea.

"Poor lamb," she said, noting my reaction. "First you come home drenched, and now this *awful* news. We must both go to bed early. Neither one of us can afford to be taken ill."

"I'm all right, Auntie," I assured her. "What I don't understand is why Jeremy should know anything about the accident. Did Mrs. Pardy explain?"

Mrs. Pardy had been at the infirmary when Dr. Leach returned after examining the body and had been the one to bring the sad news to Windmill Cottage.

"Have you forgotten, Victorine? It's Wednesday. Eva has a standing order for Wednesdays...*had* a standing order," Aunt Julia corrected herself, "as she wanted supplies in stock for the Thursday council meeting."

The hand holding the hanky dabbed at the corner of one eye. "Poor lad! He was so fond of her. It must have been a shock to find her lying at the bottom of the vicarage stairs. Her death, coming so soon after his mother's... He must be devastated."

"Was she dead when he found her?"

"Yes... No! To tell the truth, I'm not certain." A frown rumpled her otherwise smooth forehead. "There'll be an inquest, of course. We'll know everything then. In the meantime, the entire village is being kept in the dark."

"Perhaps that's as it should be."

"What nonsense." My remark was waved aside like an offending gnat. "Eva's death affects us all. We have a right to know."

"We have the vicar's feelings to consider," I reminded her. "You know what it's like in Braxton. People feed upon gossip. A detail here, a snippet there and suddenly a mountain of hearsay has risen. We wouldn't want that, would we?"

Aunt Julia nodded her agreement, being protective of the one man she admired almost as much as her brother. "You're right, my dear. We mustn't say or do anything that would add to the poor man's grief."

Suddenly, she sprang to her feet as though having seen a mouse scurry across the carpet. "What the man needs at the moment is sustenance! A shepherd's pie. And some hot rolls." That said, she marched into the kitchen, leaving me to sit alone by the fire.

Staring into the burning coals, I tried to imagine Jordan's state of mind. I hoped our bliss, his and mine, might overcome the pain he would be feeling, or would serve as a balm, at least. Still, it must be acknowledged that Eva Flemming had been a dutiful wife, and though bland domesticity could never entirely satisfy him, he owed her some allegiance. He would grieve, but how much, I wondered.

Under similar circumstance, I had suffered when my parents died, especially with regard to my father. Indeed, I was almost destroyed by regret. No matter that in my mind he had decided to betray me, to send me away to an accursed institution far from home; the moment he was irretrievably lost, my fury dissipated and I was visited by a host of happy memories that were far more torturous than my despair. Oh hateful, happy memories. They can char the soul.

That no similar self-loathing should taint the love that Jordan felt for me was my first concern. He must be made to see that Eva's death was no judgment against us, but a providential act that removed the sole impediment to our happiness. Neither of us was to blame. Neither of us!

Fourteen

I AWOKE IN A cold sweat the following morning. If I had dreamed, I had no memory of it, but I felt disoriented, like someone too quickly snatched from one place to another. Seconds passed before the shadows of my room became familiar, and not until I was reacquainted with my surroundings did I become aware of voices rising from the parlor below. Dressing quickly, I ran downstairs to learn if there was any news regarding yesterday's tragedy.

A bedraggled Mrs. Pardy was seated by the hearth, having just emerged from the pouring rain. Aunt Julia was bent over the fire, stoking the coals with wads of paper, struggling to get the flames going. She turned to greet me as I entered.

"You look tired, dear. Come sit down. The room will be warm soon."

Turning again to her task, she went on with her back to me. "I confess I didn't sleep well myself. I kept thinking about poor Eva and how the vicar will cope with her gone. Such a tragedy. But Cordelia's brought a bit of news. Good, in a way. The inquest has been set for Tuesday. This whole, sad affair will be behind us in a few days. Not that we'll forget Mrs. Flemming. There'll always be a place for her in our hearts; but I rather think it's better to bare the facts early so a healing can begin."

"Sir Ian Dunbar will be presiding," piped Mrs. Pardy who, dressed in a somber gray, looked like a titmouse.

"Such a nice man," she chattered as I settled on the settee. "Not stuffy like some with titles. Personable to everyone. I confess our paths have seldom crossed, but I do have a client or two in his vicinity who hold to that opinion." The eyes of our seamstress sparkled with expectation, as if she wanted me to guess who those clients might be. Apparently she thought they might impress me. If so, my response was a disappointment.

"Sir Dunbar? Why do we need a magistrate from the neighboring shire? What's wrong with Mr. Cowley?"

"Have you forgotten, Victorine? He's away on business.

138

Something to do with his family's estate. Won't be back for a fortnight. We couldn't wait, could we? It wouldn't be seemly, would it, Julia?"

My aunt sighed as she sank into her armchair, successful at last in her efforts to draw the fire. "Of course, it wouldn't. Not seemly at all."

Each of us paused to consider the question of what was and what was not seemly, but these reveries were soon broken by the sound of the kettle's whistle as it steamed in the kitchen. Aunt Julia rose to answer its call. Her disappearance was followed by the requisite sound of china being lifted from the cupboards and when at last she reappeared, it was with all the accoutrements of a morning repast: tea, toast and a pot of marmalade. This we ate hungrily.

"I only hope we shan't have to look for a replacement soon," she remarked when the tray was empty. Her tone was matter-of-fact, as though a conversation had preceded it.

Mrs. Pardy and I looked up like startled birds.

"Replacement? For what? For whom?"

"Why, for the vicar, child. I suspect he'll want a change..."

"But he's done nothing wrong!"

"Of course, he hasn't! No one said that he had. But the memories are bound to be painful. And living in that drafty vicarage now that she's gone... It will seem so empty."

"He could always take lodgings."

"And where would that be?" My aunt raised an eyebrow skeptically. "Here with us?"

"Why not? He could have the guest parlor. And he loves your cooking."

A faint chuckle followed my remarks. "Victorine, be reasonable. Our cottage is too small and so are most of the dwellings in Braxton. I suppose he could move to one of the farms, but that would be so remote."

"What about the pub?"

The two older women stared at me aghast, their mouths hanging open.

"I hardly think The Crown would be suitable, not as permanent lodgings. Anyway, even if a place could be found, I doubt he'd want to stay."

"Why not? He has friends here."

"Well, new friends, such as we are, may not be enough. But you mustn't upset yourself so. You've gone all pale at the mere mention of his leaving. I promise you, I haven't the slightest notion of what the vicar's thinking. I doubt he's given the future any thought at this stage. I was ruminating out loud. That's all. When the question arises, if it does, I promise, I'll do everything in my power to encourage him to remain."

"As will I." Mrs. Pardy nodded, smiling at me.

Later that afternoon, Aunt Julia donned her porkpie hat, stuck with her favorite ruby colored pin, and made ready to leave for the vicarage. I had wanted to go, too, but was denied because a delivery was expected from the green grocer.

"But you said Jeremy wasn't making his rounds," I objected, throwing her a churlish glance.

Nothing was made of my protest. Aunt Julia continued to struggle with her gloves, her fingers being stiff, all the while barely looking at me.

"Yes. But it's not as though the world's come to a halt, has it? Someone will arrive or else Arthur would have sent word. Anyway, we mustn't overwhelm the vicar with too many visitors. I'll convey your condolences. You may be sure of it."

That said, she hurried out the door and down the gravel path. I stood watching her as she headed for the High Street, my eyes narrowed in resentment, until she disappeared past the row of trees that bordered the lane.

A quarter of an hour later, I realized my good fortune in being left behind. Jeremy was making deliveries after all. The ring of his bicycle bell brought me running to the kitchen as though the cottage were on fire.

"Thank heaven's it's you!" I cried, pulling him inside. "I've been so worried."

After sliding the groceries on the table, he put his hand on his hips and stared at me. "Worried? Why?"

"Aunt Julia said you were hiding, because of what's happened—"

"I wasn't *hidin'*. Why should I? I been down to the station, that's all."

"How awful for you. I suppose they asked you lots of questions. If you'd have asked me, I'd have gone with you for support. What's happened is terrible."

I pulled out a chair, hoping he would sit down. He looked at it but remained standing.

"Thanks, but I didn't need any help. Anyway, you needn't pretend with me. I know you never liked Mrs. Flemming."

"What a mean thing to say! I never wanted the poor woman

dead. I hope you haven't been giving anyone the wrong idea."

"That's right. Put yourself first, like always. You needn't worry. I never said nothin'. You flatter yourself, anyway, if you think people dote on *your* opinions."

"Why are you being so horrid? I'm trying to be sympathetic."

"Come off it, girl! You want to know what I saw. Everyone wants to know that. People have been plyin' me with their sympathies all mornin'. Well, I can't say nothin'. Not till the inquest. That's what I been told."

"Fair enough." I shrugged, feeling the heat of Jeremy's anger as if it were a hot iron. "I won't ask. I wasn't going to anyway, though you may think it. I was worried about you. I wondered how you were feeling. They say you were the one who found her. It must have been quite a shock."

"They? Who's they?"

"Mrs. Pardy and some others."

"It's all gossip. Nobody knows except Constable Mills, the doctor and me."

"Then you weren't the one to find her?"

"Stop wheedlin', Victorine! I said I wasn't talkin'. I got to go, anyway. I'm needed at the shop."

His body twisted in the direction of the door, but I caught his arm and spoke softly to placate him.

"Don't be angry. I really am trying to help. Stay and have tea with me, why don't you? The kettle's on."

"I don't feel much like tea...."

"Not even a bit of trifle? With raspberry jam?"

"Did your aunt make it?"

I could see him weakening. "Of course, she did. Why should the best cook in Braxton buy baked goods?"

"True enough." He straddled the chair I'd pulled out for him. "There's no one bakes like your Aunt Julia. Don't see how you stay so skinny. I'd be the size of a horse if I lived here."

"Skinny? Is that how you see me?" I peered down at my waist to make my own assessment. "I don't think I'm skinny. I could lose a few pounds, in fact."

"Where? Inside your ears?" Jeremy flashed a smile that led me to believe his indignation had passed.

"There! That's the face I'm longing to see. Not those horrid frowns you've been giving me lately."

"And who's fault is that, I wonder?"

"Is it mine?" I set a large slice of trifle in front of him.

Jeremy looked down at the fork I had hastened to provide; then I stood watching as he took his first bite. Raspberry jam and cream oozed from the sides of his mouth.

"Is it?"

"What?"

"Is it my fault?"

"What d'you mean?"

"That I make you frown? Be honest with me."

"I didn't mean anythin' by it, Victorine. Forget what I said. Nothing's changed. We're still friends. Aren't we?" He looked up with the question reflected in his eyes.

"What a stupid thing to ask. Of course, we're friends. As you said, nothing's changed."

"I meant my feelin's for you—you're not the same."

"What do you mean? I haven't altered all that much. We're growing up, that's all."

"I'm not talkin' about growin' up. Ever since *he* came..."

"The vicar? Honestly Jeremy!" I didn't mean to sound exasperated, but I couldn't help myself. "Talk about me and Mrs. Flemming! What about you? You've been critical of him from the moment he arrived. I don't know what's got into you."

Jeremy put his fork down and looked at me as though I were a bug specimen. "Let's just say, I've had my eyes opened. I seen you with him on the moor. Lots of times."

"You mean to say you've been spying on me?" Anger constricted my throat so that I was fairly growling.

In the past, Jeremy would have walked away from an argument. He didn't like to upset me. The penalty was that I might not speak to him for days or that I might have a seizure. But lately those considerations weren't enough to hold him in check. His anger easily matched mine, as though he had no control over himself—a hazard I found to be more and more intimidating.

"I got a right to be on the moor same as you," he shouted, rising from the chair and shoving his trifle across the table with a force that caused it to skid off the plate. "Besides, from the way you was actin', it didn't seem to matter *who* was watchin'. Cavortin' and battin' your eyes the way you did!"

"I *never!*"

"It's not right, Victorine. He's a married man...or *was.*"

Jeremy's words hit me like a slap in the face. I was stung by the unspoken accusation. A cool head would have served me better under the circumstance, but a dread that was swishing its tail inside me made that impossible.

Stamping my foot, I shouted back at him. "I won't have you spreading rumors about me or the vicar. We met by accident. If you say otherwise you're a liar, and I'll never, ever speak to you again."

"Met by accident? Do you take me for a fool? I seen how you was holdin' hands. Like a pair of lovers, you were. You ought to be ashamed, Victorine. You ought to be hangin' your head and prayin' for forgiveness, not standin' here makin' a brazen face."

"I tell you I've done nothing to make me ashamed. And who are you to judge? You used to follow Mrs. Flemming around like a sick puppy."

"It's not the same—"

"It is! Only you want to pretend otherwise."

Jeremy's shoulders slumped. I could see his distress but I showed him no pity. "I'm not the one who's changed. *You* have. All this anger, this hatred for the vicar. It's so unlike you. You're not the boy I grew up with. You're a stranger."

"Victorine, I'm sorry. I don't mean to hurt you. I'd never want that. But someone's got to open your eyes. I'm tellin' you, this vicar you dote on isn't what he seems. He's...he's *evil*."

My arms and limbs trembled when I heard him. Jeremy saw his effect and came around the table, but I backed away.

"Leave me alone. I don't want you here. Don't touch me!"

My protest was ignored. Jeremy gripped my shoulders as if he were about to shake some sense into me.

"Don't talk rubbish, I can't leave you like this. You got to lie down. Now! Right now!"

I struggled as I was forced to the floor, weeping with unspent rage. But my tears were from more than anger. I was mourning our lost childhood, Jeremy's and mine, and terrified for our future.

Fifteen

S O MANY SPECTATORS crowded into the Leland refectory on the day of the inquest, that a visitor to the High Street might have mistaken Braxton for a ghost town. A smaller gathering had attended Eva Flemming's funeral, death being a common sight, but an inquest was a rare spectacle that could not be missed.

Aunt Julia, using her influence as a church elder, had arranged that we be seated near the front. An aisle down the center of the room bisected the rows of chairs, and of these, the front seats, to the right and left were reserved for those required to testify. They were empty when we entered, as was the desk placed to face the assembly, which the magistrate was to occupy.

The interval before the proceedings was a time to see and be seen and Aunt Julia made the most of it, taking sorties through the crowd and generally behaving as if she was the hostess of the affair. I took my seat in a nervous state.

Voices passed around me like disembodied spirits. Once or twice, laughter rose above the buzz of conversations that vied with one another within the cramped space. The din was almost at a carnival pitch when the vicar and the other witnesses appeared, moving down the center aisle. They were followed by a sudden silence that was, itself, deafening.

Jordan, tall and gaunt in his black attire, looked so like a spectral figure that those in his path immediately made way. Unimpeded, he soon reached his designated chair and perched himself on the edge of it with his fingers digging into his knees. He looked neither to the right nor the left but stared straight ahead, rigid as a portrait painting.

Dr. Leach joined him, his gray beard flowing to his chest, and to his right sat Constable Mills, a boy by contrast. The last seat, at the end of the row, was Jeremy's. I could not see him clearly, only his shock of blond hair that glistened in the reflected sunlight.

Sir Dunbar entered. He was a man in his late fifties with a rosy, kind face. He stopped to offer his condolences to the vicar before taking his seat behind the dark oak desk. Then, he nodded to his clerk for the proceedings to begin. He looked a bit impatient as his eyes scoured the room. Word was that he'd been reluctant to serve as magistrate because on this day his daughter, son-in-law and their two children were returning home from a lengthy trip aboard. Being one who doted on his family, Sir Dunbar found it hard to be away. Robert Cowley's absence, however, had left him not choice.

Constable Mills was the first witness. He rose and took the chair to the right of Sir Dunbar. People coughed or blew their noses during the interval, in a last minute flurry to make themselves comfortable. Sir Dunbar waited.

On several occasions during his testimony, Constable Mills consulted his notes. His remarks were dry and factual. He said he'd been intercepted during his rounds somewhere around four o'clock on the afternoon of the fourth of September by Jeremy Simones. He was informed there'd been an accident at the vicarage, and he'd followed on foot behind the boy's bicycle. When he arrived at the house, he found Mrs. Flemming lying at the bottom of the parlor stairs. She was not breathing. It appeared that her neck had been broken. Dr. Leach, who was attending the vicar in the guest parlor, came out to speak with him and confirmed that Mrs. Flemming's neck appeared to have snapped during a fall.

"Did she say anything to Dr. Leach before her death?" Sir Dunbar stared over the heads of those gathered as he asked the question.

"No, sir. He told me she was gone by the time he arrived."

"By 'gone,' I presume you mean dead. Go on then. Who found the body? The vicar, I presume?"

"The vicar was home at the time, sir. In his study. He said he ran to the landing the moment he heard his wife scream."

"So he did not see the fall?"

"No, sir. But he saw Jeremy Simones emerging from the kitchen about the same time he reached the landing."

"What reason did the boy have for being on the premises? Was he a frequent visitor?"

"He's the green grocer's son, sir. Mrs. Flemming had a standing order on Wednesdays."

"So she must have heard him and was hurrying downstairs to let him in?"

"It's possible, sir, though Jeremy usually lets himself in. There aren't many locked doors in Braxton."

The magistrate smiled. Coming from a small community, he

understood.

"So he was already in the house at the time of the fall, is that correct?"

Constable Mills consulted his notes, then read aloud from Jeremy's statement. "'I was in the kitchen when I heard Mrs. Flemming cry out.' Yes sir. That would indicate he was on the premises."

"Very good, Constable Mills. Now, if he was in the kitchen when he heard Mrs. Flemming, I presume that means he didn't see the tumble either. Or did he?"

"No, sir. I mean yes, sir. That's correct. He didn't see the fall. He found her at the bottom of the stairs, but she was still alive."

"How did he know that?"

"He heard her moan."

"Did she say anything?"

"No sir. She just moaned. Seeing her condition, the boy went straight away for the doctor, then came looking for me."

The magistrate nodded to indicate the reaction was proper. "And when you arrived, could you determine the cause of the fall? Was there a defect in the stairs? A loose bit of carpeting, perhaps?"

"No sir. I saw no physical explanation. The stairs are unusually narrow, though."

"Was Mrs. Flemming in good health? Not suffering from dizzy spells or the like?"

"I couldn't say, sir. You'd have to ask Dr. Leach as to that."

The magistrate waved his hand, conceding the point. Then a pause followed and after that, a frown. The next line of query was one Sir Dunbar had to address, though he loathed doing so, which was plain to everyone by the gravity of his expression.

"Think carefully before answering, Constable Mills. Then speak plainly so that all may hear... When you examined the scene, there was no sign of a struggle, was there? No unusual marks on Mrs. Flemming to indicate her fall might be anything but an accident?"

The question outraged those who heard it so that a whispered protest permeated the hall. It floated above the heads of the spectators and gained strength, row by row, so that Sir Dunbar was forced to raise his gavel. Not until he had rapped several times was order restored.

The silence that fell was a churlish one, reflecting more of a desire to hear the constable's reply than a respect for the magistrate's authority, a man largely unknown to the assembly.

"I-I..." The officer looked uncomfortable and squirmed in his armless chair. "I'm satisfied, sir...that is, in my opinion, there's little evidence of foul play."

"*Little* evidence?" The magistrate rapped his gavel at an involuntary gasp of surprise. "Surely you mean *no* evidence?"

"Well, sir, a button *was* torn away and there were scratch marks along the throat..."

"Not surprising, Constable? After so great a fall?" Sir Dunbar's voice grew impatient and purposefully loud in order to quell the murmur rising from the back of the room. "I, myself, took a tumble off my front steps last week. Only two steps, mind you, yet I had to have stitches. Imagine falling down a flight of stairs. Was there anything remarkable about these scratches?"

"Wh-what do you mean, sir?"

"Heaven's man, you're an officer of the law! I mean were they deep? Did she look as if she'd been attacked with a knife or some dangerous object?"

"No, sir."

"An axe?"

"No. Of course not, sir."

"Of course not? It's been known to happen, you know. Apparently not in this case. Mrs. Flemming's scratches were small, I take it. Consistent with a fall? Is that what I'm to understand?"

The man in the blue uniform curled in upon himself as though he'd received a blow to his stomach. "Yes, sir. The marks would be consistent with a fall."

"That's all I'm asking, my good man. You may step down."

Dr. Leach was the next to testify. He had little to add except that Mrs. Flemming's health had been robust and without so much as a sniffle during her tenure in the parish. As for the scratch marks, like Sir Dunbar, he considered them to be injuries in keeping with the accident.

Jeremy followed. Rising, he shuffled to the front of the room like a prisoner in leg irons. Friends and neighbors, seeing how pale he looked, murmured in sympathy. Even Sir Dunbar felt compelled to inquire if he felt strong enough to testify. Jeremy said that he was, but avoided the magistrate's eyes and those of everyone else in the hall.

"According to Constable Mills, you found the deceased lying at the bottom of the stairs. Is that correct?"

"Yes, sir. It is."

"You came rushing in because you heard a cry. Is that correct?"

"Yes."

"And prior to that you heard nothing out of the ordinary?"

"I-I don't know what you mean, sir. There was a storm blowin'."

"So it was impossible to hear much of anything, except Mrs. Flemming's cry." Sir Dunbar turned to his clerk. "Underline that, please."

Jeremy's head swung in the magistrate's direction. "Underline what, sir? I-I didn't say I heard nothin'. I said the storm was makin' a racket."

"Yes. That's what I just said, didn't I?" The interrogator looked impatient. Like the rest of us, he must have felt a prisoner of this stuffy room.

"I might've heard somethin'," the grocer's son persisted.

Sir Dunbar sighed. A new line of questioning had opened, one that had to be pursued.

"Might have? What does that mean, exactly? What is it you think you might have heard?"

"Dunno for certain." Jeremy stared into his hands while the magistrate choked on the reply.

"Don't know! Don't know? Then what is your objection? I can hardly record that you *may* have heard something, but you're uncertain. That's not very helpful, is it?"

Jeremy considered the matter while Sir Dunbar pulled out his pocket watch and studied it, most likely imagining the arrival of his family. By now his grandchildren would be tearing though the manor in search of him, believing him to be hiding, laughing and calling, "Granpa! Granpa! Read uth a thory. Pleath do!"

His impatience troubled the row upon row of Braxtoners who cared little for his disquiet. They were eager to hear the lad's testimony. He'd been wandering in and out of their cottages for years, had grown tall under their watchful eyes, and they knew him to be true as a plumb line. If he was troubled by something, they wanted to know what it was, and whispers to that effect rose above the silence.

Sir Dunbar gave a rap with his gavel and the room came to order. But outside, in a tall tree, the continuous cawing of a crow seemed to mock the proceedings, which put a smile on the faces of those who thought it was a judgment against the magistrate.

"Well, young man, do you or do you not have anything to add?"

"I-I'm sayin' it's hard to know, sir, on account of the storm."

"*Yes, yes, we've established the presence of a storm. We've got that down.* But have you *anything to add*? It's not a difficult question is it?"

"No, sir..."

The crow's caws grew louder.

"Do you mean 'no,' it's not a difficult question, or 'no,' you have nothing to add?"

"As I said, because of the storm..."

Sir Dunbar's gavel came down with terrible force, enough to snap it in two. "*Let the record show that the boy heard the storm, only the storm and nothing but the storm!*"

The man in black robes took a sip of water to regain himself and in the interval seemed gratified to observe that silence reigned both within and without the hall. The crow must have flown away. That being the case, he turned an almost affable gaze upon his troublesome witness.

"Now then, we've heard testimony that Mrs. Flemming was alive when you found her. Is that correct?"

Jeremy looked crestfallen, but nodded. "I-I heard her moan, sir."

"Then she was still alive. Good. Now we're getting somewhere. Did she say anything? How she had fallen, perhaps?"

"No, sir. She was in pain so I went to fetch the doctor."

"She said nothing and you went for the doctor. That's your testimony, is it?"

"Yes, sir."

"Thank you for being so clear. Now, Constable Mills has stated that when the vicar heard his wife call out, he rushed to the landing. Did you see him there?"

"Yes, sir."

"Did he say anything to you?"

"He didn't say nothin'."

"Did you say anything to him?"

"No, sir."

"Why not?"

"There weren't time. I had to get help."

"So you left the vicar standing on the landing and ran off. How long was it before you returned? I mean, did you find Dr. Leach in his surgery? Or did you have to go looking for him?"

"No, sir, he was in."

"So you both ran back to the vicarage."

"I was on my bicycle, sir."

"All right, you rode your bicycle and the doctor came on foot. Did you arrive together?"

"Yes, sir. He kept pace with me. It weren't far."

"So you were gone for how long?"

"About ten minutes, maybe."

"And what did you find when you returned?"

"The vicar was kneeling beside his wife. He'd put a blanket over her."

"And what was his state of mind when you found him?"

"I don't get what you mean."

"You said earlier that he was in a state of shock. How was he when you found him again?"

"I didn't say he was in shock, did I?"

"Yes, you did! Well, *someone* did."

Flipping through her record, the clerk leaned forward and whispered in the magistrate's ear.

"I stand corrected. Constable Mills testified that you had said the vicar was in shock."

"Maybe so. I don't remember."

The striking of three on the church bell tower forced a sigh from Sir Dunbar. His right eye twitched with annoyance, and it seemed he held the whole of Braxton in the same regard.

"All I want from you, lad, is some estimation of the vicar's demeanor. Was he happy? Dancing a jig?"

Jeremy looked shocked. "No, sir. He was cryin'."

"*Crying.* Thank you! That's very direct. Very clear. Now, tell me this. When you returned, did you notice if anything about the scene had been altered?"

"Yes, sir. The vicar had thrown a blanket over his wife—"

"Yes, yes. I know. I mean, was anything else changed, any sign of tampering..."

"I don't understand."

"Fair enough. That will serve as a 'No.' I've no further questions."

Jeremy returned to his seat, the picture of abject misery.

The last witness was the vicar. As he was sworn in, Sir Dunbar observed the gaunt man with compassion, and what followed were a few discreet queries, meant to confirm the established facts.

After that, the ordeal ended quickly. A verdict of accidental death was rendered and everyone looked relieved. Smiles and handshakes went round, as though this had been a festive occasion.

Like many others, Aunt Julia rushed forward to offer the vicar words of comfort, as did Sir Dunbar, who dashed away immediately afterwards...likely in the faint hope he might yet enjoy a glimpse of his grandchildren.

Unlike the many, I struggled against the tide of well-wishers in search of an exit, emerging at last into the sunless air with my bonnet and gown awry. Jeremy, to my surprise, stood next to me, having been driven, it seems, by my same desire to escape the hurly-burly inside. We were so close, we were almost touching, but there was no time to speak. He bolted past me, like someone remembering he'd left a kettle on the fire. Watching him go, I was filled with a mixture of sadness and fear. Our friendship was unraveling. I was losing him. And worse! That dissolution, I knew, would threaten any happiness I might dare to seek with Jordan.

Sixteen

THE ORDEAL OF the hearing took its toll on Jeremy. He turned inward, lost the vivacity in his step, and looked upon the world with eyes as vacant as fogged mirrors. Aunt Julia diagnosed his condition as acute melancholy brought on by the death of his friend, Eva Flemming.

"Give him time," she advised Anthea Clemmons who had commented that his testimony at the inquiry seemed confused. "He'll come 'round and be his old self again."

But time passed, first one month then two, and all agreed that there were no signs of a recovery. Eventually, Dr. Leach was consulted, and though he could find no physical cause, he suggested a few months rest, free from any responsibilities. Even school was ruled out so that like me, Jeremy became a home student.

Barred from meaningful activity, the grocer's son wandered across the countryside like a gypsy. Once or twice I saw him on the moor, but from a distance. He lived in solitude and made no pretense of his desire to remain in that condition.

The same was true of the vicar. The day after the inquest, he departed for London, leaving Aunt Julia to make his excuses to the congregation. Stunned by his action, I vented my anger the only way I could, by accusing him of abandoning his flock, a charge that Aunt Julia easily swept aside.

"He had to leave, my dear. He has his wife's affairs to settle. Apparently, though she was careful not to boast of it, Eva Flemming was a wealthy woman, involved in a number of charities. Those responsibilities now fall to her husband, so it's only natural that he should have to meet with her solicitors. He'll be back soon. In the meantime, Charles Harriman, the young curate from North Staffordshire, will assume his duties. He's quite handsome, I'm told." My guardian gave me a sidelong glance. "Very handsome, indeed."

Rejecting the olive branch that was offered, I continued to sulk, particularly as I'd had no word from Jordan. Under the circumstance, an interval of reserve might be prudent but I never imagined being cut off entirely.

For me, the days passed endlessly. For others, Jordan's absence posed no hardship at all. Charles Harriman proved to be all that Aunt Julia had made of him: tall, fair and bestowed of an aquiline profile. His arrival caused a stir among the eligible young ladies of our village. They flocked to his side like hummingbirds to a fuchsia, a sight I found at once comical and indecent.

He, to the contrary, was not the least offended by the attention, even gave the impression he thought it was his due—though why, I cannot fathom. His frayed frocks and linens made it clear that he was penniless and could only hope to make his fortune by marrying well.

To my dismay, there were a number of parents, those who should have known better, who condoned their daughters' mild flirtations. They thought him personable and amusing and sent him frequent invitations to their homes. Aunt Julia suggested that we should do likewise, but I was adamantly against it.

Whether my aloofness intrigued him or he feared to lose my guardian's patronage, I do not know, but Mr. Harriman went out of his way to burden me with his company. I could appear nowhere in the High Street without his getting word of it; then suddenly he was there, at my side, offering to carry a package or soliciting some trivial advice with regard to his sermons. As this was the baldest form of flattery, I gave it no credence and noted that if I remained in his presence for even the briefest time, the conversation turned to him: what balls he had attended while in London, the great houses he'd been invited to, and the number of politicians, dignitaries and the like that he professed to have met— though I suspected the acquaintanceship was no deeper than having stood by one or two of them during a passing parade.

Of art and literature he knew little. He was a Cambridge graduate, but our conversations bore no evidence of that; and beyond a smattering of theology and a good opinion of himself, I was loathe to discover any benefit he'd gained from his attendance at so august an institution. Indeed, his vapid monologues made me long for the wheezing of Vicar Soames.

In time, discovering that my disinterest had no effect upon his good relations with my aunt, the young curate turned from me to her—a neglect for which I was grateful, especially as he seemed to bear me no ill will. Like a bee in search of pollen, failing to find it in one blossom, he searched in another.

My greatest concern was for Jordan. Two months had passed and still I'd had no word from him. Was he ill? Had he met with a mishap? Convinced that some dire fate had befallen him of which others were aware but which was being kept from me, I grew sullen. Aunt Julia knew something. The very mention of his name seemed to fluster her and she would change the subject posthaste. Why? Surely her fondness for him could not have grown cold in a scant two months. Or had Charles Harriman made greater inroads in the community than I could have imagined, for he left little doubt that his permanent posting to Braxton would be welcome. My heart hardened toward them both.

The weather did nothing to assuage my melancholy. First rain, then snow oozed between the cracks in the windows and permeated Windmill Cottage with a chill no fire could remedy. This was the season of deep winter when residents burrowed into their homes like squirrels.

Christmas came and went without much public fanfare. The tragedy at the vicarage continued to hang like a pall over the village so that the church, the traditional center of festivities, was quiet. A few parties were given, the invitations to which I stubbornly declined. Aunt Julia protested, of course. "Eva's gone, dear. No amount of brooding will bring her back. What harm can it do to accept the hospitality of a few friends? None, I should think. Indeed, I suspect the dear woman would wish you to enjoy yourself."

When these pleadings had no effect; when, to her dismay, each newly arrived envelope was thrown, unopened, into the fire, she eventually fell silent and retreated to her needlework. There, among the embroidered pansies and coral bells, she took some solace.

I should have done more to comfort her. Anyone less self-absorbed than I would have seen that she was grieving. Her sighs were numberless and she would sit at the window for hours, staring into the garden, its bones laid bare like the contents of a violated grave.

With both of us dispirited, our conversations were limited to the barest essentials: what to have for supper or whose turn it was to fold and lay away the laundry. Once these filaments in the web of ordinary life were connected, we disengaged and spent the greater part of each day drifting aimlessly in and out of our rooms, waiting. Waiting for who knows what.

On a particularly dreary afternoon, with icicles everywhere

so that the world outside seemed to be made of glass, Aunt Julia joined me in the kitchen. She looked the picture of misery. Her nose was red, her hair disheveled, and she was so bent by a bronchial cough that the afghan thrown about her shoulders formed a misshapen hump. She headed for the stove and warned me not to get too close.

"I wouldn't want you to catch whatever I've got," she explained. "Nothing seems to keep me warm. Even my water bottle's of little comfort. I thought maybe a hot toddy..."

Filling the kettle with water, she peered from the window. If she hoped for a sign of spring, she was disappointed. Winter's grip was ruthless. Her herb garden was blackened, and enough limbs had been snapped off the trees to make them seem more like rows of amputees than a peach orchard.

As always, she took what solace she could.

"I suppose this cold spell will keep the pests down. And the peonies should do well come spring. They like the cold. Still, I find it hard, don't you? All this ice. Snow I don't mind, but ice! It's not safe to walk about. I feel like a prisoner."

She turned to face me, being reminded of how I detested confinement.

"Oh, my dear. This will soon pass and, like my peonies, your beloved moor will be all the better for it. But how are you feeling? Any nasty headaches? It hasn't been a good year, has it?" She went on, not waiting for a response. "You've been so ill and then the accident... I know there's a purpose in what's happened, but that doesn't make it easy to bear, does it?"

Seeing her lips tremble and that she was on the verge of weeping, I suggested that we sit together in the parlor. We hadn't made ourselves a proper tea in several days. Now seemed a good time as nothing cheered my guardian so much as a hearty fire and my company.

She nodded without speaking, afraid her tears might break through. Seated together in the parlor, she handed me a cup of steaming brown liquid, then locked her gaze on me as if to ask a question.

"Robert Cowley's had a letter from the vicar," she began.

"The vicar?" I sat bolt upright, making no pretense of disinterest. "What does it say? Will he be back soon? Is he coming here, to the cottage? Tell me, Auntie. I want to know everything."

"Calm yourself, my dear! I'd no idea the news would be so affecting. You mustn't make yourself ill."

Ignoring her admonition, I continued to press for information. "When is he expected? This week? The next? Why have you said nothing till now? If you say it slipped your mind, I think I shall scream."

Her hands flew up in resignation. "Heavens! What a fuss. I'm almost sorry I said anything. It did slip my mind. Why shouldn't it? There've been other things to consider: Eva's tragedy, for one, worries about the damage being done to the garden for another, and now this dreadful bronchitis. Besides, how was I to know his letter would be of such importance? The last time you spoke of him, you laid some very hard charges against him. I was afraid you might still be miffed."

"I could never stay miffed with him. No one could. Could you?"

"No, I could not, but mine is a more forgiving nature. Youth can be cruel in its demands for perfection. But if you must know, he'll be here in three days, and you're not to upbraid him with your opinions when you see him. Remember, the man is recently widowed."

"I won't, Auntie. I promise, I'll be as good as gold. You must invite him here. At once! The moment he arrives."

"I doubt it shall be as soon as that," my guardian chuckled. "But it will be soon."

"When?"

"Soon! Goodness, so much impetuousness, and all for a man whom last week you condemned as scurrilous. I shall never understand you, though I will give you credit on one account. You were right about Mr. Harriman. He is far too ambitious! I shall be glad to see the last of him."

"Ah! What's his misstep?" I smiled conspiratorially. "Did he forget to compliment you on your floral arrangement for the chapel?"

"Nothing so trivial as that, Victorine. Give me some credit. No, it's his conduct of late I'm talking about. Did you know he's been courting Robert's niece, Samantha? Rather shamelessly, in fact. Last week he took her for a carriage ride and made a show of it by driving right through the High Street. Then there was that box of chocolates he bought her. I don't know where he's getting his money, but I know he's after hers. It can't be her stubby neck and limp hair that attracts him. What with their farm interests and their commerce in the potteries, the Cowley family is one any man might dream of marrying into. I only hope the vicar sends him packing before the foolish girl loses her head."

As the source of her bitterness was the curate's apparent neglect of me, behavior that I had encouraged, I ought to have come to his defense. I failed to do so, however, partly because his reputation was no concern of mine and partly because Aunt Julia's prattling allowed me to engage in my own ruminations without further comment.

Under what circumstances would Jordan and I meet, I wondered. If we found ourselves alone at Windmill Cottage, I'd chide him for having sent no word; after which, I'd subject him to frequent sighs and long periods of silence. Anything to force an apology was fair in that he needed to admit his error and be punished.

A public setting would require the use of other means to exact the same effect. Perhaps I would greet him forthrightly but with a show of indifference. Or, keeping my distance, I might force him to come to me, an idea that struck me as immensely pleasurable: to bend his will to mine.

But what if I failed? What if he treated me with equal reserve? Would his behavior be merely the dictates of discretion or a sign of something more ominous? And if I reversed myself and went to him, how should I be received? His eyes, would they reflect the love of which he dared not speak or would they turn away after the briefest show of recognition? If so, I would be destroyed, set adrift on the sea of despair, tormented by the certain knowledge he no longer loved me…if he ever had.

To consider this last possibility was to plunge a dagger through my heart. My arms and limbs fell useless and I could feel the warmth draining from my body. Aunt Julia ceased her monologue, peered at me a moment, then hastened to my side, her pinched face hovering above mine. I could see her lips move. She was barking out instructions I could no longer hear. My emotions had come upon me too swiftly. I was overwhelmed by them and lay inert as she tucked her afghan about me to prevent my thrashing. That was all I remembered before slipping into the dreaded darkness.

Mercifully, the spell was brief. Nonetheless, I awoke to find my collar unbuttoned and my throat laid bare to facilitate breathing. My skin felt tight and my extremities tingled, but no other harm had befallen me, thanks to my guardian's vigilance.

Relieved to see me conscious, she collapsed into her chair. Her eyes closed, as if to enable her to gather strength, and in that interval I observed how much the strain of my care affected her. True, she had always seemed old to me. I guessed her to be near sixty, though she was never specific about her age, and she used a concoction of sage, rosemary and tea to darken her hair. Still, the transparency of her skin, the blue veins protruding beneath were not, I surmised, the effects of time only, but those of constant worry.

I was sorry to be a burden to her and said as much. Instantly, her eyes popped opened.

"Burden? You've never been anything of the kind. A perfect joy, that's what you are. I used to say the same to your mother when she was sharp with you. She didn't like to hear it and often came back at me: 'You know nothing about children, Julia. If you did, you'd know that Victorine needs a firm hand.' Firm hand, indeed! 'She needs a hug, that's what she needs,' I'd say in reply. Sometimes your mother would get so cross with me, she'd stomp out of the room and leave us to ourselves. I was glad then. I could wash away those little tears and cuddle you. Anyway, it was better for her to be angry with me than with such a dear child."

I rose and planted a kiss on her soft cheek. "You've always been my guardian angel."

"Oh, you mustn't make too much of what I say." She blushed as she broke into a smile. "It isn't as if your parents didn't love you. They did. And I know they'll always come first in your heart, as is proper."

"I don't see why," I said matter-of-factly, sitting down again. "I didn't come first in theirs."

Aunt Julia flinched when she heard me. "That's not true, dear! You mustn't say that. Why would you even think it?"

"They intended to send me away, didn't they?"

"Wh-who told you that? Nothing was ever settled. Not as far as I know."

"Father told me. I don't suppose he was teasing because that would be cruel, and anyway, he looked so sad."

"I shouldn't wonder, if it's true. Sending you away was never his idea. It was Edwina's."

The pain of old memories came flooding back. "Why? Why should she want me sent away? It's not as if I could help being ill."

"Of course, you couldn't. You're not to blame."

"Then I must have done something to make them stop loving me—"

"Hush now! I won't have you thinking such thoughts. I've told you. Your parents loved you very much. It couldn't have been easy for them to consider parting from you. But, they wanted you to have proper care..."

"You've cared for me all these years and you never thought of sending me away, did you?"

My guardian shook her head and looked perplexed. "It's no good brooding about the past, Victorine. Your parents had their reasons. Part of the problem was Edwina's impatience. She loved you, but she wasn't a young woman anymore. You were born years after she and James had given up hope of a child. When you came, it was a shock, as well as a surprise."

"You're older than she was. Anyway, if I was so much trouble, I don't see why she didn't hire a nanny. My parents could have afforded one."

"True, but it mightn't have looked right. Too pretentious for a vicar in a village like Braxton. We're down-to-earth people here. Anyway, a nanny wasn't necessary. I was there to help. It's just that, in time, Edwina began to resent me. Perhaps she became a trifle jealous as you and I got on so well. I don't know. Maybe she just didn't like having an old spinster underfoot."

"You're more a mother to me than she ever was."

"Oh, my dear! The pleasure I get from hearing you say that makes me feel positively guilty. Still, I thank you for it. We mustn't be too critical of Edwina, though. She did her best. She really did. Truth is, she had a talent for making life difficult. That's why we seldom saw eye-to-eye. Of course, I didn't have a tragedy in my life, like your mother did."

"What do you mean? What tragedy?"

My guardian blinked as though she'd taken a misstep.

"I'd forgotten. You never knew your Aunt Augusta. She died before you were born."

"I had another aunt?"

"Yes. Your mother's sister. She was sixteen when she died."

"Why? What happened? Was she ill?"

My aunt paused as if weighing the consequence of my being told the sad details, an interval in which a patch of sunlight flooded the room. She must have taken it for a sign.

"I suppose you have a right to know. She was family, after all. The best face I can put on it was that she had an accident. That's the official record, anyway—though your mother called it a suicide."

"Suicide!" I fell backwards in my chair. "Why? How?"

"A fall...from the cliffs...."

"Here in Braxton?"

"No. Where Edwina grew up. Outside Scarborough."

"But why?"

"She'd been unwell for some time, hearing voices and the like. I don't know all the facts. Edwina didn't like to talk about it."

"You mean she was insane?"

"That word was never used, but yes, that seems to be the case. Certainly she couldn't be left to herself. Once she got hold of a knife and cut slashes the length of her arm. The cook had only been gone a moment, but when she found Augusta, she let out a scream that brought the entire family running. They found blood everywhere, on the floor, the table, under the stove. Her brother had quite a struggle to take the blade from her, I understand. Got a nasty gash on his arm for his efforts. Such a waste, She was bright and quite lovely, I'm told."

"It's a wonder they didn't watch her more closely after that. How did she get away?"

"One would need eyes in the back of his head to watch a person every second. And most of the time, she seemed lucid. She tricked them, I suppose. Anyway, by the time she was missed, the sea had claimed her. Her body was found by a fisherman not far from where she was presumed to have jumped."

"The family must have felt dreadful."

"Of course, they did! She was loved in spite of her affliction. On her good days, I'm told, she could be very sweet."

"Did they ever think of sending her away where she could be cared for?"

"According to your mother, her parents struggled with the notion, but they never came to a decision. One deterrent was the shame it would bring. Edwina's family was prominent in Scarborough. The bulk of your inheritance, as you know, comes from them. But to be more charitable, I suspect they hoped she would grow out of it. A foolish hope, but when a person is loved, it's difficult to admit frailties. They must have suffered a great remorse after the accident. So, you mustn't judge your mother too harshly for wanting to be cautious with you. Of course, the situation wasn't the same. There are two nice sanatoriums not far from here. If you had been sent away, most likely it would have been to one of those. But for Augusta there was only Breckenridge."

"Breckenridge?" I sat upright in my chair. A memory flickered across my mind of a long ago quarrel between my parents.

"Yes dear. Breckenridge is an insane asylum."

Seventeen

THAT NIGHT AS I lay in my bed, I was assailed by black thoughts. Any doubts that my parents had planned to betray me were erased. My mother had argued to send me to Breckenridge. Worse, she'd brought my father to the same persuasion. Had they survived the conflagration that killed them, I'd have been forced to live out my days in quiet desperation, banished to a place where the only means of escape was by suicide. Any remorse I might have felt for their untimely deaths evaporated. Theirs had been a heinous plot against me. But why? I admit to the invention of imaginary playmates but my loneliness as a child drove me to it. Surely my mother perceived the difference between that and madness. Or was it as my aunt surmised? A gloomy outlook, perhaps even an imbalance, had condemned me.

My heart went out to Aunt Augusta, a girl unseen, unknown, but to whom, by the mention of Breckenridge, I was inextricably bound. I longed to speak to her, to take consolation from her experience, for neither among the living nor the dead was there anyone with whom I felt more accord.

At what hour I eventually fell asleep I do not know, but when I did, I dreamed of my parents. They materialized as apparitions, hovering above my bed. Many times, they had appeared in such fashion, but that night their grimaces had no power to send me shrieking against my pillow. The depth of their treachery was enough to free me from the shackles of guilt.

But one face, pale in death as it had been in life, maintained a hold over me. Eva Flemming formed an unholy triad with the ghosts of my parents. Like them, she wore an accusatory expression. Like them, her lips formed soundless curses that, though unheard, were powerful enough to make me shudder.

I cried out and Jordan appeared. To my horror, his was a visage that brought no comfort. His eyes burned like living coals and his lips were frothed with blood. Even so, I longed to cling to him and feel his kiss. But the spirit ignored my importuning and turned away as though I were rotting carrion.

Shivering and alone, I awoke with my eyes swollen by a surfeit of tears. How I stumbled through my toilet, I barely remember, but when I descended the stairs, it was with all the forebodings of a condemned prisoner. In such a mood, I was unprepared for the scene that awaited me.

"Scones for breakfast and sticky buns for the afternoon!"

Aunt Julia had taken possession of the kitchen and like a conquering army was leaving it in shambles. Cookbooks and utensils were strewn everywhere, as was a quantity of flour. The stove fairly glowed from its fire as it belched yeasty aromas into the air. Apparently, the toddy of the night before had worked its magic. The mistress of Windmill Cottage was her former self again and so full of enterprise that I barely had time for a cup of tea before I was shanghaied into service.

Slapping a lump of dough upon the tiles, she began kneading it, her sleeves rolled back far enough so that her plump, shiny elbows were exposed. I was sent to fetch raisins and bits of orange peel, and these I added to the sticky concoction at my aunt's direction. She leaned her entire body into her task, swaying in a rhythmic dance that was vigorous enough to make her complexion rosy. Watching her and that puckish smile, I was almost happy.

As she shoved the last row of buns into the oven, she confessed that, in part, our endeavors were to celebrate the vicar's return, which, she reminded me, was imminent. "I've sent round an invitation with his name printed boldly upon it, lest Mr. Harriman should make a false presumption." She sniffed with an air of displeasure as she mentioned the poor man's name.

I couldn't help wondering, as we at last sat down for our meal, what he had done to provoke such ire. Whatever his transgression, my aunt's bad opinion of him was so deeply entrenched I doubted he would ever again stand in her good graces. Perhaps his neglect of some detail regarding the church calendar had annoyed her; or he may have forgotten to consult on an order of supplies. Whatever the omission, it had been a grave oversight.

Vicar Soames had been guilty of such a folly and had paid for it. When he allowed some boys to set up a botanical study at the south end of the churchyard without telling her, Aunt Julia had been horrified.

"Think of it, Victorine! There are headstones in that corner of the grounds. The little scamps are bound to steal their specimens from the graves."

The study group ended the moment her feelings were known,

but by then, the damage had been done. The old man's apologies, which were profuse, had seemed only to make matters worse; and, I suspect, that was the incident that set the wheels in motion for his retirement.

No doubt the departing vicar had left a word of warning to his successor, for Jordan had been careful to solicit my guardian's opinion on every occasion. Knowing his solicitous treatment of her, I was confident that his visit to Windmill Cottage was fast approaching and the certainty of it banished all my forebodings.

Two days later, my confidence was rewarded. He appeared on our doorstep and when I entered the parlor, choosing to be late, I found him nodding his head in agreement while Aunt Julia made disparaging remarks about the weather.

"Sometimes, when it's severe like this, I begin to doubt I'll ever see my camellias again..."

The sound of my footfall turned both sets of eyes in my direction. Aunt Julia's eyebrows lifted with some surprise that I was wearing the lilac dress that had been made for last summer's prize giving. She made no comment about its inappropriateness, however, merely urged me to come and sit near the fire.

The vicar rose as I came forward to offer me his chair, but I sat, instead, upon the settee. After several months with no word from him, I hardly dared meet his gaze. I was even afraid the pounding of my heart could be heard. Aunt Julia saw nothing of my disquiet. She smiled upon us both like a hen glad to have her chicks come safely home to roost.

Soon after, there came an outpouring from the kitchen, the result of the work of the past two days. It was gratifying to see how our guest laid siege to the assortment, as though he'd not eaten for some time, but more probably because he was aware that we'd outdone ourselves to honor him.

In either case, the three of us fattened ourselves like Christmas geese, Aunt Julia pausing only to bring the vicar up-to-date on the latest gossip. One story, regarding Mr. Pounder, brought a smile to Jordan's lips:

Apparently, on the eve of Chapman's winter recital, the music teacher had taken it into his head to kidnap the rooster from across the road and lock it in his hall closet, a space that would admit no ray of sunlight. By this means, he hoped to obtain a good night's rest before an event that always put a strain on him. This year had been particularly difficult as the number of untalented boys with no interest in Mozart was on the increase. Plagued by thoughts of certain disaster, he'd broken out in boils, the most prominent being on his backside. That fact he'd confided to Miss Clemmons, who had confided to Mrs. Pardy, who in turn had informed my aunt.

The theft went off without difficulty. The chicken allowed itself to be stowed away and Mr. Pounder, secure in the knowledge that sunrise would break unheralded, drifted off into a deep sleep. Unfortunately, the latch on the closet door was faulty, a fact unknown or unremembered by Mr. Pounder, so that the rooster had little trouble pecking its way to freedom. After that, it proceeded to explore the cottage leaving feathers and less savory deposits in every nook and cranny.

The kitchen proved to be of special interest as Mr. Pounder, usually a tidy man, had left the remains of his supper in the sink: a smattering of corn and mashed potatoes. The chicken made short work of the refuse, and then, as it was a cold night, sought the comfort of a warm roost: In the end, Mr. Pounder served admirably. They slept together, man and bird, like newlyweds, until sunlight pierced the horizon. Then the rooster woke and performed as nature intended.

What followed next was bedlam. Mr. Pounder catapulted from his bed, flinging blankets as he went, so that the frightened rooster squawked more loudly than before. Indeed, the cacophony of barnyard noises escaping from the teacher's cottage alerted his neighbor, who came running to see what fate had befallen his prized breeder. Before long, the two men were shouting at one another and shaking their fists.

Constable Mills, who lived nearby, came to investigate. Whether his lack of uniform or lack of a nightstick robbed him of authority is unknown, but clad in his nightshirt, he was unable to resolve the argument. Both men were too livid.

In time, the weather and the hour took their toll upon the usually good-natured constable. He wanted his bed, he wanted his tea, and most of all, he wanted these two fools to stop shouting.

Tucking the chicken under one arm, he issued a warning to both of his neighbors, promising that if the matter wasn't settled by sunset, a magistrate would be called.

The threat worked its magic. That evening, Mr. Pounder presided over his recital and the rooster was returned to his brood—though not before the former had forfeited a guinea for having laid insult to the latter.

The striking of four on the hall clock resounded like an alarm.

Hearing it, Jordan shot up from his chair. He appeared confused as he gathered up his pipe and other belongings.

"My goodness, where has the time gone?" said Aunt Julia, rising also.

The vicar shook his head. "I don't know, dear lady, but I'm late! Carillon practice starts in half an hour. I must hurry. Thank you for a wonderful afternoon. I should like to come again. Soon, if I may. No one prepares a tea to compare with yours, Miss Ellsworth."

Pleased by his remarks, Aunt Julia threatened to send him off with remnants of her chocolate trifle, but the offer was declined. She'd done enough damage to his girth for one day, her guest observed with a smile.

He headed for the hall, but not before making a slight bow in my direction. If he hoped to read some message in my gaze, what he found was surprise. I, too, had been unaware of how swiftly the afternoon was passing. Aunt Julia had beguiled us with her tea and cakes and prattle. Now Jordan was leaving and neither of us knew what the other was feeling.

Aunt Julia rejoined me in the parlor after he was gone, looking pleased with herself. "Such a lovely afternoon. Just like old times. I'm glad to have him back. He looks well, doesn't he, considering?"

"Yes, yes. But I forgot to ask him something. Excuse me, Auntie, but I must go. I *must!*" I brushed past her with no further word of explanation. Alarmed to see me in a heightened state, she called after me, warning against the consequences of too much excitement; but I paid her no heed. Snatching my cape from its hall peg, I burst into the frozen air even with her footsteps in pursuit.

"Child! There's a storm brewing. You're not dressed for it. Come back. Come back at once!"

Not till I'd obtained the footpath did I dare look around. Mercifully, no one was following, but I knew I had only a few minutes' head start. Aunt Julia would stop to prepare herself before venturing out, but she would follow. My hope was to find Jordan and draw him to a secluded place before she could intercept us.

To my relief, he appeared not fifty paces ahead of me. The incoming storm had slowed his progress. With one hand he was anchoring his hat and with the other clutching at his lapels as he leaned into the wind. I had no difficulty catching up with him, though it was a moment or two before he realized I was at his side.

He looked startled, then, even frowned, knowing I'd behaved impetuously and afraid of the impression it had left. A lecture might have followed, but the storm broke in earnest and we were forced to take shelter in a nearby grove. We'd barely reached its perimeter when the air exploded with the sound of a tap, tap, tapping, fortissimo at first, but modulating to softer music as the vicar and I stood together under the trees.

As a child, I had always felt a singular affinity with nature, not the communion experienced by others, but as if I were suckled by the elements. Rain, snow, thunder, each held a wisdom for me. Yet, as I stood observing Jordan, his eyes closed, his face uplifted in that cathedral of bare branches, he too seemed to receive a benediction.

Before long, the downpour transmuted itself into snow. White powder carpeted the woodland floor and made marble of the trees. The sweet scent of earth invaded my senses and a stillness fell that was of a holy order. In that sacred place, I confessed my feelings.

"I love you, dearest. You are my bliss, my life!"

I admit, I hadn't truly dared to expect a similar display of emotion, though I had hoped for it. Jordan was the darkness against which the candle of my devotion glowed. When I heard his moan, so deep, so shuddering, it pierced me to the core.

There are times, in dreams or when tossing in the dead of night, that the soul is visited by a loneliness more frightening than death. For me, this was such a moment. I heard that moan and sank to my knees, weeping unrestrainedly. Snow fell like petals from the sky. My consummate wish was to buried by it, to fall into an endless sleep, without dreams.

Once in my childhood I had known a similar despair. One would think it was the day my parents died, but it was not. There was a logic to their demise, if not a justice. What I refer to is an event that left its mark upon me because of its sheer, inexplicable cruelty.

I remember I was playing in the garden the day that it happened. The sun was a bright ball overhead and the earth so warm that it seemed winter would forever be banished. I'd taken off my shoes and socks to walk upon the cool grass, though doing so was forbidden.

Suddenly, the back door slammed and fearing my mother had seen me, I hid among the flowers to escape a scolding or worse.

But she was not searching for me. She was headed for the pond that skirted our property, her lips set in a grim expression, a weighted sack in one hand.

Afraid of what she might say when she returned, I struggled to put on my socks and shoes. I had to act quickly if my offense was to go undetected. Then I heard a sound that banished all thoughts of personal safety, a sound at once so pitiful and so frightening that it set my unshod feet to flying.

"Mama, Mama! Please! Don't hurt my kitty! Please, please don't hurt my kitty!"

Mother neither paused nor turned to look at me, but reaching the water's edge, hurled that sack with its precious cargo far out across the pond. It sank in an instant. Little bubbles were floating to the surface by the time I caught up with her.

I wanted to throw myself in after that hapless creature, caring nothing of the consequences, but Mother prevented me. "Stop it, Victorine!" She shook me hard as I struggled. "You're not allowed to have pets. You know what the doctor said. Your father's wrong to concede to your every whim then leave me to do what's right. It's not my fault. It isn't." I heard the anger in her voice, but it meant nothing compared to my grief.

Kneeling in the grove with my dark angel standing above me, all the pain of that childhood memory came flooding back. To lose again what I loved most was inconceivable. I would rather die than endure it. I tore at my clothes in the hope that heaven and the cold would end my misery.

This frenzy had its effect. The man for whom I would have given my life forced me to my feet. His strong arms crushed me to his bosom and as if to breathe new life into me, his lips brushed against mine.

"Victorine! My child. My dearest."

Finding ourselves alone, in a world curtained by falling snow, Jordan and I felt free. Both of us sensed it and our bodies trembled. Each kiss grew more bold, each touch more bruising. We were being consumed by love and were no more in charge of ourselves than is the tide when the moon is full. Falling to earth as lovers, we laid upon sheets of purest white. My breasts were exposed, but the trees peering down on me made no judgment. This nakedness, unsullied by pangs of modesty, was my natural state. I needed to feel no shame even as Jordan caressed me. I was his to do with as he liked and my joy was limitless.

Yet, even as we climbed toward the heavens, a single voice had the power to send us both plummeting headlong into hell.

"Victorine! What's happened? Are you all right?"

Aunt Julia was a speck on the horizon. Even so, hers was a progress too swift for one poised on the brink of ecstasy. Conflicted by desire and the need to avert discovery, I froze and in that instant a familiar lethargy descended. The panic in Jordan's eyes was palpable. He rose and urged me to comport myself, but it was too late. I closed my eyes and let the world go black.

Eighteen

"Are you awake, dear?" Aunt Julia peeked round my door before entering, her lips bowed in a foolish grin as though she were about to hand me a present.

Two weeks had passed since my collapse and during that interval I'd been plagued by bouts of fever and delirium. In all that time, my room remained darkened, the curtains parted slightly to admit the barest slant of light.

During the times when I was ill, Aunt Julia always took precautions to avoid upsetting me. To that end, no mention had been made of my outrageous behavior, though there was a crispness to her manner which led me to know that she disapproved. A girl in my frail condition should not go cavorting in the snow—for 'cavorting' was how she interpreted what had happened. Today, however, she looked neither worried nor disapproving but decidedly happy.

"See who's come," she said, stepping to one side to reveal my visitor.

Jeremy stood with a nosegay of yellow crocuses held in one hand. He was clutching them hard enough to make the petals droop. Aunt Julia rescued them by placing them in a nearby vase.

"There," she said stepping back to admire the arrangement. "Aren't they lovely? Spring is almost here." After that, she went on to describe the winter camellias and hellebores that were lifting their budded heads outside in the garden.

Our guest remained standing, saying nothing. After a time, he was pushed with some impatience toward the chair beside my bed. "Sit down, child, for heaven's sake. Victorine won't bite, you know."

Jeremy did as he was told though he looked uncomfortable, like a seagull perched on a sparrow's nest. My guardian shook her head, unable to accept that two young people who had known each other all their lives could be so reticent in one another's presence.

She left us soon after, assigning me the task of putting Jeremy at ease. I began by thanking him for the bouquet and telling him how well he looked, though that was a lie. He appeared haggard and there were dark circles under his eyes.

"I've been wondering about you lately," I went on, probing for an explanation. "I've not seen you in so long. I was beginning to think you were avoiding me."

Jeremy looked dour. "D-don't know what you mean. I wasn't avoidin' you. Do you think it's right that I come bustin' in here when you was burnin' with fever?"

"No, of course not. But you have been making yourself more absent than usual. Don't pretend to deny it. I know you too well."

"Maybe you do and maybe you don't. But if I've been keepin' to myself, it's because I haven't felt like talkin', that's all."

"What? Not even to me? I thought we were friends."

"Maybe. I'm not always certain."

I could feel myself bristle. "Well, if we're not friends, why have you come? Why bring me these flowers?"

Jeremy took pains to correct himself. "'Course we're friends. I don't mean it the way it sounds. But you have to admit, it don't always seem that way. Sometimes, you shut me out."

"You're talking nonsense. When do I do that?"

"When you don't want to hear what I've got to say. When you know it's the opposite of what you want to do."

"I've a right to a mind of my own, don't I? Anyway, why go on about something if you know I don't want to hear it? That's not being a friend."

"But it is!" Jeremy insisted, leaning forward as he did. "A friend's got a right to warn you. Not only a right, but a *duty*. You may be bright and all, Victorine. But outside of books, you don't know much about the ways of the world."

The remark was so pretentious that instead of becoming angry, I was amused by it. I tossed a pillow at him, half expecting Jeremy to throw it back. He looked at me, disapproving, which made me realize how much I had misjudged his mood.

"I know a bit more than you'd like me to know," he went on in tones sober enough to blacken the sun. "I'm not as dumb as you think —"

"I never said you were dumb. You're putting words in my mouth."

"Not dumb, then, but gullible. That's what you believe, isn't it?"

"Well, you must admit, you haven't always shown the best of

judgment. I never got lost in a cave looking for buried treasure."

The stirring of an old memory did its work. My visitor cracked a smile, though still protesting.

"That's not fair. I was only eight—"

"Yes, and so was I, but I'm the one who rescued you. Good thing, too. You hadn't even taken a lunch."

"I coulda lived off the land."

"What nonsense! Nothing grows in a cave. Anyway, you hadn't even so much as a knife with you, not that I can imagine you killing a rabbit."

"Go on, laugh. I know you think it's funny."

"I didn't then. I was worried. Something bad could have happened. You might have died."

Jeremy eased back in his chair, his hands resting on his knees. "I admit, I owe you. But that was a long time ago. I'm not talkin' about when we was kids."

"But I am. I'm saying that if we were friends then, we still are. Nothing's changed, has it?"

I flashed him my most appealing look and was pleased to see that it could still work magic. He took hold of the hand I was offering and squeezed it.

"'Course not. You know it hasn't. I'd never turn against you, Victorine. Never."

Aunt Julia returned at that moment and, finding us reconciled, beamed her approval.

"There! That's how I like to see things stand between you." She set down her tea tray and began cutting the cake she had brought without a pause in her remarks. "I don't know what's come over the pair of you, lately; but you've been acting like strangers. It troubles me when I see that, you being such friends. I'm glad you've put an end to it."

She meant nothing sinister by what she said. The observation was made in passing and would have been forgotten if Jeremy hadn't taken pains to contradict her. "I don't know what you mean Ms. Ellsworth. Nothin's wrong between Victorine and me."

His vehemence made her suspicious. I could see it in her gimlet eye. How foolish to lie to her. Certainly he'd been acquainted with her long enough to know that she abhorred deceit as much as canker on a rose.

I remembered how painful it was to make that discovery. I'd been ten at the time and had arrived at Windmill Cottage a scant three months before, orphaned and afraid. Because of the fire that killed my parents I'd brought little with me except a few clothes. I suppose it was natural to reach out for objects that would comfort me and I recall being enamored of one of my aunt's hat pins: a silver cube studded with a square of ruby-colored glass. It was large and shimmering, an object intended to mesmerize.

One day, while my aunt was out among her flowers, I removed it from its place in her jewel box and hid it where I was certain it would not be found, in the far corner of my wardrobe. My guardian had so many baubles. Surely *one* would not be missed.

To my sorrow, its disappearance was noted almost at once. The hat pin had been a gift from an unnamed admirer, a man for whom she apparently still had affection. The object, therefore, was dearer to her than I could have imagined. I hated to see her so distressed and longed to return the accursed object; but I did not dare. If she thought me a thief what would become of me? Would she cast me out? The risk was too great. My best course was to say nothing, allow her to think she'd been careless, and hope that in time, all would be forgotten.

A week went by, then two, and when there was no further mention of her prized possession, I congratulated myself for having weathered the crisis. What a fool I was! On Friday of the third week, I came home from school to find my world undone.

Aunt Julia was in the kitchen, rolling out a pie for our supper. Nothing was untoward in this, but on that day, the first day of spring-cleaning, her customary housecoat and apron had been augmented with a pork pie hat. What's more, it was secured with a pin whose ruby fire gleamed in the afternoon light like a maharaja's gem.

Seeing it, my lips quivered and I felt myself grow red in the face. A thousand, thousand reasons...excuses...apologies exploded in my head, but I had no voice, having been struck dumb. I was capable only of tears and a torrent of these dashed themselves upon the white bib of my uniform until it turned gray as ashes. Even my limbs betrayed me, trembling as they did, not from an external cold, but from a bone marrow chill no fire could assuage.

Flesh became stone. And I? A study of despair! Though it may be difficult to believe that a person could gaze upon such misery, hear my sobs, observe my tragic expression and not show pity, my guardian was one. She cast not a single glance in my direction, but continued to roll out the thin crust that was for our supper with an indifferent air, as if cooking in a hat was as normal as sleep.

The rest of the afternoon was marred by much the same silence.

All efforts to engage her were doomed. No tears, no pleadings, no avowals short of a confession could end my predicament. Nonetheless I endured, dreading the unknown more than my present suffering. But, as the day waned and my aunt grew more morose, often glaring at me with her arms crossed, her eyes the size of pinpricks, my resolve eroded and with more contrition than I would have thought possible, I confessed my sin.

The repentance I felt on that day was genuine. But more than guilt, I dreaded banishment. What if Aunt Julia were to send me away, as my parents had almost done? I could not bear being discarded, like refuse, in some institution. That was tantamount to being buried alive. I would have done anything, promised anything, rather than endure it.

When she heard why I'd kept my silence, my aunt gaped in amazement.

"Send you away? My own dear brother's child? Why, you're as precious to me as my right arm. This is your home, Victorine, for as long as there is life in me."

The oath was delivered with a bone-crushing hug and was so reassuring that, when I was sent to bed early and without my pudding, I considered the punishment more than just. That night I slept sounder than I had in weeks. Not that the ordeal left no mark upon me—it did. I vowed never again to lie or steal... without sufficient invention.

"Never quarreled? You expect me to believe that?" Aunt Julia had Jeremy squirming in her line of fire. "You think I don't have ears? Eyes? That I haven't observed the number of times you've stormed from the cottage, leaving poor Victorine on the point of tears? We both understand that you're grieving, dear boy, and we make our allowances. But you mustn't lie. That would be a sin."

Jeremy's chin sagged into his chest and he looked for all the world like a Christian soon to be fed to the lions. "I-I'm sorry, Miss Ellsworth. I didn't mean to... I don't know what's come over me. I haven't been thinkin' straight, not since the so-called accident..."

"'So called'?" The knife Aunt Julia held in her hand thudded to the floor where it was allowed to remain. "It *was* an accident. You were at the inquest. You heard the decision."

If she meant to chasten Jeremy with the force of her objection, she failed. He fired back at her with a stubbornness that was unexpected.

"Hogwash! That weren't no inquest. The magistrate asked a few questions, that's all. Then it was over. Truth is, no one knows what happened. No one except the vicar. He's the one who *says* it was an accident."

"Which should be word enough for anyone."

Aunt Julia stooped to retrieve the cake knife. The frosting it had spattered she daubed with a wet napkin. Her demeanor made it clear that it was better to be tidying up than to be arguing with a peevish boy.

Jeremy buried his head in his hands. "Ah, what's the use! You don't understand a word I'm sayin'. Not a word."

"I *do* understand." Aunt Julia rose with her eyes flashing. "But you're talking nonsense. You've no call to impugn the vicar. And believe me, you'll be in a pack of trouble if you persist. Besides, if you thought something was amiss, you should have said so before. At the inquest. That was the proper place. Not now. Not like a traitor, slandering him behind his back."

She regretted her words the moment she saw the damage they had done. Jeremy slumped as though he'd been landed a blow to the stomach.

"Oh, my dear, dear boy. I know how you're suffering. But it won't do to lash out at others. Especially not the vicar. She was his wife, after all."

A pair of red-rimmed eyes answered her. "How can you be so blind? He's makin' a fool of you. *All* of you. Mrs. Flemming was too good for him. Why, he hadn't got a penny to his name till he met her—"

Aunt Julia's plump hand flew upward in objection. "That's enough, Jeremy. Keep talking like this and people will do more than think you've gone a little strange. They'll cart you away!"

"Mad, am I? Is that what you think? Maybe so. If a man like that can pass himself off as a preacher!"

The bitterness of her godson's retort caused my guardian to pause. Never, till now, had a harsh word passed between them. She'd always thought she understood him better than she did me. And now this rift existed. How had it occurred? What was tearing at this innocent boy? She turned to me with eyebrows lifted.

The question was one I, too, might have asked and was more than eager to have answered. But for that, Jeremy and I would have to be alone. I communicated this need with a gesture. Fortunately, my guardian understood. She withdrew almost at once, but not before casting a wan smile in my direction to thank me for my intervention.

"I don't know what come over me just now," Jeremy muttered

once we were alone. "I never meant to speak to your aunt like that. I think the world of her, you know."

"Not to worry. She's fond of you, too. She'll make allowances."

Jeremy raised his head to look at me. "You think I'm crazy, too, don't you?"

He looked crazed, but I knew that he was not. The torment in his eyes was no aberration of mind, but one of spirit. Whatever had driven him to this excess, it had to be exorcised. Otherwise he might become more desperate. Nevertheless, I feared there was a danger to myself.

"Aunt Julia is right, of course," I began carefully. "If you thought something was amiss, you should have said as much at the inquest...though what it could be, I can't possibly imagine—"

"God's blood!" Jeremy interrupted. "Did it never occur to you that I was protectin' someone...someone I cared about?"

If he meant me, I was anything but flattered! What did he know or think he knew? I felt trapped. Angry.

"You're talking nonsense, you are. How could you be in a position to protect anyone? You weren't in the room when Mrs. Flemming fell. That's the truth, isn't it? That's what you swore."

My companion's face grew ashen. Whatever he expected to hear from me, it wasn't outrage, and when he did, he fired back with outrage of his own.

"Where was you, Victorine? Don't lie. You was with him, at the vicarage, wasn't you? *Wasn't* you?" Jeremy had taken hold of me by my shoulders and was shaking me.

"Let go of me! Of course, not. I was on the moor. Everyone knows that. Who are you to say otherwise? Let go, at once!"

"I will when you tell me the truth. When you stop these *lies*."

"I'm not lying! Why do you accuse me? I've done nothing!"

"Because *this* was in Mrs. Flemming's hand when I found her. How did she come by it, if you wasn't there? Answer me that!"

Jeremy reached into his shirt pocket and threw a shiny object onto the bed: the seagull with its wings outstretched in flight.

Nineteen

IMAGES OF EVA Flemming's final moments have haunted me
since the afternoon of her death. Each visitation is marked by
exquisite clarity. I am made witness to the victim's gape, her eyes
and mouth opened wide as she teeters on the stairs; her hands
clutching at vacant air. Grotesque truths freeze in the mind. How
else could it be that the memory of her terror has never faded?

Jeremy's visit to my sick bed forced to me realize how much
one's fate depends upon chance. If I had not caught myself as I
stumbled, if the vicar had been less quick to react—pushing me
into hiding when the grocer's son appeared—how different the
inquest might have gone. The return of the silver pendant made it
clear that I stood on a razor's edge.

Happily, Jeremy's doubts about how it came into the victim's
possession had been easy to satisfy. Indeed, he was all too eager
to believe my story: that the seagull had been borrowed; that Mrs.
Flemming had wished to examine it before making a request of
him. I found his desire to acquit me quite touching. But would
it last, I wondered. My fiction had been made on the spur of the
moment. Concerted probing would bring it down like a house of
cards. To keep him preoccupied, I agreed to join him on an outing
as soon as I was well enough.

That February, temperatures were well above normal. So, on a
particularly fine day, Aunt Julia packed a lunch for us and Jeremy
and I headed for the moors to test his new kite.

The wind nipping at our heels put my companion in high
spirits. He ran ahead of me on numerous occasions, coaxing me
to keep up. We came to rest on the high cliffs where the winds are
most blustery. My companion looked intense as he unwrapped the
parcel that contained his creation. Gusts made the task difficult.
More than once, I had to retrieve a stick or errant tissue while
Jeremy clung to the rest. The work made us breathless and we
laughed.

"You make a good apprentice, little Roughskin."

I must have looked surprised when he called me that. He

hadn't used the name in years, not since we were six or seven. I often wondered why, as "Roughskin" was a favorite story of mine. I never asked, though. I assumed someone had told him this fairy tale went against nature: a king, grieving for a dead wife, could never marry his daughter.

If so, I envied him his scruples. Though a clergyman's daughter, I was none too sure of mine. For me the world seemed not so black and white but more a pallet composed of shades of gray. Certainly, Jeremy could never understand the dark forces at work in me, so I never trusted him, entirely.

On that day, however, with the wind blowing a fresh breeze at our backs, our differences seemed unimportant. We were children at play again, working hard to send a paper seagull high into the air. And finally, we succeeded!

"Take hold of it, Victorine. See how she feels."

Jeremy stepped to one side and allowed me to take control the moment the creature was airborne. I was humbled by his trust, for we both knew that kite flying was largely a mystery to me. Still, with him at my side, I felt confident.

Overhead, a pair of a multi-colored wings, red, green and white, hovered. They looked so beautiful, so transparent against the sun that I hardly dared breathe. "What if the kite falls?" I cried, seeking reassurance.

Jeremy ignored the question but was already coaching me. "Not too tight on the string. That's it. That's it. Give her some line. Gaw! Look at that bird fly. She's halfway to heaven, she is."

Jeremy tugged at my arm, urging me to run. Already the colored ribbons were making streamers in the sky. How alive the creature seemed, bobbing and weaving on the currents. And how fragile, too. A change of wind, a sharp yank of my hand, and its fortunes could be reversed. Poor, dumb seagull. Lose yourself in the clouds but remember this, a slim thread holds you prisoner.

How long we skirted the cliffs I don't recall; but neither the breeze nor the paper wings faltered and so we were allowed to play at our game until the sun was more than halfway across the sky. Then hunger forced us, by slow degrees, to bring the bird down.

Our appetites were sharpened by the weather. We fell on the contents of the basket my aunt had packed for us as though this was our first meal in several days. Jeremy devoured two of Aunt Julia's pork pies and did not hesitate to accept a third when I offered it. Satisfied at last, he fell on his back and looked up at me.

"What a great day this has been. I haven't been so happy in ages. Are you happy, Victorine? Are you?"

I assured him that I was, which seemed to please him all the more so that his face broke into a broad grin.

"Let's come out tomorrow! Especially if it's nice. What d'ya think? Miss Ellsworth won't mind. Bet she'll even pack us another lunch."

A second outing seemed doubtful. Aunt Julia was too cautious where my health was concerned. She'd probably want me to rest instead.

Jeremy brushed aside my misgivings. "When she sees how you look, what the fresh air's done for you, she won't object. Honest. If you could see yourself. How your eyes sparkle, how your cheeks glow!"

"She'll accuse me of running a fever."

My remark brought a chuckle. "Even so, you look beautiful."

"Do I? Is that what you think?"

"Me and the whole of Braxton. You're the most beautiful girl in these parts. Maybe even the world."

I could feel myself blushing. "That's silly and you know it."

"I don't. When I look at you and see those dark eyes, that thick black hair...how could anyone be more perfect? That's what you are, Victorine. Perfection."

He pulled me toward him and brushed his lips against mine, an homage so natural that I took no offense. Even the gentleness of his caress was pleasing. To feel adored is an emotion too intoxicating to resist. More kisses fell along my throat and upon the curve of my ear and I closed my eyes, refusing to admit any sensation save the sweet frenzy of Jeremy's touch. I was carried away by him, far, far away, to a place unlike the holy ground I'd found with Jordan. Here was a bright, shimmering jungle.

"I love you, Victorine. There'll never be anyone else for me. No one. You're my life."

I kissed him back, hard enough to make his lips bleed. Then I felt him shudder and the dam of his inhibitions broke. He tore at my clothes, touching me in secret places, forcing sweet moans to rise in my throat. The ecstasy, the bliss of surrender set me adrift. My body rose and fell upon a sea of velvet waves while the sun pulsed within—a universe so complete that the cries that answered mine seemed blown from a distant shore.

"Victorine! My god! My god!"

Twenty

IF I'D BEEN lacking in hope or ambition, I might have gone to bed happy after my day on the moor with Jeremy. My suitor was handsome, had prospects, and had been my friend my entire life. Many a country girl would have snuggled against her pillow with a smile upon her lips. But I was unhappy. What I'd done was not for love. Call it curiosity as much as passion, but do not call it love. How could it be? My heart was already given, though I had betrayed it and the man I adored.

That night, I slept fitfully, ashamed of what I'd done and cursing myself for having agreed to return to the moor with Jeremy the following day. No one in my state of mind could have slumbered. It should come as no surprise, therefore, that by the wee, small hours of the morning my bed clothes were in shambles: the sheets in knots, the blankets strewn across the floor like carrion left to rot upon a field of battle. Yet, elsewhere the cottage was still, like the midnight world of owls and foxes. How was it, then, that beyond the raging of my conscience, I felt a presence, as if I were being called to the window?

Rising, I pressed my face against the glass. Nothing stirred, though the trees seemed to be thrusting their claw-like fingers into the sky. I admit that it was difficult to see. Save for the moon, the clouds were inky black and the garden was a web of shadows.

Shivering in my thin gown, I was about to return to bed, when I heard my name called out. The voice was husky, though soft enough to be barely above a whisper.

"I know what you did," it accused. "I was there. I *saw*."

I froze, like a hunted animal that hears a twig crack in the forest, straining to penetrate the shadows. Nothing moved. But someone was in the garden. That voice was not of my imagination. It was too cruel, too menacing.

A cloud drifted across the moon, blackening its face. All else remained still—a silence that made my hair feel as though it stood on end.

"Who's there? What do you want? Show yourself!"

Though I dreaded an answer, the hush that followed was far more frightening. To be visited by a phantom who could see and yet remain unseen, who could attack and not be exposed—this was the stuff of a haunting. But why?

My mind raced for an explanation. I could find none. Even if Jeremy and I had been seen, it was inhuman to taunt in this way. Chide me. Admonish me. But in mortal form. Not as some disembodied voice sent to hound me from the grave.

How long I stood at the window I don't recall, but I kept my vigil until my arms and limbs grew cold as marble. Then, defeated by the silence, I checked to see that the window lock was secure and stumbled back to bed. My sheets were icy but no matter. I could not sleep. Those whispered words stung like nettles in my ears.

"I know what you did. I was there. I *saw*."

✪ ❋ ❋

Morning broke with a diamond's brilliance. The sun, bright on the horizon, painted the world in hard edges and as the day grew warmer, my memories of the previous night dissipated. By the time Jeremy arrived, no one could tell I'd tossed and turned till dawn. Ebullient at the prospect of another perfect day, my companion behaved with such care and thoughtfulness toward me that my aunt remarked upon it as she walked us to the door, carrying yet another ample basket. This she handed over and as she stood chatting with us, her eyes grew soft with affection.

I, too, was moved. Seeing the two of them together, the mutual regard they held for one another and the ease with which they carried on their conversation, they seemed more related by blood than friendship, though no physical similarities existed. Jeremy was tall, slim and fair while my aunt was quite the opposite. Their dissimilarity aside, there could be no doubt about the tenderness they felt for one another, a bond which, since the death of Mrs. Simones, had intensified. I thought it strange, this connection she felt toward the Simones family.

Aunt Julia continued to fuss as she said her goodbyes, clucking like a plump hen over one of her chicks, warning of the weather and urging Jeremy to keep his collar turned up against the chill. What a pity, I thought, that she'd never married, for her every instinct was bent upon nurturing. It showed in the loving care she gave to her garden and in the faultless shine of her silver. All that was hers she lavished with attention. But neither tulips nor tea services could satisfy so expansive a nature. For that, a dozen offspring were required. Indeed, it struck me that had I been but one of a brood vying for her attention, life at Windmill Cottage would have been less onerous.

"Enjoy yourselves," she sang as we headed up the path. "Such a beautiful morning. But mind the weather. These are early days as yet. If it rains, come home. I won't have either of you catching colds."

She continued crooning instructions until we could no longer hear her, having disappeared behind the trees that lined the footpath. The moment we were out of sight, I discarded caution to the wind, unloosed my bonnet and let the sun fall warm upon my face. How good it was to be out-of-doors, to feel the breeze kiss my cheeks. Jeremy was of the same sentiment, though unlike the previous day, he controlled his exuberance and remained steadfastly by my side.

The absence of a parcel or any wrappings that might contain a paper bird made my heart sink. Apparently, there was to be no kite flying on this occasion. My misstep of the previous afternoon had given Jeremy other expectations and, when we reached the same spot as before, he was quick to spread out the blanket Aunt Julia had provided.

Watching him, I grew furious and refused to help as the wind played at its old tricks so that he was forced to anchor each corner with the staples at hand: apples, oranges, the picnic basket itself. Imagine his surprise when, after all this, I refused to sit down and strode off in the direction of the cliffs, without a word of explanation.

"You don't have to come," I snapped as he came trotting up beside me. "I should be glad for some time on my own. Honestly."

My companion frowned, his noncomprehension continuing as he marched beside me. What had happened, he must be wondering, to so change the atmosphere? We'd been talking amiably moments before. I'd even complimented him on his new jacket. My behavior now made no sense to him; and I chose not to explain. How could I make him see that his happiness meant my oppression?

We may have grown up together in Braxton, had the same neighbors and knew their eccentricities, yet this tiny village, choked by a green belt, was to each of us a different world. If yesterday's folly were to become known—if someone really had seen us—it would mean my ruin. I'd live as a pariah in respectable society. Not so for Jeremy. Having behaved according to the dictates of his male nature, he was bound to be forgiven, even to be admired by some.

"That's him. He's the one what done it to the Ellsworth girl."

My skin crawled with humiliation and Jeremy was to blame. He'd professed love for me, but love exacts no dishonor. I'd been used to satisfy his lust and realizing this, my anger became unbounded.

Unable to control these emotions, I stumbled as I walked, though I knew the terrain as well as my hand. Jeremy offered to be of help, but each time I rejected him as I would an adder's sting. I needed to get away, away from him, away from the voices in my head, away from myself, if possible.

I tore across the bracken, hoping to make the world a blur and by so doing, to distance myself from it and all contained therein. What a fool I'd been. What a bloody fool!

Alone, half-conscious, exhausted—for a moment it did seem as though the earth fell away. I sensed that I was rising toward the sun. The beams that bore me turned my skin golden, and though they burned more and more bright as I ascended, there was no searing pain, only the sensation of sinking into a warm, milk bath. Music poured into my ears. Such music. If the world's greatest paintings had been transmuted into sound, their beauty would have been crude by comparison. My soul vibrated with the chords, and as I peered into the source, a vision greeted me—one so sublime, that even now, though its memory has faded, I weep to think on it. I can only say that if a thousand, thousand dervish dancers, each jewel encrusted and lithe beneath their glorious armaments, were discovered dancing in the desert, their glittering spirals would be nothing compared to the ecstasy of my apparition. It was at once dreamlike and yet more real than when I walked upon the earth. Here was beauty. Truth. Flashings of the eternal.

My soul longed to rest at the center of this infinity. Dear God! What peace I felt. My soul! My soul! And then there came a snap, dry like a twig breaking. Mind and body stiffened as I reached some barrier that could not be crossed. Then, like Icarus, I plunged earthward from the skies.

I opened my eyes. The ground beneath me was cold and damp. My limbs were shivering. That Jeremy was nowhere in sight was of no consequence. I was beyond his ministrations. Around me the landscape faded and grew bright like a cosmic pulse. And overhead, a seagull kept its vigil. Its feathers, white and black, stretched far across the sky. Did it know how beautiful it was? Did it know?

I considered the question while a blanket was being tucked around me. Jeremy had returned, I supposed, but I didn't look up to make certain. I didn't care. My eyes were fixed upon the seagull. There's where I wanted to be. High overhead. Free and alone. But the hands commanding me were relentless. I was forced to sit up so that my arms could be bound as well. Cocooned in this fashion, I no longer imagined myself a creature of the air. The world became its dreary self again. Tears of recognition stung my eyes and I wept uncontrollably.

"Marry me, Victorine." That's what Jeremy whispered. "I want to take care of you. I want you to be my wife."

Had I been of ordinary mind, I would have clung to my childhood friend and sought salvation in his love. But I was not so blessed as to be ordinary. My spirit was dark; my passions unholy. He and I were kindred spirits only in this: that we both suffered. I broke into a peal of laughter—as though Salome had dropped her final veil to reveal a eunuch. Life was absurd!

Alarmed, Jeremy shook me. "Stop it, Victorine. Stop it!"

He was weeping. I was weeping. In our despair, we clutched at one another like babes abandoned in the woods.

When my lips sought his, he returned my kisses with those that were lingering and bittersweet.

"I don't care what's happened. I know it weren't your fault. It was him. Him! I want to marry you. That way you'll be safe!"

My eyes popped open. If ever tenderness was raped, it was at that moment.

"What do you mean? Keep me safe from what?"

My companion shook his head, sadly. "It's no good, Victorine. I wanted to believe you. I tried. But that laugh... I remember now. You was at the vicarage. You was there when she fell."

As quickly as we had made peace, we'd become strangers again. Jeremy's eyes were pools of despair. Looking at him, at the pain creasing his face, I knew that nothing would dissuade him: no stories, no pleadings, no whispered promises. He'd been robbed of his innocence and I was to blame.

If I felt pity for his heartache, the feeling was surpassed by a desire to save myself.

"I wasn't at the vicarage, I tell you. I wasn't! Why do you accuse me? Do you think I can be frightened into accepting your silly proposal? I'll tell everyone that you made up this wicked story because I rejected you. Everyone knows that since the inquest you've been acting crazy. They'll believe me, not you. *Me.*"

Without another word, I rose and stumbled in the direction of Windmill Cottage with Jeremy at my heels. My heart was pounding. My tongue was swollen as if it lay on a bed of sand but I would not stop. I had to be free of him and the shadows that were gathering.

Jeremy took hold of me again, demanded an explanation, but I resisted.

"Go away! I don't want you here. If you care about me at all, then leave me alone. I tell you I was on the moor that day. *On the moor!*"

"You're lying, Victorine. I can see it in your eyes. But it don't matter. I promise you, I'll never tell anyone. Never."

"Never? You mean if I marry you! Otherwise, how could you be trusted?"

"Not trusted? Wh-what about them voices? I never told anyone..."

"You mean when I was a child? You weren't the only one who knew about them. Mother knew, as well. She heard me one night. Nightmares is all they were. Everyone has nightmares. You can't threaten me with that."

"I'm not tryin' to threaten you. Why do you keep actin' as if I am? I said I loved you. Wanted to marry you. Does that sound like a threat?"

Would that I had been capable of compassion as Jeremy faced me with pleading eyes. The course of our lives might have been altered; but I felt nothing, only that I was suffocating.

"You don't know the meaning of the word *love*. If you did, you'd have never used me so selfishly."

"Used you? When? Yesterday? B-but I thought that was what you wanted. You said—"

"You *seduced* me."

Stunned, Jeremy took a step backwards. "I never... I wasn't tryin' to... My God! I thought you loved me. I thought we'd be married and—"

"Married? What happiness would there be in that for either of us? We've nothing in common. I want more from life than to be buried in Braxton as a shopkeeper's wife. Besides, you think me a monster."

"I never said—!"

"You said I lied about being at the vicarage. That I laughed when Mrs. Flemming fell backwards down the stairs. Maybe you think I pushed her? Yes, by the look of you, I believe you do—"

"No! What you're sayin' is crazy!"

"Maybe I am crazy. What then? Would you still want to marry me?"

Jeremy's hands flew to his temples as though he was wracked by pain.

"I love you, Victorine. More'n my life! That's all I know. That's all I care about."

"You say that now but in time, you'd come to hate me. In time, you'd give me away."

"*Never!* I'd *die* first."

"Words! Puffs of air!"

"I tell you, I would!"

"You couldn't even stand at the edge of the cliffs over there and peer down. You wouldn't go that far—because you haven't the courage!"

Jeremy looked to where I pointed. His face went blank. Why would I make such a challenge? He didn't understand, but it didn't matter. Without another word, he headed toward the precipice, trotting at first, then running at full speed. I followed after, surprised at how easily he acceded to my will. Of course, he would never stand at the edge, the very edge as I had meant; but what if I were wrong? What if I found him teetering three hundred feet above the roiling sea? Would I call him back? Or would a darker force overtake us both?

There are moments when the scent of death becomes intoxicating, when some dormant impulse awakes and tempts us to our doom. Rational minds may shudder, but I have tasted such an impulse. Would he, standing on the brink of oblivion, feel it, too?

For one delicious moment I allowed myself to consider that our positions were reversed. I was the one poised on the precipice. The wind was tugging at my cloak. *My* lungs were filling with a last gulp of salted air. Would I renounce the universe? Perhaps I'd hear the seagull's call and with arms outstretched, heed to it. What a joy to be set free. To become airborne. To soar, if only for a moment, upon the wind currents. But would it be worth the price, after such ecstasy, to find myself pitched headlong into the white waves, and after that, the dark?

"Fall backwards, you say? What makes you think that? Nothing was said at the inquest." Jeremy had stopped in his tracks. His cheeks glowed red as though they'd been slapped. "I imagined she'd tripped goin' down the stairs."

I felt myself being shaken once more.

"What d'you know, Victorine? What is it you're not sayin'? Tell me. *Tell me!*"

"Stop! You're hurting me. I don't how she died. It was a figure of speech. It doesn't mean anything. I tell you, I wasn't *there.*"

"I don't believe you. You're lying again, but this time I mean to have the truth, the whole of it!"

I was being rattled so hard that blood trickled in my mouth where I'd bitten my tongue. The pain made me angry.

"What right have you to question me? You're only a shopkeeper's son. I don't have to answer to you."

"A shopkeeper's son with a clear conscience," came his hoarse reply. "Can you say the same? Can you? It's him you're protectin', isn't it?"

"What? First you accuse me, and now the vicar? You're mad, you are. Mad and jealous, because he's twice the man you'll ever be."

"You're a fool, Victorine. A bloody fool. You don't know the first thing about him. You see what you want to. It's all in your head."

"I see him well enough and you, too. How could you imagine I'd marry you? You're not fit to wipe his boots."

Jeremy's eyes narrowed. "You think you're in love with him, don't you? Worse! You think he loves you back. Don't bother to deny it. I've seen that soft look of yours whenever he's around. Makes me sick, what he's done to you. Turned you into a tramp."

"That's a horrible thing to say. How dare you!"

"Gettin' high and mighty won't do no good. I seen you with him on the moor. You should hang your head in shame. But you don't see the sin of it, do you? He's got you so mesmerized—"

"He doesn't! And you're a fool to say so."

"Then why lie about the vicarage? What is it you know about Mrs. Flemming's death? Tell me. Or shall I guess? You're scared 'cause it weren't no accident, was it? *Was it?* One of you must of killed Mrs. Flemmin'."

Jeremy's eyes were wild as he pulled me to the ground. I remember crying out, surprised and in terror as my arms and legs were pinned. What did he mean to do? Was he going to kill me?

His hand was at my throat.

"Jeremy, please. *Please!*"

Kisses, brutal and unwelcome, reigned down upon me. My breath came in gasps and I felt myself grow weaker. What must I do? How could I free myself? Was there no one in that vast expanse to hear me? My mind snapped. Overhead I could see that the sky was a river of blue. Birds drifted in its currents as did the clouds, white and tall as schooners. Along the ground, a salt breeze ruffled the heather, which in turn exploded more scent into the atmosphere. And yet, none of this mattered: the beauty of the universe, my present predicament. I viewed it all with catatonic indifference—which was not peace but a shrugging off, as if to ask, "What has life to do with me or me with it?"

I have stood on the brink of dissolution before, but by my own hand, never as a victim. The ignominy of my present circumstances, the unseemliness of it, pricked me, kept some small candle aflame, and with the advent of pain, palpitating and glorious, I awoke to fresh anger.

"Let go of me, Jeremy! Let go!"

My graceless prayer was answered. I heard a voice overhead.

"In God's name, what goes on here?"

Jeremy was thrown from me and a sweet surge of air filled my lungs. I was saved, though being dazed, I failed to recognize my deliverer. Pain was my first preoccupation and then the cold. I started to shiver.

A cloak was thrown over my exposed flesh and after I'd been helped to sit up, a silver flask handed me. I recognized the initials at once. My heart sang as I drank the brown liquid that seemed to burn life into me.

Jeremy remained where he'd been deposited and was rocking to and fro, his arms clenched to his ribs. The sun, at its zenith, etched a sorry picture of a mind turned inward. Words were being murmured but inaudibly, as though meant for an inner ear. Only when touched did he react like a wild thing. He leapt to his feet, his eyes staring from their sockets, and made a sudden leap in my direction, but the vicar interposed.

"Leave the girl alone! Can't you see what harm you've inflicted? Thank God I came along when I did. Now sit down or I swear, I shall knock you down!"

The threat was brave indeed. The grocer's son stood nearly a head taller than his opponent. Jeremy's youth and muscular frame would serve him well in any altercation. Nonetheless, the older man stood at the ready, his hands squeezed into fists.

"I just want to talk to her. To explain—"

"Explain to me! I'm the one who demands an answer."

Despite his trembling, Jeremy's lips curled back in anger.

"What's happened here's got nothin' to do with you. I don't owe you no explanation."

"There, I'm afraid, you're wrong. You'll speak to me and to no one else. Is that clear?"

"In a pig's eye!"

Jeremy's attempt to push past the vicar met with a blow that sent him reeling. He looked surprised, then fell to his knees with his hands splayed out in front of him. For a moment, he remained kneeling in the mud, collecting his senses; but when he rose, the fire in his eyes sent a message no one could have mistaken.

"So it's a fight you're after. Come on, then. I'll give as good as I get—though I thought it was only women you raised your hand to."

"What?" The vicar's mouth fell open as if a blow had been landed. "What's that you said?"

"You heard me well enough. You know what I'm talkin' about."

"I don't, you ignorant boy!"

"You hit her, hard. Twice. I was outside the vicarage. I saw you."

"You were spying on me?"

"I was makin' a delivery. But I stopped when I heard the argument. You didn't see me, 'cause you was too busy beatin' your wife!"

"That's a lie!"

"It's not. I should've told someone. But Mrs. Flemmin', she wouldn't let me. She made me promise. I'm sorry I did. Maybe if I hadn't, she'd still be alive!"

The vicar's face went a mottled shade of purple. To be confronted by an upstart boy, one so far beneath his station, must have stung his dignity. But more than pride was at stake. Jeremy's charge, even without proof, was likely to do much harm. Suspicion would be sown, rumors spread, a reputation sullied. I could hear this calculation in the vicar's reply as he gave answer to the charge.

"I begin to fear for your mental state, dear boy. Accuse me? Do you imagine people will believe you when they learn what you've done? Till now, people have made allowances for you: your moods, your isolation. But this attack—of course, you must give account. And it would be far better given to me than to Constable Mills, don't you agree? I may be in a position to help."

The sight of an outstretched hand set Jeremy's blood to boil.

"You be of help to me? I spit on your offer!"

"I'd rather hoped you'd show more sense." The vicar sighed with genuine disappointment. He would have said more, importuned more, but Jeremy swept his words aside.

"I am showin' sense and I know my duty. It's to that girl over there. It's her forgiveness I want, not yours."

"You expect her to forgive you? Look at her! Look at what you've done. She's in a state of shock."

Jeremy could see the truth in what the vicar said and his eyes were swollen with grief. "I-I'm sorry, Victorine. So sorry."

If I could have answered him, I don't know what I might have said, but a part of my brain had shut down and I was incapable of it. I only know that I went pale and that the vicar, seeing it, came to my side and offered me another sip of brandy.

With his back turned to him, Jeremy seized his opportunity. Grabbing the vicar by his collar, he flung him to the ground. "Leave her be! You'll not have her, you devil. I'll kill you first!"

A cloud passed over the sun, plunging the landscape into shadows. In the darkness, both men paused to glare at one another. "Take care," the Vicar warned, rising to his feet. "You've proven yourself unfit for polite society. Do nothing more to alienate what friends may be left to you. You'll need them once all this is known. Have you never seen the inside of an asylum, Jeremy? I have. It's a soulless place. Men lie shivering on their cots while the rats run free. I met a man once whose nose was half bitten off because he slept too soundly. As for the beatings, they occur daily, administered by the guards or the inmates who do their work for them. And the smell. The smell! All the sulphurous fumes of Hades would be sweet in comparison. Excrement everywhere. Sometimes even in the food. You can complain, of course; but then you'll be tossed into a windowless cell, forced to remain until—how shall I put it? 'Until you've come to your senses.' Think on it, Jeremy. *Think on it.*"

Delivered in such solemn tones, the vicar's threat had the power to deflect his adversary and force him to consider his precarious position. Jeremy knew the vicar to be evil but how was it to be proved? The villain was too clever. Too agile. Too well-respected by most in the village. He, to the contrary, had acted the fool, certainly in his conduct with me but in his general demeanor before that. Hadn't he made a show of his moods? Abandoned his friends? Refused Dr. Leach's sedatives? He'd even quarreled with his good friend and godmother, Miss Ellsworth, senior. She'd warned him against excess and she was right. If a trap had been laid for him, it could not have produced a more harmful effect than the damage done by his own hand.

For the first time in his life, I could see Jeremy was afraid. His world was in tatters and he had no way of mending it. So much had happened. So much revealed! I knew he couldn't take it all in. He needed to think. To put some distance between himself and what he'd done. I was not surprised when he turned and ran...ran as fast as he could, without looking back.

Twenty-one

Your aunt's bound to raise questions. She'll see your clothes, your injuries. Have you considered what you'll say?" Jordan was gathering up the blanket and the picnic blanket in preparation for the walk home.

"What's there to consider?" I shrugged. "I'll tell her the truth."

The man with dark eyes cast me a sidelong glance. "Normally, that would be the thing to do. But in this case, I wonder..."

"What do you mean?"

"Well, that rash talk about me, for example. It's nonsense, of course, but he might gain an audience. Who knows what he'll say if he becomes desperate. What set him off in the first place? Why did he attack you?"

For a moment, I hesitated, afraid of how Jordan would react. But, there being little alternative, I screwed up my courage and told him the truth.

"He knows I was at the vicarage—"

"Did you tell him?" he cut me off, frowning.

"No! My pendant was in your wife's hand."

"It was? Good Lord! But surely you made some excuse."

"I told him she borrowed it."

"And he believed you?"

"At first."

"At first? What changed his mind?"

"When he proposed, I'm afraid I laughed at him."

"He proposed? Well, well. That comes as a bit of a surprise. But I don't see the connection."

"He heard that same laughter at the vicarage."

"When Eva... You convinced him he was imagining, I hope. That he was hearing the storm."

"He didn't believe me."

"No." The vicar shook his head slowly. "I don't suppose he was of a mind to after your rejection. That must have hurt. But to attack you so viciously. It doesn't make sense..."

"He suspects her death wasn't an accident."

"What?" He swung around to face me.

"He thinks she was pushed."

"But why? What did you say to him?"

"Nothing! I'm not a complete fool. He hates you and wants to think the worse."

"So that's what he meant when he said, if he'd spoken out she might still be alive. He blames *me*."

"Yes... Is it true what he saw?" My voice was timid, tentative. "D-did you strike your wife?"

"Victorine! What a question! And one that's no business of yours, I might add—"

"That means you did."

"It doesn't! And that's not the point. We have a larger problem on our hands: what to do if Jeremy decides to spread these insanities."

"You said it yourself, nobody will believe him."

"Don't be such a child. That was a bluff. The sad truth is that in the minds of many, an accusation is as good as the facts. There'll be gossip, suspicions." The vicar threw me another hard glance.

"What's become of the pendant? Does he have it?"

"No. He returned it. It's in my jewelry box. I haven't felt like wearing it."

"Good." He looked relieved and resumed walking. "Then there's nothing to link you to the vicarage. It's your word against his. We're free to put some other face on this afternoon, if it becomes necessary."

"What do you mean? What's happened is bound to come out. As you said, Aunt Julia will see my condition."

"You can say that you fell."

"Why should I? After what Jeremy's done!"

I felt slapped by Jordan's suggestion. Where was the outrage of the man who'd rescued me? Suddenly he was all logic and reason. What did he fear? If Jeremy aired his suspicions, and if, somehow, my presence at the vicarage was proved, the visit could be explained. I'd come for a book, or for a lesson, or to find sanctuary from the storm. The fact that Eva Flemming had returned early from her shopping and found us in one another's arms was unknown to anyone except ourselves.

Jordan looked annoyed when I argued thusly. "Have you forgotten? Your name was never mentioned at the inquest. What would people make of my silence?"

"Jeremy said nothing about the pendant. You were both trying to protect me. People will understand."

"Yes, but I had no reason to want to do so. You could have corroborated the accident. You were a witness. My keeping silent makes our being together look suspicious."

"Then why did you push me into the bedroom? Why force me to hide?"

"Because *you* were hysterical, you silly girl. Because *we'd* had no time to agree upon a story."

Tears I thought were already spent welled into my eyes. The man I loved had never spoken to me so sharply. "You needn't shout," I complained, squaring my shoulders. "Anyway, what if he does say I was there? As you observed, it's Jeremy's word against mine."

"Can you be so certain you'll be believed?"

My mouth fell open. I could hardly believe my ears. "What do you mean?"

"Isn't it obvious? If you make his attack public, he'll have to defend himself. Even if he suspected nothing about your presence at the vicarage, he'd be bound to make *some* excuse."

"Like what, for example?"

"My dear girl, have you learned nothing from reading the history of Elizabeth Dernwood? When a man is desperate, he can do or say anything to save himself. Like Nathan, Jeremy could convince himself that you trifled with him, teased him beyond reason. In that frame of mind, he might think it right to seek revenge."

"That's a lie. I *never* led him to think I cared."

"But he has friends enough who will believe him; and it will be made worse if the charge is compounded by the suspicion that you had something to hide. The really vicious minds will say that you toyed with Jeremy to gain his silence. That *you* are responsible for what happened."

"Ridiculous!"

"Is it? Think Victorine. *Have* you done nothing to encourage him? *Are* you entirely blameless?"

I felt my cheeks go red. Why was Jordan accusing me, examining me as though he wished to penetrate the secret corners of my mind? Perhaps he already knew or had an inkling of what had happened yesterday on the moor. If so, it might be prudent for me to make a full confession—which I had longed to do as the knowledge of my treachery sat like a pustule upon my soul. To expunge my sin, to throw myself upon Jordan's mercy—that was the catharsis demanded by my transgression.

I should have fallen to my knees at once. And yet, cowardice held me back. If Jordan knew, I reasoned, then it was folly to confess. The tardiness of it would condemn me further and he was bound to become more miserable. But what if he did not know? Then his question was an idle one and I would be a fool to condemn myself. If I'd been guilty of cowardice only, I might have gone to bed happy that night, but a second, more ominous thought was forming from the dark matter of my brain, one which I instinctively feared but had no power to deflect.

Something in Jordan's question, be it the timbre of his voice or its plaintive tone, caused me to recall that on the previous night I had been tarred by a similar charge. I remember thinking at the time how strange it was that an adversary would confine his complaint to me when it carried far more worth as the coin of common gossip. Unless someone wanted me to suffer—wanted me, awake or dreaming, to agonize over the hour of my undoing.

Was Jordan my avenging angel? He and he alone might find justice in such a plan. Being wronged, it was his right to punish me. Or so he may have thought. Perhaps he'd come upon us, Jeremy and I, by chance. At first, he'd refuse to believe his eyes; then, when there was little doubt he was betrayed, his fury must have fomented, overflowing at last as he stood in the dark, there beneath my window. Perhaps jealousy had goaded him to follow us on the second day. If so, that would account for his timely appearance.

These perfidious ideas horrified me even as they expressed themselves. Behavior of this kind was the product of a sick mind. Jordan was not guilty of it. He couldn't be! We loved each other too much. But... Oh! I must renounce these doubts or drive myself mad!

To purge myself, I gave air to one venomous thought, the least rancorous among them. That way my pride was appeased; my fears diverted; and the least harm done. I accused Jordan of being a fraud. His solicitous concern for my reputation was nothing but a veiled attempt to protect his own.

When he heard the charge, a thin smile played about his lips. Not so with his eyes. They flashed a warning that I should not go too far.

"Neither of us can afford a scandal, can we?" He spoke quietly, forcing me to listen. "You've seen the consequences of society's rebuke once before. Am I to be cast out like your poor teacher, Mr.

Huddleston? Is that what you want?"

That he could make such a charge stabbed at my heart. I hastened to assure him. "No, dearest! No!" Then a second notion followed. Would such a fate be so bad? He had money now. With wealth, he needed no position. We could go away together. To Italy! France!

When I suggested that we flee, Jordan's eyebrows lifted. A look of surprise and scorn spread across his face. "A man does not live well in this world without his good reputation, my dear. It's a cruel truth, and one which applies even more so to a woman."

"I care nothing about reputation. You think me weak like Elizabeth Dernwood? Try me. I'll leave this very moment, if you agree."

"I've no doubt of it," came the melancholy reply. "But that's because you're ignorant of all that you stand to lose."

"If I'm such a fool, how can you care for me?"

"I both care and am flattered by your offer, but I cannot allow you to be so rash. To sacrifice yourself? And me? No, my dear. We must find a better way and avert the shame."

"You think I'm responsible for what's happened today. But I'm not."

"No? Not even a little? Just as you are not responsible for Jeremy?"

"Why do you go on with these insinuations? What is it you think I've done?"

"I? I accuse you of nothing. My wish is that you consider this business with fresh eyes. Nothing more. Imagine how this affair will seem to others. *We* know Jeremy to be capable of violence. But as yet, few do. If we fail to be cautious, we may jeopardize our future happiness."

Though it pained me to agree, what Jordan said was reasonable. Little would be gained and much could be lost if I exposed Jeremy. But what if *he* confessed? That would be the honorable thing to do and he was still capable of honor. How would my silence look then?

"I'll go to him at once," Jordan offered. "He won't have had time to do anything yet, not with his anger still at work. I'll tell him that you're shaken by what's happened, but not seriously injured; that you forgive him, we both do, because we're aware of the strain he's been under—"

"Forgive him? Never. I hate him for what he's done."

"Victorine, listen to me This is no time to be emotional. We must keep our heads."

"Will Jeremy keep his? Will he even listen to you? He despises you and always has."

"That may be, but he still loves you."

I laughed at the notion, but the Vicar remained unruffled.

"You are, as yet, not fully schooled in the ways of men, my dear. I tell you he loves you to the point of distraction."

"You can say that after he assaulted me? I feared for my life!"

Again that thin smile presented itself. "You mistake his intent, I think. Even so, was not Desdemona loved to such a degree?"

"You speak to me of Shakespeare? Now? This isn't some fantasy. It's my life!"

"*Our* lives. Let's not forget why I make this proposal. We must convince Jeremy that he is forgiven—unless you hate him more than you care for me."

The charge was more than I could bear. I rushed forward and threw myself into Jordan's arms. "Oh, dearest! Never say that. Never, ever think it."

"Then you agree on what must be done?"

"Yes! Yes! Anything. But make it plain to him that he and I are never to meet. I couldn't bear it. You will say as much, won't you?"

A sigh escaped Jordan's lips. "If you wish it, my dear. But consider. How is such a promise to be kept in a village of this size? Your paths are bound to cross. Jeremy will make his deliveries. You and your aunt will shop in the High Street. In which case, your public conduct must be ordinary or it will give rise to suspicion. Private meetings, I agree, are out of the question. Under the circumstances, I think he'll see reason."

"I pray that you're right, dearest. But Jeremy's conscience can be formidable."

"In this case, I think not, my beauty. In this case, 'conscience does make cowards of us all.'"

Pleased with his literary allusion, the vicar bent down and kissed me full upon the lips.

Twenty-two

THAT NIGHT I was sent to bed early to rest from my "accident" but was unable to sleep. Around midnight, a storm broke and a fierce wind rattled through the attic and at the windows. Lightning flashed across the sky. It entered my room with a blue glare, transforming all that was familiar into shapes that were transitory and unreal. Being alert, it was natural that I should hear when a trio of visitors came pounding at the cottage door.

Aunt Julia was slow to answer. Her slippers made sleepy, padding noises as she crossed the hardwood floor; but when the pummeling grew more and more insistent, they broke into a trot.

"Hang on a minute. I'm almost there!"

With the latch clicked and the door flung open, a dank breeze made its way up the stairs. A jumble of masculine voices followed, all talking at once so that their words were indistinguishable, like boiled rice when it clumps. Something was said about going into the kitchen. I heard footsteps and then the voices became muted. From my window I could see the silhouettes of three bicycles leaning against a tree. Tarpaulins and ropes were lashed to these, together with other paraphernalia that I was unable to identify.

Below, in the kitchen, the kettle's whistle rose in concert with the clatter of china. Conversation grew more animated but no more intelligible—except for Aunt Julia's cries of, "Oh dear!" and "How frightful!"

I could hardly believe the little time that had elapsed before the men departed, regrouping a moment under the tree. Their rain gear kept me from seeing their faces, but by his nightstick I knew that one of the men was Constable Mills. He made broad gestures in his attempt to communicate against the wind. Then, apparently having settled upon a course of action, our visitors faded into the night.

I was still at the window when Aunt Julia rapped on my door. She looked nervous as she entered. Her eyes flitted about the room and she kept playing with the belt of her dressing gown. When at last she found her voice, the news came in a rush.

"Jeremy's had a breakdown. He's run away and Arthur fears he may do himself harm. I was hoping you might know something. He came home in a terrible state after the picnic. Wouldn't answer any questions. Just locked himself in his room. His father decided to let him be, thinking the boy'd come round; but when he heard glass being shattered, well, naturally, he ran upstairs and threatened to break the door down when Jeremy refused to answer. The poor man was halfway down the stairs again, going for his axe, when he heard the latch click and his son bolted from the room. It happened so quickly, he was almost knocked down. If that wasn't shock enough, he said the boy looked frightful. His hair stuck out all over his head and his eyes were the color of pomegranates!

"Poor Arthur tried to follow, of course, but Jeremy was too quick for him. He disappeared like dust in a storm. Now it's half past midnight and there's still no sign of him. That's why I've come to you, Victorine. Did you two have another quarrel? Is that what those bruises are about? Be honest with me. The truth's bound to come out. One can't keep a secret in a village this size."

My guardian looked so pathetic, with her hair falling in wisps over her face, that I urged her to sit down, which she did, sinking into a nearby chair with a sigh. Her ankles had swollen during the night and a nagging rheumatism seemed to have attacked her right arm as she favored it a little, holding it closely against her side. Pulling the eiderdown from my bed, I placed it round her before sliding back under the covers, using this interval of time to consider how I would reply to her questions.

My preference would have been to tell the truth; but I dared not, being unsure of the reason for Jeremy's behavior. At least two possibilities presented themselves, each requiring a different set of answers. If Jordan had managed to intercept Jeremy and laid out our proposal and if it had been rejected, then the truth would serve me well. The assault upon my person would so incense the minds of those who learned of it, that any charges against Jordan and I would be discounted as calumny. But, if as yet he'd not been briefed, which was the more likely, then my silence would give Jordan time to sound him out. What to do? What to do?

"Wasn't that the vicar with you just now?" I asked, deciding to parry a question with a question. "I thought I recognized one of the voices as his."

Aunt Julia nodded and said that it was. The two men with him were Arthur Simones and Constable Mills. They'd come to say that a search party was being formed and to ask—as ours was the last house before the moor—if the cottage might serve as a nerve center for the operation. Mrs. Pardy and some other women had already agreed to supply sandwiches for the volunteers who would take respite here.

"They think he's on the moor then?"

"Very likely. At least it's one of the places they intend to look. And the woods, too, though there's little refuge to be found there, either. Poor Arthur. Poor, poor Arthur."

No sooner had she spoken than a gaggle of women was heard entering the garden. We flew to the window to catch a glimpse of them. They were jostling against the wind, five figures, their dark cloaks flapping like wings so that it seemed as if a coven of black birds were gathering.

"That'll be Cordelia and the others. I must go down at once." Aunt Julia turned and headed for the door, pausing just long enough to refuse my offer of help.

"Six women will be more than enough in so small a kitchen. I'd rather that you rested, dear, really. I know that you're worried, and I promise, if there's any news, I'll come up and tell you."

The latch fell behind her with a note of finality, but if she truly believed I would lie in my bed waiting for events to unfold, she sorely misjudged me. The moment I was alone, I began struggling to put on my rain gear. If anyone was to find Jeremy, it must be me. The trouble between us had to be put to an end before it became a public scandal.

Happily, the noise of the storm was my ally. Neither my footsteps on the stairs nor the opening and closing of the front door brought anyone to investigate. I was as free as the wind that shook the trees.

Outside, light from the kitchen window fell like a golden tablet across the herb garden. Silhouettes of my aunt and those of the other women scurried to and fro within its frame. It would be hours before any of them would notice I'd gone. In the meantime, the rain offered a welcoming tattoo.

I'd brought no torch with me, but I reached the moor in good time, aided by flashes of lightning and my familiarity with the terrain. To the west, the lanterns of the search party flickered. Men were combing the adjacent woods, a quest that was pointless, as Jeremy would never go there. I headed south to where the surf carved lesions into the cliffs. Some were barely large enough to house the summer birds, but others could shelter a man or a pack of wild dogs.

The moon, breaking through the clouds, made diamonds of the rain, and these fell in such quantity that the ground beneath my feet glittered like a jeweled highway. I took it as a happy portent and was gratified when, not twenty minutes out, I came upon my quarry.

At first he seemed no more than a shadow suspended between earth and sky. Then lightning flashed and his outline became distinct, though the blue haze surrounding it gave him the semblance of an apparition. I called out his name but there was no answer. All I could hear was the tap, tap, tapping of the rain.

"It's all right!" I persisted. "I'm not angry. I'll keep my silence. It'll be just like before. Only, come home, *please*. The whole village is looking for you."

I had continued to inch forward as I spoke, though I was soon brought up short by a voice that was both hoarse and derisive.

"Aren't you afraid to be alone out here? Afraid of what I might do? Or is your precious vicar nearby?"

"I came by myself. I'm not afraid. You didn't mean to harm me. You're unwell—"

"Stop talkin' to me like I'm an idiot!" came his sharp reply. "I can see right through you. It's a game you're playin'. You'll keep silent if I'll keep silent. That's it, isn't it? You and that vicar of yours have cooked up this sorry scheme, and now he's sent you after me in the hope you can twist me round your little finger. The man's a coward. Don't you see that? He sends a girl to do his errand. He's not man enough to face me. How can you love him, Victorine? How can you?" Jeremy covered his eyes with his hands. "I wish to God I was ill, like you say. I'd rather be ill than to see you as I do now."

Hearing the tremor in his voice, my instinct was to run away, back to the sanctuary of Windmill Cottage; but retreat was foolish. I could never be safe unless I turned Jeremy around.

"What do you mean? I haven't changed." I took another step forward. "I swear to you, I've done nothing wrong."

"Don't swear, Victorine. You've got enough lies on your conscience."

"I don't understand. Why do you accuse me? Are you still thinking about the vicarage? What does it matter if I was there or not? It was an accident. You were present. You saw."

"I *saw* nothin' and you know it. But I heard. Dear God! I *heard*. It's all come back to me. The angry voices. Yours. His. Mrs.

Flemming's. She kept sayin' over and over, 'I can't go on like this, Jordan. Not again!'

"He tried to calm her down, but you was all over her like a wasp, sayin' she weren't good enough for him; that he didn't love her. He tried to stop you. 'Victorine, enough! Enough!' But you wouldn't listen. You laughed! Then I heard a scream and someone went tumblin' down the stairs. I was scared to death that *you'd* fallen. That's when I come runnin'. But it wasn't you. It was her. It was *her!*"

The memory sent Jeremy to his knees. "She looked so pale. So helpless, like a child with her hair fallin' across her face. I wanted to pick her up, but I didn't dare, she was moaning in so much pain. I didn't know what to do. The vicar was hangin' over the rail, but where was you, Victorine? You'd vanished. I thought maybe I'd imagined you was there. Then I saw the pendant and I *knew*. If what happened was an accident, why did you hide? Why? A part of me guessed, but I couldn't bear to think on it. I was that afraid for you. But the memory wasn't lost, was it? It was buried inside me, tearing me apart. And now that it's back, I can't forget it, much as I want to!"

I knelt down beside Jeremy, my heart full of pain. I hadn't meant to hurt him. I really hadn't. If I could undo all that had happened, make some recompense... But it was too late now. My only thought was to take him in my arms and rock him to and fro as though he were a child. He did not resist and seemed glad for it as he buried his face in my bosom. For a timeless moment we were innocents again, finding solace in one another's company and letting the rain wash over us.

"I love you, Victorine. I can't help it. I love you so much!"

"I know, dearest. Don't cry anymore. Please don't cry. I'm your own, true Victorine, just as before. I'll tell you what happened, if you want me to. Then you'll see. I'm not to blame. It was the vi—"

"What a touching scene. I almost hate to interrupt but the next lines belong to me, I think."

Jeremy and I looked up in shock. The vicar was standing above us, a black figure against the gray sky, his cloak billowing at his sides. Seeing him, I shuddered.

"We've some unfinished business, the three of us," he went on. "That's why I remained behind in the shadows of Windmill Cottage, waiting for Victorine to come looking for you. I knew that she would and that she'd succeed. Much better than running around blindly in the dark, don't you think?"

"You followed me?"

"Of course!"

Jeremy leapt to his feet, pulling me with him. "Leave us alone! We got no unfinished business with you. You can go to hell! That's where you belong."

"You may well think so, after watching Victorine's performance just now, but—"

"I wasn't going to say anything, Jordan. I promise I wasn't—"

Jeremy staggered back from me. "*Jordan*? You call him that?"

I went blank, being so unexpectedly confronted, but the vicar was quicker than I. "Oh rarely, dear boy. No, more often she calls me 'dearest' or 'sweetheart'..."

Jeremy bristled and took a threatening step in the vicar's direction. "That's a lie! She wouldn't. She'd never!"

"Come now. Surely you've guessed? Victorine attends us both! Or is it the other way round? Yes. The latter, I think."

Jeremy looked as if he'd been smashed in the face by a brick. "Is it true, Victorine? You and him? T-together?"

"No. He's lying. We've never been together. You of all people should know that."

"He 'of all people?' That's a curious phrase. What power makes Jeremy privy to information regarding your virtue? Is he clairvoyant? Omniscient? Or is there some other reason, I wonder?"

"Please Jor— Vicar? Leave us alone. If not, you'll spoil everything."

"What more is there to spoil, my dear? My reputation is in peril. Jeremy is half-mad and you were about to accuse me of something dastardly, I think. You see, dear boy?" The vicar gazed at his rival. "We are more alike than you realize. Victorine has made fools of us both."

Hearing him, a sweet, sickly panic seeped into my mouth and ears. Misfortune was about to overtake me. Jordan was scrambling to save himself while much the same undertow was tugging at me. I was petrified by it. Was it possible that we would really betray one another? That all of our vows of love were no more than dainty ornaments to be smashed at the first stirrings of adversity? The idea struck as a dagger at my heart and yet I knew that it was true. To save myself, I could sacrifice anyone and never count the cost.

If these had been my final thoughts, I cannot say what would have become of me. I might have thrown myself over the cliffs in desperation or run across the moor until my heart stopped. But, having peered into the darkest recesses of my soul, the sins revealed there, black though they may be, gave me hope—not because they were anything less than horrible, but because, once I recognized them, I had power over them. I could change!

If I valued love, then I must *be* loving. If loyalty was breath to me, then it must reside at my core. All and each goodness existed when my action was its accomplice. Let Jordan abandon me; I refused to abandon him. *My* conduct was what mattered. Despair was pointing to the path of my salvation. I would walk it freely, happily and even bless the man who would betray me.

Taking Jordan's hand in mine, I placed it over my heart, so that he could feel it beat in earnest, and swore that I would destroy myself before doing or saying anything that would bring harm to him. By such assurances, I had hoped to gain good effect, but the opposite proved true. Jordan's jaw fell when he heard me. His eyes stared wildly as though he feared I'd gone mad or that this was some trick he had yet to fathom.

"Now here's a pretty subterfuge," he cried, snatching his hand from me as though it were on fire. "Do you not see the twisted cunning of her brain, Jeremy? She swears she'd rather die than betray me. But what have I done to require so great a sacrifice? Nothing. Absolutely nothing. Yet by these vows she would have you think otherwise. It's a trick! A shameless guile! As God is my witness, she knows better than I what treachery befell at the vicarage."

Jeremy, who'd stood transfixed as the scene before him unfolded, suddenly found his voice.

"S-so it's true, then. There was some mischief. I knew it. I was sure of it. My God! Why didn't I come runnin' when I heard the shoutin'? Why eavesdrop in the kitchen like some useless busybody? I should've said somethin'. If I had maybe...maybe..."

Unable to complete his thought or even bear it, he crumpled forward and vomited into the wet earth. His hands he used as a prop against his knees, though they did little to stop his quaking.

He remained in that position for several seconds while Jordan and I looked on, uncertain of what to do. Certainly, I felt pity for him, but any offer of help was resisted, and at the first sign of movement the poor wretch stiffened, rose and backed away.

"Don't pretend you cared about your wife!" he shouted, his eyes boring into the vicar. "You may fool others, but not me. All you wanted was her money. Well, it's yours now. So you can go away, and good riddance. God'll deal with you in His own time. But as to Victorine, leave her out of your wickedness. She'd never do anything wrong. Never."

A flash of lightning illuminated our faces as he spoke and oh, what a dreadful tableau was revealed then: three blue-white grimaces like those chiseled upon the faces of gargoyles, the outward show of an internal hell. Jeremy's eyes, in particular, glowed with a phosphorescent fire. He wanted absolution. His. Mine. But I could do nothing, say nothing to save him. My innocence had long since flown.

Reading the truth in my eyes, he uttered a deep, mournful wail.

"No-o-o-o! You aren't to blame. It's him what brought the poison. *Him*."

Jeremy turned on his heels, his eyes ablaze with suffering, and ran in the direction of the cliffs. Neither Jordan nor I could be sure of his intent but ahead, members of the search party had begun to gather, their torches forming a halo against his fleeing silhouette. He would be upon them in a matter of minutes, though it was doubtful they had seen him, yet. Their movements were too random and without purpose. The boy veered away when he saw the lights, and made for the dark, apparently not wanting to be found. It occurred to me that if he were brought down now, no one would be the wiser.

Of one mind, the vicar and I took off in hot pursuit. Though the mud and bracken tugged at us, nothing could slow our pace. We ran knowing our lives depended upon it and as such, we soon cornered our quarry near the edge of the cliffs, two hundred yards from where the searchers were gathering. He turned to face us, his complexion as pale as marble. His gaze flew from mine to Jordan's then back again, assessing our purpose.

"Don't come any closer, Victorine. I warn you. Let this be between him and me."

With legs astraddle, Jeremy stood, his hands knotted into fists. Then an awful silence fell. Whether the cause was that of our concentration or Nature's pause to observe the unfolding drama, I do not know, but certainly the calm was eerie.

We began to move slowly, noiselessly, like players in a pantomime, forming concentric circles with Jeremy at the center and Jordan and I at his sides. To the uninformed, it might have seemed an underwater ballet; but ours was no artistic endeavor. We meant not to create but to destroy.

If this confession is shocking, so be it. Yet, consider a moment how mayhem serves the universe. What is life without death? Meaningless. Abundance without annihilation? Impossible. A crop without a harvest. Folly. The universe is poised between these disparate forces: to murder and create. In choosing one above the other, I am no monster, but a child of the eternal order. I saw this truth so clearly that night, in the pouring rain with Jeremy's blood dripping from my hands. The knowledge that I was neither good nor bad but an instrument of fate gave me stamina and, though my cohort hung back while I was thrown to the ground again and again, each time I rose with a greater purpose and delivered such blows that my victim, unwilling to defend himself further, fell at my feet, his wounds weeping, his sides heaving in that pause between life and death.

How I came to curse that interval. Words, deeds, actions, these are the dissemblers that keep us from our deeper thoughts. But silence offers no such opiate. It is the portal to conscience. I awoke to a question. Why had Jeremy not dealt me a disabling blow? How easy it would have been for him, being so much stronger than I. He was capable of violence. Had I not once suffered at his hands? Why, then, when I meant to do him harm, did he refrain? Was it guilt from before, a horror of repeating his brutality? I thought in part that it was. But, coming at him as I did, he had every right to defend himself. Why then was he weeping at my feet instead of taking his vengeance against me? Surely he must hate me. Or was I wrong again? Could it be that he still cared? Was ever a mortal born so true?

I saw at once that it was so. He loved me better than I loved myself...*if* I loved myself. Certainly, at that moment I felt nothing but a loathing as each insight paled before some fresh ignorance. My life struck me as no more than a series of tunnels, an underground that I was free to create but from which I could not escape. I had lived blindly, pledging myself to this or that virtue, and even now, imagined I was acting out of loyalty to Jordan. But these avowals were no more than the ornaments of intellect. Jeremy acted from his heart. He was capable of sacrifice. I, only of demanding it.

And still he loved me.

Naught's had, all's spent,
Where our desire is got without content.
'Tis safer to be that which we destroy,
Than by destruction dwell in doubtful joy.

I fell to my knees struck dumb by humility and the terror of a life without him. Was it too late, I wondered? Too late to be forgiven?

"Jeremy, dearest," I wept as I took his face into my hands. "You do love me, don't you? Don't you?"

That night I heard a sound which I shall never forget: a cry that seemed a distillation of all human suffering—as if the earth had opened and the dead from centuries past had stirred, awakened by the fresh scent of air. Who could hear that wail and keep his sanity?

※ ※ ※

The inquest concerning Jeremy's death went smoothly enough, except for a letter sent by Vicar Soames. His name being raised at the proceedings came as a surprise to many who, like myself, had presumed him dead.

His remarks were intended to corroborate that Jeremy had been in a disturbed state of mind for some time. He wrote that he'd received a communication from the boy prior to the inquiry concerning Eva Flemming's fall. In the note, he said that he had some concerns regarding the manner of her death and wondered what counsel the vicar might provide. As he offered no evidence to support his feelings, the old man replied at once, advising that he should answer only those questions put to him and do no harm. After that, he received no further correspondence but had kept the letter as it had disturbed him greatly.

Doubtless the old man meant well, but I'd have preferred that he kept his silence. His comments, together with Jeremy's letter, cast a pall over the minds of some. A connection was made between the first death and the second. Whispers began to the effect that two violent mishaps in the space of a year was extraordinary in so small a village where death was usually visited upon the very old or the very young and for understandable causes. Still, there was no evidence to refute my testimony that Jeremy had leapt to his death and the verdict was so ordered, though a malaise lingered.

It might have been my imagination, but I felt myself being shunned—nothing overt, merely public encounters with friends and acquaintances that were all too brief. Social contacts became negligible, and likewise Jordan, by report, worried that attendance at church services was down.

A month passed, then two, and when the numbers failed to improve, he submitted his resignation. What reason he gave, I do not know, as I had not spoken to him since that night on the moor. Our separation was Jordan's idea. I thought it a hard stricture, but he promised me it was a temporary one so I agreed. When he left without saying goodbye, I was surprised, desolate. Wicked thoughts assailed my mind. I even considered raising fresh questions about Jeremy's death or about the death of Mrs. Flemming. If I could raise enough suspicion, the authorities would have to investigate. They'd have to bring Jordan back to me. I would stand as his accuser and he would be forced to beg my forgiveness. Would I forgive him? Could I?

In the end, of course, I came to see the wisdom of his departure. Mistrust continued to taint the minds of the villagers. Only his absence could absolve us of any doubts pertaining to our reputations. Later, we would find our way to one another. But not now. Our duty was to wait. Needless to say, during this interval it rankled me to listen to Charles Harriman droning each Sunday from the pulpit.

Epilogue

SEVEN YEARS HAVE passed since Jordan left Braxton. I have yet to receive a letter. Occasionally, rumors about him reach my ears. One has it that he is married to an Indian princess and lives in Calcutta. Another places him on a cattle ranch in America. The story that persists most, however, is that he lives in a splendid villa somewhere in Tuscany. These are lies, of course. I expect him to write any day now. He may have done so already and failed to reach me, not realizing that I no longer reside at Windmill Cottage. Less than a year after he left us, Aunt Julia arranged for me to live in a quiet setting several miles from Braxton. I am well cared for here, monitored frequently by a young Dr. Nathan Childers. I do believe he has taken a fancy to me and without much effort on my part, I might become his obsession, his Elizabeth Dernwood.

It amuses me to play with the idea, as there is little else to divert me. Aunt Julia is my one constant link to the outside world; but since her marriage last year to Arthur Simones, her visits have become infrequent. When she told me of her marriage plans, she assured me there was nothing impetuous in it. If she'd had the courage of the first Mrs. Simones to ignore the difference in their stations, she would have married the green grocer when he proposed long ago. Instead, she had turned him away—the man who'd given her the ruby hat pin. I'm glad she's been given a second chance for happiness.

As to the others of our village, I hardly think of them, except for Jeremy. Why dwell upon the past when there's little to be gained by it? What sustains me is the future: the certainty that one day Jordan will carry me away from this place. Or if he does not, or cannot, then with my inheritance, I shall find him!

I am no Elizabeth Dernwood, no Juliet, no Desdemona—those marrowless heroines of Art. Let them die for love. I mean to live for it! Jordan is my destiny. I will admit no impediment. 'Heaven hath pleased it so, to punish me with this, and this with me.'

Caroline Miller

Caroline Miller has published numerous short stores in publications as diverse as CHILDREN'S DIGEST and GRIT. Her short story "Under the Bridge and Beneath the Moon" was dramatized for radio in Oregon and Washington.

In addition to writing, Caroline is a silk painter whose pieces have been sold in galleries in the Portland area. Her work has also been included in a number of juried art shows.

Caroline has taught English at both the high school and university levels, headed a labor union for five years and successfully ran for public office three times. She holds a B.A. and M.A.T. degree from Reed College and an M.A. in Literature from Northern Arizona University, where she graduated with honors.